CHICAGO TIME

RICHARD HELLINGA

ISBN: 0985393629
ISBN-13: 978-0-9853936-2-5

DEDICATION

For Stephanie

CONTENTS

CHICAGO TIME

1   HOW THEY MET

If La Ville Venteuse had not been closed that morning in 2003, Robert and Elise would not have met. Robert arrived first, eager for a cappuccino, only to discover that the entrance was locked and the CLOSED sign up. There was a hand-written note taped to the inside of the glass door, which read,

> *"Dear loyal customers,*
> *"It is with mixed regret that I must tell you that La Ville Venteuse is closed as of this Monday. It has been a wonderful 7 years here in the Ravenswood neighborhood.*
> *"Sincerely,*
> *"Jean-Claude Beaubien."*

Robert read it once more. Almost every morning for nearly four years he had stopped at La Ville Venteuse for a cappuccino and either a chocolate or almond croissant. The shop was only a few doors down from the Montrose L station, making it a convenient stop on the way to work or home. Inside the darkened shop, the glass cases that were normally filled with dozens of different pastries in sweet shades of red, white, blue, green, dark brown, and golden brown, all organized into neat rows on inclined shelves, were empty. Once or twice a week after work Robert would stop in and get something for his after-dinner dessert; a slice of cheesecake, flour-less chocolate cake, or a fruit custard. Robert had loved everything he had ever eaten there. The now former owner had always seemed very French to Robert; proud, confident, informed, and rude. A few customers seemed to have a strong personal rapport with him that Robert could never figure out how to gain, despite how often he patronized the place. A few had even spoke to the man exclusively in French.

"No, no, no!" exclaimed a female voice to Robert's left. "This can not be."

Robert turned and saw a black-haired woman with light white skin. He had seen her many times before in the shop having long conversations in French with the owner. She looked to be in her late twenties, possibly thirty.

"You speak English?" said Robert.

"Of course I do. I'm an American," said Elise Callahan in an accent-less voice to Robert's growing surprise.

"You're American?"

"What gave you the idea I wasn't?" She thought the nearly sun-burned-faced guy standing next to her, whom she had always thought didn't look too smart to begin with, was even dumber. She thought any man who wore golf shirts with khaki slacks didn't have a proper sense of fashion. Didn't he know that not all shirts with collars were meant to be worn with khaki slacks to work?

"You were always talking to the owner in French. I never heard you speak English," said Robert.

"Well, I'm not. I studied French in college and then lived in France for awhile."

"Is that what it took to get the guy to be nice to you. I've been going to this shop for years and never got anything more than a 'thank you.' Now, I'll never get anything more than that, or his pastries for that matter."

"Did you ever say hello to Mr. Beaubien when you came in?"

"Sometimes. I think so. Why?"

"It's impolite to a French person not to greet them in their own shop."

"And that's why he was so rude?"

"He considered it rude when someone entered his shop and didn't greet him. He considered his shop a part of his home. That's how they do things in France."

"How was I supposed to know that? I'm not in France. I'm in Chicago. I don't assume that when a guy's at work he wants to talk about everything under the sun but the business at hand, especially if there's a long line of people behind me. I assume he's working."

"I have to get a hold of Mr. Beaubien. He had talked about closing the shop, but I didn't think it would happen so fast. This doesn't seem possible."

"Why would he close?"

"He wasn't making much profit on the place. But he was making a lot on the catering end. A lot more. My guess is that's what he's going to focus on...So you liked La Ville Venteuse?"

"Oh yeah," said Robert. "Everything was delicious here."

"And now it's gone. One less thing for me to like about this city."

"My whole morning routine is screwed. Where am I supposed to go now? There's nowhere else around here to get decent coffee, let alone great pastries."

"Well, I wish I knew the answer, but I need to get to work." Elise turned away and headed towards the L tracks.

Robert followed. "Me, too."

2   CHICAGO TIME

As Robert and Elise got near the station, Robert noticed the headlines displayed in the two newspaper dispensers just outside the entrance: *The Chicago Sun-Times* declared, COUNCIL DEMANDS MORE OFFICE SPACE; *The Chicago Tribune* reported, MAYOR CALLS COUNCIL 'CUCKOO.' There are 50 members on the Chicago City Council, one representing each of the 50 Wards in the city. Chicagoans refer to them most often not as "councilmen" but as "aldermen." Thirty-one aldermen had stormed out of the council chamber in defiance of the mayor. It was the first time the City Council had ever even defied the mayor, who was respected and feared more than loved. What had started as a dispute between one alderman and the mayor over allocating a small amount of money for a Chicago Park District study had escalated into an all-out media war. For nearly a week and a half insults and accusations had been thrown back and forth between Mayor Patrick Nash, his supporters, and the striking aldermen.

Robert thought that only the Chicago City Council could do nothing and make people think that it was something on their behalf.

Elise entered the station and walked through the turnstile. Robert was not too far behind. The station was the original one built when the L line first opened. It was small and made of brick, looking always as if it was huddling due to its placement directly underneath the tracks. The bricks were painted white. Because of the application of so many layers through the years, the paint looked as if it was a plastic cover, its thickness smoothing over the indentations where the mortar had been applied between the bricks.

Robert knew the station had been selected for demolition, and a new station was to be built on the south side of Montrose.

Up on the platform, Robert looked at the sky. Seeing that it was devoid of clouds, displaying a blue that was searing in it's clarity, he thought he should be okay without an umbrella. He brought his attention back to the L platform. A small crowd, all dressed in casual or formal business attire, was waiting for the next train. Elise was standing a few feet from him.

"Hey, do you know if there are any other places like La Ville Venteuse around?" Robert asked Elise.

"No. And I don't care. I've got other plans and they don't include Chicago."

Robert had asked what he thought was a simple question and was annoyed that he hadn't received a simple answer. "Like what?"

"I'm moving to Paris at the end of the month."

"Gee, that's original."

"What do you mean by that?"

"Exactly what I said. It's not an original idea. It's been done and written about to death."

"Because it's the city."

"It's a city, a beautiful one no doubt, but not the only city in this big world of ours."

Elise was about to reply but the shiny steel-gray L train turned the corner from the West, screeching through the turn and heading South. Each car gleamed then disappeared behind the lead car. Seconds later the eight cars came to a stop at the platform without so much as a jerk. Lucky for her, she thought, that the CTA finally got its act together during the last few weeks before she was leaving the city for good.

For the past week the L trains had been running without delay, full of passengers, but not packed uncomfortably. There were none of those random stops in the middle of the tracks that occurred on almost every rush hour trip, annoying the riders. There were also no musicians on the platforms playing and asking for money. No one stepped on any wads of gum stuck to the floors of the trains. No one tried to witness entire L cars full of people with warnings that the End Times were near and that you could not be saved by your job, money, girlfriend, car, wife, TV, stocks, bonds, husband, boyfriend, house, dog, or anything else but Jesus Christ the Son of God Himself sent to Earth to save us all.

The doors opened and Robert boarded the nearest L car, wondering why someone would want to live such a cliché, no matter how attractive a cliché it might be. Elise thought about getting on a different car to end the conversation. But she couldn't let him dismiss Paris as just any beautiful city.

Who did this guy think he was? No one talked to her that way about her plans. Nearly everyone else had been complimentary or envious. Everyone!

Elise stomped into the car. Robert was standing by the opposite doors, holding onto one of the poles. She strode to the other side of the pole and grabbed it. "What is wrong with you? How can you think such a thing? Let alone say it to someone you've just spoken to for the first time."

Robert would have loved to move to Paris at that moment rather than go to work with a caffeine headache and deal with whatever new dumb decision his boss Perry had made regarding the QA Department. Since he had neither the job prospects, the necessary will, nor the language skills to pull off a trans-Atlantic move, it was easier to continue the argument.

"Moving to Paris isn't original. That's all I'm saying. Even Prague got done. All those American, Gen-X, ex-pats went to Prague after the fall of the Berlin Wall thinking for some strange reason that it was going to be like Paris in the '20s. God knows where that idea came from. But it turned into a whole lot of nothing."

"Prague is the Golden City."

"When I was there in the mid-'90s it wasn't so golden. Plenty of homeless and a lot of bad Communist-era architecture. Not to mention all the restaurants trying to charge you for bread and other stuff you didn't ask for."

"Such an American."

"I am what I am."

"I can't wait to get out of here."

"Chicago doesn't care."

Elise tightened her grip on the pole. Her hand was about a half-foot below Robert's. She thought about slapping him. Why this indifference? Why was he being so infuriating? The last time she could remember someone being able to get her so angry was in Paris, with her ex-boyfriend Patrick. But at least for awhile Patrick had shared her Parisian dream.

"You've probably never even lived anywhere else," she said.

"For your information, I lived in the Bay Area for most of the '90s."

"Well, la-dee-da," she said. Elise turned her head away from him and looked though the windows on the opposite doors. Flat black rooftops and gray light poles blurred by. A crew-cut young man in a suit was talking on his cell phone about how drunk he had been Saturday night at a bar called Hi-Tops.

Robert didn't want to say anything more to the attractive woman with fierce blue eyes whose hand was just below his on the pole. There were no rings on either set of fingers, he noticed. If she wanted to leave Chicago for Paris, then good riddance. When he had traveled through Europe years before, he had met a number of U.S. ex-pats who hated the U.S. He would strike up a conversation and whatever world event was dominating the news would eventually come up. The angry ex-pat would recount the same litany of sins that Robert had quickly become overly familiar with: CIA-backed coups in Guatemala, Chile, and Iran, the creation of Panama and the building of the canal, an irrational stance against Cuba, unconditional support of Israel, Sexism, Racism, horrendous public education that left U.S. citizens less-informed than their foreign counterparts, especially when it came to world history, rampant Consumerism, a pop culture that was really no culture, unrestrained capitalism, the arrogance in believing the U. S. is exceptional and unlike any empire that existed before it. When Robert would point out that atrocities and invasions committed by old colonial powers such as England, France, Belgium, and Spain were far worse, and that as empires go, the U.S. was much more benevolent, and that whenever the population of a country like France or Germany became five percent people from "somewhere else" there were protests, the argument just went round and round again. Robert felt there was no point arguing with people like that. It was as pointless as arguing about corruption with a Chicago machine hack like his father. They had an irrefutable belief, a mind closed to self-doubt and introspection.

Elise watched the brick buildings pass by. She couldn't wait for the day when this was no longer her view. When she would be on the Paris Metro and able to reach every part of the City of Lights, or to a station where she could catch a train to anywhere in Europe, and where she wouldn't have to deal anymore with that particular brand of provincialism known as Chicago boosterism. She'd had it with people like the man whose hand was too close to hers and their constantly pointing out how Chicago invented modern architecture, modern comedy, modern theater, and how the local TV news was always looking for the so-called "Chicago Angle" in any major news story that didn't emerge from Chicago. But by far the most annoying facet of life in Chicago was everyone's reference to things happening on so-called "Chicago Time," as if the city had its own special time zone. The city was actually in the Central Time Zone but you'd never know it talking to people in Chicago. It was a perfect example of the city's own warped sense of itself. No wonder her father left the city to go to college and never came back.

Through the train windows, the passing rooftops began to disappear, replaced by taller and more taller buildings. After stopping at the Merchandise Mart, and passing through the concrete and steel canyon created by the river, the view inside the Loop was of the large-windowed office buildings on Wells.

The train stopped at Washington. Elise looked back at Robert. She wanted to say something more definitive than "la-dee-da" to make her point. Noticing that she was looking at him, his frowning glance met her frowning glance. He wondered what she wanted now, with his dull headache approaching a pile-driving thud with every throb of his heart. She squinted slightly. He squinted slightly back. Elise realized nearly everyone who was getting off at the stop had already gotten off. The doors would be closing soon. Who knew when she would see him again? This might be her last chance to win the argument. Though it was probably a waste of time and breath. So forget about it. She let go of the pole and walked out of the car. Robert watched her short fast steps. The doors closed behind her and the train continued on its route. He turned his head and his eyes caught sight of a copy of the day's *Chicago Sun-Times* on a nearby seat. He reached over and grabbed the paper.

3   IF HE WAS IN CHARGE...

Robert exited the train at the next stop, Quincy. He hurried down the steps, taking two at a time, to the sidewalk. He walked East, around the Fourth National Bank Tower to Lasalle Street, where he jaywalked across and headed into the Gloria Jeans Coffee in the first floor of the Lasalle Bank building. The fact the line was long only added to his agitation. He took his spot at the very end and was pleasantly surprised to find that the line moved at a good pace. When it was his turn at the register, he ordered a double cappuccino with a double-shot of espresso. "Quad in a double!" shouted the young clerk.

While Robert waited he thought that he wouldn't have to be in such a hurry if someone else was running the department instead of Perry. Like Robert. If he was running the department it would be run much more efficiently, openly, and happily. All of the petty, annoying, unproductive things, like writing up testing summaries in addition to the bug reports, would never be part of any Quality Assurance Department he would run. In fact, if he was in charge, the department would be a much better department and there would be less rancor with the programmers in the Software Development Department. Of course, that would never happen because the bank would never let a big mouth like him be given important responsibilities. But just what had upper management been thinking when they had put Perry in charge of the QA Department? The man had previously been a consultant with Arthur Andersen in some vague capacity as an Efficiency Engineer but had never written a single test case in his life.

Robert took his cappuccino, added some RAW sugar, stirred it in quickly, and tasted it. He liked it almost as much as the cappuccinos from La Ville Venteuse. He took another sip then pushed open the glass door to the sidewalk. He jaywalked back across Lasalle and through the revolving doors of the Fourth National Bank Tower.

Robert's gray cubicle was located on a center aisle on the eighth floor. He set his bag on the floor next to his chair, and peeled off the white plastic cover to the cup. He was about to take a tentative drink when Karen Washington, who occupied the cubicle next to him said, "Robert! You're here! We've got a department meeting starting right now."

Karen was the other Lead QA Engineer in the department. Two years older than Robert, her cubicle was devoid of pictures. She was black and a lesbian who was out only to Robert and a handful of other people within and outside their department. Robert's cubicle was also devoid of personal photos. There was a black sign that read, in white letters, "White Sox Fan Parking Only" hanging on one wall. On another was a calendar of Lake Michigan light houses his parents had given him as a Christmas gift. Robert was not enamored with lighthouses. He merely thought it was useful to have a calendar in his cubicle.

"Did Perry email us the agenda?" Robert asked

"No."

"We don't know what it's about?"

"No."

"Crap." Robert thought the reorganization, rumored about since the merger between BMC and Fourth National Bank had been finalized less than two months before, was finally taking place. The rumors had been constant about which departments were going to be consolidated, which branches would be closed, and how many people were going to be laid off. The rumors had stopped nearly two weeks before, making some people feel relieved and others more paranoid. Robert had been through this sort of thing before. The rumors often reached their highest and most absurd the day before the reorganization. But it was Monday, and reorgs never happened on Mondays. They were always on Fridays. So whatever Perry wanted, odds were it wasn't related to any reorg. Which was good in a way but annoying in another. Robert had never had a clear idea of what it was Perry spent his time doing. Perry would mention all kinds of projects with acronyms like PALS, COMS, and WAL, that were always "about to be ready" but never implemented in the department.

"Come on!" Karen nearly shouted.

Robert, with a yellow legal pad and blue pen in one hand and the cappuccino in the other, followed Karen up the elevator to the 10th floor, out the door to the right, passing a few rows of light gray cubicles and the sounds of typing, copying, and faxing, to the Wright Conference Room. Inside the large conference room, everyone else from the department was already seated: Nikolai, Anna, Katrina, Timur, Rakesh, Dipti, Sanjay, Wen, Gary, Jeff, and Bob. Seated at one end of the long table was Perry Billows, the QA Department Manager.

Perry always told himself that attitude was something you decided to have. He was middle-aged with the gray starting to overtake the light brown in his hair. He was still married to wife number two after nine years and was quite content to being the step-dad to his wife's two sons, but still smarting after all those years for not getting joint custody of his daughter Michelle from his first marriage.

Perry had been in a foul mood all weekend. His daughter had gotten engaged three months ago to a stockbroker she had been dating for a year. Perry had been overjoyed at the news. Then Friday evening she had informed him that her step-father was going to give her away at the ceremony.

"It's not like you were ever really there for me," she had said.

"I couldn't be! I was too busy working in order to pay alimony to your mother, child support for you, and then support Mary, the boys, and myself. I'm still paying for your college loans!"

Perry decided he was most certainly not going to spend his Monday morning thinking about his ungrateful daughter. He had a meeting to run, decisions to make, emails to answer, and more meetings to attend. If he was going to ensure that he had a job after the reorganization resulting from Fourth National's merger with BMC, he had to be on his toes, keep his eyes and ears open, play his cards right, and go with the flow.

"We were waiting for you, Robert," said Perry as the door shut behind Robert.

Karen took the open seat near the middle of the table on the door side of the room. The only available seat remaining was the one to Perry's right.

Robert sat in the chair next to Perry. "Sorry. I needed to get a cappuccino."

"We do provide free coffee in the kitchen."

"That stuff will give you dysentery."

"No need to be crude, Robert."

"Sorry."

"Speaking of complaints, that's why I called this meeting. As many of you know, there have been a lot of complaints about our performance as a department. With the merger, there is talk about downsizing and/or outsourcing some of the services our department provides to make room for BMC's QA Department. Now, you all know that I would love to keep each and every one of you. But I can't guarantee that, unfortunately. We have to take a long hard look at ourselves, evaluate our performance, and see where we can make improvements. For example, let's take Robert, here."

Robert raised his eyebrows. "He was late, and as a result he made us start this meeting late. Do you have something to say to your co-workers, Robert?"

Despite a few drinks of his cappuccino, Robert's caffeine headache remained strong. He knew he was one of the best workers in the department. The previous Department Manager, Lisa Timoshenko, had hired him. A year later she left to become a consultant. Perry was hired shortly after that. Robert thought it was Perry who antagonized the software developers by withholding QA resources for petty reasons, which had in-turn caused the very real possibility of the department being cut and most of its services outsourced to a consulting company. So Robert was damned if he was going to be used as a scapegoat. He took a sip of his cappuccino, licked the foam off the top of his lip and said, "I sure do, Perry." He turned, looked around at his co-workers, and said, "Aren't you all tired of working for this jackass?

4   DIRTY BITTER COFFEE

Inside the law offices of Tinker, Evers, and Chance, Elise was sitting behind the long, wide mahogany-brown reception desk next to Carol Wolker, who was the other receptionist. With long, straight, light brown hair, gleaming blue eyes, a warm smile, and a calm clear voice, she made an excellent face for the firm. Carol was on the phone with a woman who wanted to sue the Mayor of Chicago for planting a tree on the street median in front of her house, thus blocking her view of the park across the street. Carol was calmly explaining that Tinker, Evers, and Chance didn't handle those kinds of cases. When Carol had first begun working at the firm seven years ago she had been annoyed by those kinds of calls (people who wanted to sue the President or the U.S. Government for such heinous crimes as manipulating the weather to flood their basement or having men in black cars follow them around). Now, she found them entertaining.

Elise's French skills were one of those things about her co-worker that Carol had found interesting. Though, as Elise's final day got closer, Carol thought Elise's fixation on France was unhealthy and that Elise would be better off staying in the U.S. and finding someone (man or woman) with whom to settle down. It was one thing to be fluent in a language. It was another thing to be obsessed with an entire country. She hoped her son and daughter, ages 12 and 10, would do exciting things like travel to Europe, but she did not want them getting hung up on moving to some foreign country, especially at an age when they ought to be thinking of settling down and furthering their career.

As Carol was politely extricating herself from the phone conversation with the Woman with the Obstructed View, Elise was reading a story in the French newspaper *Le Figaro* on her PC. It was about the French actor Vincent Cassel, but she couldn't get past the first paragraph telling about him posing in a studio for promotional photos. She was still annoyed that the guy she had met in front of La Ville Venteuse didn't think moving to Paris was original.

In between answering phone calls, guiding clients to the right office, and avoiding questions from Carol about her personal life, on a typical day Elise read French web sites on her computer. She also cursed herself for having chosen to learn French as opposed to Spanish (a more employable language skill in Chicago) and cursed the French for not having immigrated in significant numbers anywhere besides Quebec, an extremely cold place; a place that referred to itself not as a country or state but as a form of winter. After having lived in France, she had to admit that the French compulsion to stay in France was probably a good one what with the varieties of wine and cheese, art, culture, the beaches on the Atlantic and Mediterranean coasts, and free health care. A compulsion that mirrored the average U.S.

citizen who also felt no desire to leave the U.S., what with 24-hour restaurants, big houses, numerous beaches, and great customer service compared to the rest of the world.

Elise had been plotting her return to France, despite her ex-boyfriend's presence in the country. She had claimed to be the first of the two who had wanted to live in France, despite the fact it had been Patrick's fellowship to study at the Sorbonne that had brought them to Paris. If she was going to be stuck the rest of her life answering a phone for lawyers, she wanted to do it in a Parisian law firm. Even Lyon would be better than Chicago, a city that prided itself on "working" and its grittiness. There was nothing elegant about Chicago, including that guy who started that argument with her on the L and his un-asked for opinions. Meanwhile, Patrick was living in Paris at that very moment in his Parisian apartment with his Parisian wife with their Parisian poodle and their Parisian infant in a Parisian stroller, with their Parisian jobs and their whole damn Parisian life, while she suffered a headache and answered phones and directed traffic for a bunch of attorneys.

Elise took a long sip of coffee, the dirty bitter coffee she had gotten in the break room and had filled with cream and sugar, wishing she had either gone to the Starbucks on the first floor or had made coffee in her french press back at her apartment. She set her mug next to her mouse and then saw Julian Foster walking very quickly toward the reception desk. He was tall, black, and lean-muscled, an admitted gym rat. He had a law degree from the University of Chicago and had just made junior partner.

"Elise, you speak French, right?" he said.

"Yes."

"How well do you speak? You're fluent, right?"

"I am. I have a Masters in French."

"Do you think you could help us out a bit? We have some people from France involved in some of the merger talks between RGB Bank and ALOI. The translator we hired canceled on us this morning. He says he's sick. I know it's last minute. We were hoping you could help out."

"I can do it," she said.

He smiled. "Wonderful. Thank you."

5   HOW ROBERT WAS PROMOTED

Sitting in a chair just outside the office of Rosalinda (Rose) Santos, the Vice-President of Human Resources, Robert folded one leg over the other, left over right, then right over left. He was wondering what the phrase "At-Will Employment" meant. What was "will" and how much of it was okay? It wasn't at a whim. This was a bank; there were procedures to be followed that had been agreed upon by the Adminisphere, after having reviewed the recommendations of a committee or task force that had been set up to study a particular area of concern. As far as Robert could tell, nothing at Fourth National happened At-Will. He was in for a reprimand at the least, maybe even a demotion or dismissal from his position. Which Robert thought would be just fine. He was tired of telling Perry all of his ideas for improvement, like buying software to automate the testing processes and instituting a flexible schedule for the department, and having those ideas rejected with Perry's stock-phrase: "That doesn't really fit with how we do things here." Maybe he would need to take that job with Derek.

Robert had taken the day off on Friday to spend the weekend with his friends Derek Jaeger and Mike Farley fishing up in Door County, Wisconsin. Derek had once again told Robert that if he was looking for a career change, his offer still stood. It was tempting to Robert. Working in real estate development in the role Derek wanted for him would eventually push Robert into the gray (and maybe even black) area of ethics in which Robert's father and two older brothers resided quite comfortably as loyal members of the Chicago Political Machine. Not to mention the pressure, roller coaster intensity, and long hours that Derek's job entailed.

The door to Rose's office opened and her head poked out. "Robert, we're ready for you."

Robert stood, took a deep breath, and walked towards the door. Rose pulled it open wider and as Robert entered, he saw Ted Allen the Chief Technology Officer (CTO) sitting in a chair to the right of Rose's desk.

"Hello, Robert," said Ted with a smile.

"Hello. Good morning," said Robert. He had not expected to see Ted there. Ted was in his late fifties and black. Robert had had very few interactions with him. He only knew what Perry had told him; Ted had served in the Marines, went to college, then worked at IBM before working in the banking industry. All of that was true. Ted had risen to CTO four months after Perry had been hired. Ted still did not understand why his predecessor had hired Perry to run the QA Department in the first place. He was a nice enough guy, but he lacked knowledge of QA best practices and talked too much. Ted didn't like people he thought talked a lot, which meant that Sales and Marketing people, along with TV talk show hosts, were among his least favorite kinds of people. He knew Sales and Marketing were necessary to the running of a successful company. He just preferred to limit his interactions with them. Straight shooters like Robert were the people he preferred to be around. Based on his reputation and his actions, Robert seemed like the right person for the job he needed done at that difficult moment in time. There were a lot of changes coming due to the merger. It would not be pretty.

"Go ahead. Sit down," said Rose motioning Robert toward the empty chair to the left.

Robert sat. "I know I was out of line with Perry–"

"No need to explain," said Ted.

"It's all right, Robert. You're not being disciplined," said Rose.

Robert looked from Rose to Ted, then back to Rose. "What?"

Rose took her seat behind the desk. "You've been promoted to Manager of the QA Department."

"You're kidding."

"No, Robert. We don't kid about things of this nature," said Ted.

"You're joking. No one who mouths off like I did this morning at the department meeting gets promoted."

"People in other departments speak very highly of you."

"I thought everyone thought I was the resident curmudgeon."

Rose, in well over 20 years working in Human Resources, had seen plenty of examples of the wrong person being hired for a job. Perry had been one of them. Robert presented an interesting case to her. She had seen his type before; smart, talented, productive, and full of potential, but lacking diplomacy and tact, the type whose loyalties remained with his co-workers and the people who worked for him, and not the company. They had names for people like Robert: "maverick," "loose-canon," and even "black sheep." Respected (and even loved) by some and hated by others. She understood why, after Perry, Ted wanted someone like Robert. Especially now with the merger, Ted did not have the luxury of time to do an outside search for a candidate for the position. He had to move quickly.

"I don't know anything about that," said Rose. "But they like and respect you, two things your predecessor didn't have going for him. Throw in your long and varied experience, and you were the logical choice to replace him."

"You'll be given a significant salary increase, an extra week of vacation, and you'll be enrolled in the MTP, the Management Training Program," said Ted.

"I thought I was going to be fired."

Ted stood and extended a hand toward him. "No. And let me be the first to congratulate you on your promotion."

Robert looked at Ted's hand. He was about to shake hands with his new boss, the man who was making him the boss of his department. Robert couldn't be the boss. No. Not him. This wasn't possible. He didn't know how to be a boss. No one had placed him in charge of anything bigger than putting together a software build...Wait!...This was his opportunity to do things his way, the right way. He could apply all the things he had learned through his decade working in QA Departments big and small. He could definitely do this. Now was his chance to run a QA Department better than the many QA Departments in which he had worked. No longer would he be saying to himself, "If I was in charge..." He was now in charge.

"Thank you," said Robert. He stood and shook hands with Ted.

Then he shook Rose's hand.

"Congratulations," she said.

"Thank you. Thank you both very much," said Robert. "Sorry, but this is a bit overwhelming and shocking."

"You're welcome," said Ted. "This is a big chance for you. I'm especially intrigued by your idea for automating some of the testing processes. I'd like to set up a meeting with you to discuss it."

"Okay."

"Meanwhile," said Rose, "why don't you take the rest of the day off. And tomorrow morning, when you come in, we'll introduce you as the new Manager of the QA Department."

6   "SOMEONE WITH YOUR SKILLS"

Elise took a bite out of her slice of deep-dish pizza. It was filled with spinach and cheese. She admitted to herself that the pizza was very good and that she would miss it just a little bit, but not in the same passionately devoted way she had heard so many Chicagoans claim they would miss it. She was sitting at the conference table in between Paul Laurent, one of the French-speaking lawyers, and Julian. Everyone involved in the negotiations was taking a break for lunch, which had been ordered in from Giordano's. People were standing, stretching, and chatting in small groups.

Interpreting for the other French-speakers had made Elise more anxious to get to Paris. Paul spoke English fluently with very little accent. But some of the French business people and the other two French attorneys spoke English with a bit of difficulty.

"Elise, thank you for jumping in on such short notice," said Julian.

"You're welcome," she said.

"You did a wonderful job," said Paul, and then he took a drink from his bottled water. He was thin, wearing gray wire-rimmed glasses. He was amazed that someone with Elise's French skills was only a receptionist. There were better, more lucrative, jobs for people like her. Could she not find one? It was a shame to see someone like her not putting her skills to use. He knew a place in Chicago where Elise would do very well.

"It was fun," said Elise with a smile full of satisfaction. Being able to deploy her French skills in such a demanding way made her feel useful.

"You are very lucky, Julian, to have someone like her on your staff."

"Elise is leaving us in a few weeks," said Julian.

Paul turned back to Elise. "Really? Where are you going?"

"To Paris."

"What are you going to do there?"

"Well, that's not completely sorted out just yet. But I have a number of leads." Elise put another piece of pizza into her mouth.

"I wish you the best of luck then...It is unfortunate in a way, because I know a place right here that is looking to hire someone with your skills."

Elise chewed and swallowed quickly. "What kind of job is that?"

"There is a French immersion school, a private school, that is looking for a teacher. For 4th grade, I believe. It is not enough to have a degree in French and a teaching certificate. The person must be totally fluent. Someone like yourself."

"There's a French school here? In Chicago?"

"Yes. Did you not know that?"

Elise shook her head no. In all the time she had been in Chicago, she hadn't heard one thing about it. She set her white plastic fork and knife onto her paper plate.

"It is quite a good school," said Paul. "Our son and daughter go there. They are seven and five. If you are at all interested, I could put you in contact with the school's principal."

"Where is it?"

"In the Uptown neighborhood."

Uptown? thought Elise. A French Immersion school in Uptown? You'd think the Gold Coast or Lincoln Park would have something like that already. She could probably take the Montrose Avenue bus every day to work. 15 minutes, tops. But she did not expect the words that came out of her mouth next. "I'll have to think about that."

"I understand. You cannot just drop a big move like the one you are taking. Moving to another country is not a small task. I do understand." He smiled and returned to eating his lunch.

7   MOISTURE EFFACEMENT

Robert put his Marshall Field's bags on the table in the dining room of his apartment. He went to the kitchen, grabbed a handful of pretzels from a bag in a cabinet, and went back into the living room. Robert thought the day had been too strange. He could not have been promoted. It was all a big practical joke that would be revealed tomorrow morning when he went in to work. The meeting would not be about his promotion. It would be the revelation of a prank that had been played on him. Perry would be there with the rest of the department. And they would laugh at him in his only suit. He had managed to get the clerk at Field's to have the alterations for his four new suits put on a rush. He would be able to pick up two of them Tuesday evening and the other two on Thursday evening.

Robert lived in a large one bedroom apartment. The dining room contained a table and four chairs, but the table was covered with unopened mail and books with pristine spines. His book and DVD collection were filled with some of the touchstones of computer geekdom (in addition to the usual reference books on QA testing, network administration, and programming in C++ and Java): Neal Stephenson, Neil Gaiman, *The Complete Hitchhiker's Guide to the Galaxy*, *Office Space*, Monty Python, *The Watchmen*, *Brave New World*, and *Do Androids Dream of Electric Sheep?* He preferred *Star Trek: the Next Generation* to the original *Star Trek*.

Robert turned on his TV to a local station, WCHI, for the noon-time news. It was a little past the half-hour. Nathan Hunt, the legendary Chicago meteorologist and weatherman, had just finished his forecast when Robert tuned in. Hunt, a 59-year-old white man, had six minutes for weather reports. His competitors were lucky if they had three. Not only did he give the forecast for the weather in the city, but he explained in detail how the weather conditions across the country moved, shifted, and combined to influence the weather conditions in Chicago. Everything from gulf moisture to arctic air, to the changing current of the jet stream, to low and high pressure systems, cold fronts and warm fronts, the types of clouds in the sky, where moisture was picked up and dropped off, the shifting winds, and how much moisture accumulation to expect was explained in his forecasts. That day he had had little to do. The weather was warm and pleasant, and was (very unexpectedly) expected to continue to be warm and pleasant for the next few days. Consistent weather was the worst thing there could be for a TV meteorologist.

In fact, the winds had stopped blowing in the city by mid-afternoon the day after the City Council strike had begun. The air was still except for the big eddies caused by cars or trucks on the streets. When the wind disappeared that August it was as if the city had been released from a vise grip of heat which had held since the beginning of July. The sun's rays did not burn hard, nor did the streets' asphalt push up heat.

"Back to you Chris," said Nathan.

"So what did happen to that big storm you predicted on Friday?" asked Anchorman Chris Giancarlo.

Robert remembered that before he had left on his fishing trip, every weather person on TV, including Nathan Hunt, had stated without equivocation that a powerful thunderstorm was heading toward Chicago. Without a doubt it was going to pass over the city and drop as much as four inches of rain in total. They had shown various satellite models of the storm's projected path. Prepare for a wet Sunday and Monday morning. Possibly even a soggy Tuesday. The rain was inevitable. Expect travel delays. Flash floods. Remember your umbrella. The beautiful day irritated Robert a little more; how, no matter how important it was that you knew what the weather in Chicago was going to be, you couldn't depend on it.

"It's gone," said Nathan.

"Gone?"

Nathan flattened his mouth and furrowed his brow. "Yes. It's an extremely rare occurrence, but not out of the range of possibilities. It's called a *moisture effacement*. It's when the moisture from a storm front spontaneously dissipates without any precipitation."

"That's interesting. I've never heard of that." Chris' face looked dubious.

"It's very interesting."

"*Moisture effacement*. That's the second time in a week that you've said that. Is that a real term?"

"Of course it is," said Nathan, straightening his back.

"Are you sure?"

"I've been studying meteorology my entire adult life, Chris. I wouldn't just make up some new piece of terminology."

"Learn something new every day."

The corners of Nathan's mouth drooped a little, looking as if he had felt a burst of heartburn. "Indeed we do."

"At any rate, this weather is wonderful."

"Like I told our viewers," said Nathan, "Enjoy this wonderful weather while it lasts. As you know, in Chicago, the weather can change very quickly."

"No kidding," said Robert before nibbling on a pretzel.

8   THE CLOUT BUSINESS

Robert picked up the cordless phone sitting on the table next to the recliner. There was a message on his voicemail. He dialed in and listened. It was from his mother. She had called and left the message at 11:07 that morning. She could have called him on his cell phone. She could even called him at work. But no. Robert knew she had purposefully called him when he was most likely to not be at home. She did this whenever she wanted to tell or ask Robert something difficult like, "your brother was just promoted again at the County Forest Preserve," or "your niece is making her first communion and I know you don't go to church anymore but...," or "your father earned a lot of overtime during the last election, so he wants to...". His mother's most recent message was to remind Robert that his father's 60th birthday party was next weekend, Sunday, and it would mean a lot to him and her if Robert would come. She was making the reservation at The Exchange and needed a final count to tell the restaurant.

Robert did not want to go to his father's birthday dinner. But since it was his father's 60th, and he had missed the 58th and 59th gatherings, he thought he ought to go. One benefit to living in California all those years was not having to attend every single family-related event. But ever since he had returned to Chicago at the behest of his almost-wife Marcia Bartolozzi, this dilemma had been placed at a primary spot in his life. Getting out of family obligations had become a matter of following a set of rules he had created for himself. First, he had decided it was not good to penalize his nieces or nephews. So if the event was related to them, he attended. Second, if it was at his mother's behest, then he attended more often than not because she often tried to mediate between Robert and his father and brothers. Third, if the event was related to his father or brothers, then it depended on how well he was getting along at that point in time with that particular family member. With his father, it was fairly easy, because he was almost never on good terms with him. So he often skipped father-related events.

Robert's older brothers Michael and David had followed their father into what Robert liked to call the "Clout Business." Robert had avoided it out of revulsion. He had seen from an early age how corruption seeped into every function of the city and county. How it was impossible to get a job in a city department without knowing someone who either already worked in the department or had clout with someone in that department. There was a comfort in it for those who had the connections; there was always someone to whom you could go to get what you needed or wanted. Having that vast network of people was a form of security. But it was not based necessarily on what most people thought of as "merit." What the public thought of as "merit" was ignored. It was "merit" wrung through the loyalties and obedience demanded by clout and the skills necessary to wield clout. To his father, brothers, and their friends there was no such thing as corruption, because corruption didn't exist. There was only clout. Those who had it used it. Those who didn't were on their own.

It was after Robert's sophomore year at U. of I. Champaign-Urbana when he decided he wanted nothing to do with that life. It started with his Computer Science degree. His father was baffled by it. Why not a business degree so he could get a good job for the city? Or why even bother with college altogether unless it was on to law school? Or what about an engineering degree of some sort? Something that makes something. As interesting as Robert found certain aspects of engineering and business principles, he did not find any enjoyment in solving differential equations or studying accounting principles or business law. Especially if he was going to be pressured to put it into the service of his father's world. He came to view the life that his father and brothers supported and extolled as a drag on the city of Chicago, reducing city services to nothing more than a jobs program for the unqualified and undeserving. If bugs and errors corrupted software, breaking or hobbling it, then his father and brothers were not just bugs in the system, but portions of a large virus feeding off the city's vitality, and slowly, ever so slowly, killing the city. Sure there were checks for those bugs. Reformers popped up from time to time who attempted to enact changes for the better that would act as an anti-virus. But clout acted as an anti-anti-virus; it was largely immune to anti-viral, anti-corruption measures.

Robert did not want to be a bug or a virus. Once he had loudly proclaimed his intentions, he had been alternately shunned and welcomed back by his family. His welcome lasted about as long as he kept his mouth shut. But with his father and brothers often bragging about their sweet jobs, their sweet deals, and on and on, Robert would end up saying something, even threatening to turn them in. To the Feds, of course. Not the city police, the county sheriff's office, or the state police. No entity in the state was going to follow through and investigate any corruption in Chicago. It had to be the Feds. It was always the Feds. Someone from outside the Clout Business. But Robert had never followed through on his threats to turn them in. He had once tried to think through how he might actually go about doing it. He had never gotten farther than looking up the number for the Chicago office of the FBI. And if he called, what would he tell them? That he wanted to rat out his family?

Robert thought it might be easier to be at the dinner if he was dating someone who could, by her mere presence, provide a shield from the usual family discourse. Even his parents liked to make a good first impression. Since the broken engagement to his almost-wife Marcia, Robert hadn't dated anyone for more than two months. There was Claire in Marketing, who was the most conventionally beautiful woman he had ever dated, with a smile that would make him feel warm all over. But when she talked it was all about work. Robert didn't mind talking about work, but that was all they ever seemed to be able to talk about.

Then there was Nicole, a friend of Sherry's and Derek's, with whom they had set up Robert. It never went past the first double-date at Brasserie Jo. They had laughed together about some of the California health fads like colonics that Robert said he had never tried. But then she made a comment about "loser geeks with no lives who play online games." Robert said he was one. He played the adventure game Ultima Online for awhile, but when he had started dating Marcia, he devoted less and less time to it. He hadn't played any other online games since, knowing how obsessive he could be about games like that. She said, "oh," and the conversation between them never progressed much beyond that.

So if Robert was going to go to his father's birthday dinner, he was going to have to face his family alone. He could call his mother and tell her, yes, he would be there Sunday, if only to find out what behind-the-scenes information his father had on the City Council strike. His father almost always knew something, or many things, that did not make it into the stories reported on TV or in the papers.

On the weekend fishing trip, Derek had asked Robert what his father knew. Derek had his own sources, but he always wanted to get as much information from as many people as possible. Robert didn't know what his father knew because he hadn't spoken to him in months, after their last argument which had erupted over his brothers using their clout to get promotions over more senior and more qualified people.

Derek complained that with the strike so many projects were on hold. All that talk by the aldermen about being on strike for the people was keeping some people from being able to go about their business the way they were accustomed to doing so.

9 ROBERT'S HOARD OF MONEY

Robert would have to decide about his father's birthday very soon and call his mother back and tell her. For now, the decision would have to wait. Curiosity about the strike or not. He set the phone back in its cradle and went over to his desk. There were two sets of monitors and keyboards on top of the desk, and four PC units underneath that were networked together. One, running Linux, he used as a server (it was also the unit he had built himself). The others ran

Windows. The oldest one was filled with MP3's, acquired both legally and through other means. One was the main computer he used for surfing the Internet and reading email. The last was his gaming computer. It was less than six months old and was the most powerful of his computers in terms of speed, memory, and graphics capabilities. He thought about checking his email and reading some Internet sites. The idea of having someone to bring along with him to his father's birthday would not slip from his mind. As he waited for his main PC to boot up, he thought of the French-speaking woman and her plans to move to France. That took guts and gumption. Picking yourself up and moving to another country. It was adventurous. It was bold. It was something many people talked of doing but few did, no matter how appealing it sounded. Most people he knew, especially those with whom he had grown up, had never left the Chicago area. There were many obstacles: language, obligations, and fear. There was also the expense. You had to have a way to make money once you were overseas. Leaving the country was something Robert had thought often of doing. Not necessarily trying to be an expat, but traveling around the world. He even had the money to do it.

When Robert had broken off his engagement to Marcia, they sold their Wicker Park condo and split the proceeds. It was a condo they had bought with money made on their Mission District place in San Francisco. After deducting the banquet room costs (which thankfully weren't outrageous since it was owned by one of Robert's uncles), Robert was left with a sum that was slightly more than one year of his salary. He did not run out and buy another home. He was unsure whether he was going to stay in Chicago. With the dot-com boom having gone bust, good IT jobs like the one he landed at Fourth National Bank were hard to come by, so he ended up staying.

The hoard of money had been sitting in an account, growing as he added to it for the past two and a half years. Robert would check his bank statement, watching the interest accumulate slowly. Every time he looked at the amount, he felt that the money was waiting for him to do something with it. Traveling had been more appealing to him than getting tied down to a mortgage. He had taken one trip by himself: a hike up Machu Picchu in Peru. It had been exhausting to climb up the mountain. It had been worth it for the exhilaration of seeing all those ruins built at the top of the world. Now that he was a manager, it felt more unseemly to him to quit his job and travel around the world with a backpack. Something you did in his new position when you were having a mid-life crisis, and at 32 surely he was too young for that.

10   THE ONLY CIVILIZED PLACE IN THE WORLD

Elise and her friend Jennifer Shapiro were sharing pints of Bass Ale together at the bar of the Duke of Perth in celebration of Jennifer's recent engagement to her long-time boyfriend Jay. Elise and Jen had been friends since they were sophomores at Augustana College. Jen had studied for a semester at the University of Glasgow and the Duke of Perth reminded her of the pubs in Scotland.

"So you met two guys today who think Paris isn't the only civilized place in the world," said Jen.

Elise thought it barely civilized, bearing only the marks of civilization but not enough of its charms. "It's not that Chicago isn't civilized. I've told you before–"

"*I have my life planned,*" said Jen, mockingly, "*And Chicago isn't part of it. I don't want to be one of those people who dreams of living in Paris and doesn't do it.* The funny thing is, you already did it."

"And it was ended for me."

"You did it to yourself."

"Nevermind. I'm not going to make those same mistakes again."

Jennifer set her beer down on the bar. "So let me get this straight. You're choosing no job in Paris versus a good shot at a job that's perfect for you right here?"

Jen worked as a law librarian for the firm Carrasquel, Aparicio, and Guillen. She was thirty years old, like Elise. But unlike Elise, and like most of their friends, Jen had a career; a job where she had progressed through training and experience to a level of expertise, and was paid well for it. Elise was still carving out an existence, under-employed with a Masters in French Literature. Did she want to get a doctorate? Find a way to get paid to study French literature and culture? That would require returning to school. Would she carve out an existence in Paris? Or would she rather attempt to become an expert about the language and culture she loved so much and gain a profession in the process? Julian Foster, who was only three or four years older than her, was a law partner. What had she accomplished? Once in Paris, what would she accomplish?

"I've been planning this ever since the day I came back to the States," said Elise.

Jennifer curled her lips in and nodded slowly twice. "I know. But you should at least consider it. Maybe talk to the people at the school."

Elise's body was turned toward Jennifer, but her head faced her beer set on the bar. With her right hand she held onto the handle of the glass. A few tiny bubbles floated up in a single stream through the amber liquid to the surface. "I've been very careful not to take on anything permanent, like a job like that or even a boyfriend. I have to get back to Paris. I haven't let anything get in the way of my plans. And I'm not about to start now. Besides, there's nothing keeping me here in Chicago."

Richard Hellinga

11   THE SIREN OF RAVENSWOOD

Elise was walking up Wolcott towards her apartment, when she heard and saw the woman that she had dubbed the "Siren of Ravenswood." She was young, in her early twenties, with short black hair streaked with pink. She dressed, Elise thought, as if she was a rockstar in search of an audience. She was singing nearly every time Elise saw her. But Elise did not mind listening to her voice, because it was a very good soprano with a raspy edge, always clear, smooth, and never off-key. She had appeared in the neighborhood in June. No matter the time of day, she would be singing with earbuds tucked into her ears from an iPod. The first time Elise saw her, it was after eleven one Friday night, and Elise was just about to enter her building when she heard the woman singing from somewhere down the street. She had been enamored of the voice, far better than what you normally heard out on the street or on the L, or even the radio. She took a few steps toward the black gate and looked for the source of the voice. She saw the woman. From the bright orange street lights, she could see that the woman was wearing a white, long-sleeved, ruffled blouse tucked into a dark-colored leather pencil skirt and black Converse all-stars. Her hair was peroxide white then and she had been singing Veruca Salt's "Seether."

This night, as Elise couldn't wait to trade Chicago for Paris, the woman was singing "Sweet Home Chicago." Elise did not think of Chicago as sweet let alone as home. Though, as annoying as it was, she admitted to herself that there was already a long history of Americans in Paris, with books and movies about it. Maybe if she was going to Buenos Aires or Istanbul, or an island in Greece...How could she be thinking such a thing? Damn, that guy! She shoved open the door to her building.

12   HOW THEY LEARNED EACH OTHER'S NAMES

Three sunny days after Elise had participated in what she was now calling the most obnoxious conversation she had ever had, she saw the man with whom she'd had that conversation. He was standing in front of La Ville Venteuse. Elise came to a stop there at the Northwest corner of Wolcott and Montrose, watching him. He put his hands around his eyes, leaned into the big window next to the door, and peered inside. Behind Elise, the corner storefront was covered in plywood. The repeated pounding of hammers and the whines of electric drills and saws were impossible to ignore. Since he was between Elise and the L station, she thought there were two choices: wait for him to leave so she could avoid him, or keep walking so she could meet up with him and restart their argument.

The man pulled back from the window. Elise crossed Wolcott. She wanted to prove to him that he was wrong to think the way he did about Paris, that once she recited her list of Great Things About Paris and her Litany Against Chicago, he would be blown away and realize that Paris was superior to Chicago, and to all American cities for that matter. Just the numerous world class museums were enough, then there was the Bocuse d'or chef's prize, the superior public transportation, the fresh baguettes, the more temperate weather, *Pariscope*, that incomparable weekly guide to that incomparable city, and the romance of strolling along the Seine, the river that Paris embraced. Unlike Chicago, a city that had turned its back to its namesake river so you couldn't stroll along it. Where was the romance in that? Not to mention reversing its flow. Yes, Chicago had a backwards-flowing river! Who had ever heard of such a thing?

The man stuck his hands into the front pockets of his slacks. Elise noticed that he was wearing a suit: a gray one with a red-patterned tie and a white shirt. His tasseled shoes were black and shiny. Hanging on his right shoulder was his usual black bag. Elise thought he must be dressed for a job interview.

When she was only a few feet from him she said, "Is this what you've been doing every morning? Standing here and staring?"

"Huh?" he said. Then he turned and saw Elise. "No. Of course not."

"Then what are you looking for?"

He looked back into the shop. "I dunno. Guess I was hoping there might be a Going Out of Business Sale or something…Anything. I'd just like one more taste."

Mr. Beaubien's note was still taped to the inside of the door.

"It doesn't look like any such luck for us," said Elise. "I hate to see the shop this way. It was like a little piece of Paris right here, in my own neighborhood."

"Well, you'll have all of Paris at your feet soon, won't you?" He said it without a touch of sarcasm.

"Yes, I will."

"Good for you." He sounded to Elise as if he was genuinely happy for her. Now that she was only a few feet from him, she could see that his face, which had been one shade of red less than sunburnt on Monday, was a vibrant brown. Coupled with the suit, he was looking rather handsome.

She pulled the strap on her black purse up closer to her neck and folded her arms. "Wow. Your attitude sure has changed."

"What do you mean?"

"You said it wasn't original to move to Paris."

"It's not."

Elise pushed out a big sigh. "All right. This has been driving me crazy for the past few days. You are the only person I've ever met who thinks moving there is unoriginal. What is wrong with you?"

"Because it started with Picasso and Joyce going there, then the whole Lost Generation in the '20s came along and made it almost a rite of passage for young wealthy people. After 80, a hundred years, a thing is old, including the idea for a lifestyle. Not to mention that a moment like that is done and gone. Never to come back. It can't be recreated."

"That's not the point. I'm not some wannabe writer-expatriate. I want to be a Parisian."

"Good luck with that."

"No one ever says, *I want to be a Chicagoan.*"

"Maybe not. But millions want to be an American. And this city is just one part of this big country that people come to and adopt as their home."

"You are the most impossible person I've ever met!"

"I find that..." Robert closed his eyes, thinking that the last thing he wanted to do was start his day with an argument. He would have enough arguments to make later that day as the boss, whether it was changing his workers' priorities or making the case about purchasing automated testing software. He opened his eyes and relaxed his shoulders. "Look, I don't know you and I don't want to argue with you every time we run into each other. The other morning I was feeling pretty cranky due to a lack of caffeine and running late, and I was probably more harsh than I needed to be. I'm sorry. It was a weird day for me. After I got done talking to you, I went into work and told off my boss in front of the entire department."

Elise unclenched the fist she had made with her right hand, only realizing then that she had even made the fist. She felt a pebble-sized twinge of embarrassment at her realization that then enlarged to a brick-sized pang when it occurred to her that every negative thought she had been having about him might have been overblown and misguided. He was much more thoughtful than she had believed him capable.

"Is that why you're looking for a new job?" she asked.

"What gives you that idea?"

"You're wearing a suit."

Robert thought that if she had noticed this was the first time he had worn a suit in awhile, then she had been paying some attention to him before. (He hadn't worn a suit since he had interviewed at Forth National three years ago.) What that meant, he did not know. But the idea of a beautiful French-speaking woman paying attention to details about his clothing made him take a much more pleasant look at her.

"So?" he asked.

"I've never seen you wear one before. I assume it's because you're headed to an interview."

Robert laughed. "No, no, no. Not at all. You wanna hear the crazy thing about my tirade? It got me promoted. Now I'm in charge of the entire department. And that's why I'm in a suit. Management isn't allowed to dress casually."

"A promotion for a tirade. Is that how you normally get promotions where you work?"

"Are you kidding? I work for Fourth National Bank. Nothing happens without numerous procedures being followed and reviewed, and forms filled out in triplicate and then signed by a number of department heads. So, it was a huge surprise."

"Congratulations."

"Thank you."

"You're welcome. So, what do you have against Paris?"

"I don't have anything against Paris! If moving there is what you really want, then I'm happy for you."

She shook her head. "But you don't even know me. I don't even know your name."

He held out his hand. "Robert."

They shook. She liked the feel of his hand; slightly bigger than hers, but with a gracefully firm grip.

"I'm Elise."

"Nice to meet you, Elise."

"It's nice to meet you, too, Robert."

Robert put his hand back into his pocket. As beautiful and intelligent as she seemed to him, he thought she was pigheaded, too. Maybe after the way he had talked to her the other day she had a right to be pigheaded toward him and he should do something to make up for it. "Look, to make up for my crankiness the other day, let me buy you a cup of coffee when we get down to the Loop."

"Sorry. I already had coffee this morning."

"Fair enough…I'd ask you to lunch today but I have to take part in what we in Management lovingly call a 'working lunch meeting.' So how about dinner?"

"Are you asking me out on a date?"

Robert's eyes went wide as he shook his head and held up his shoulders. "No, no, no. It's just a simple thing to make up for starting an argument with you."

She waved off at him. "You don't have to buy me dinner."

"If you've been pissed off at me since Monday…You did say I was the most impossible person you've ever met. Either you hold a serious grudge or I'm an impossible person. Regardless, I'd like to make it up to you. Could you let me do that?"

Elise wiggled the fingers on the hand that had been balled up into a fist. She wondered what she had to lose. She was leaving the country and he knew that. Nothing permanent or long-term could come of dinner with him.

"Okay. You can do that," she said.

"Thank you. Do you like Café Selmarie over in Lincoln Square?"

"Yeah," she said, thinking he did have some taste for suggesting one of her favorite neighborhood restaurants.

"How about we meet there at seven?"

"That sounds good to me."

Then Robert remembered he had made plans with his friend Janet to go over to her place to have a drink or two with her and her husband. He would have to remember to call Janet to tell her he was either going to be late or that he couldn't do it. He couldn't call her on his cell phone right there in front of Elise because then he would come off as tacky.

"Are you going to work now?" Elise asked.

"Yeah. Staring through these windows isn't going to make this place come back."

They both took a look at the dark inside the shop, sighed, then headed toward the L station.

13   CHANGING THE SUBJECT

On the train, Robert and Elise shared the same pole for support just as they had Monday morning.

"So how do you uproot your life and move it to another continent?" asked Robert.

"It's far from easy," said Elise. Then she related to him how she had already gotten rid of most of her furniture and was putting a number of things in storage until she could have them shipped. Her flight was leaving a week from Sunday. That she was going to stay with a friend until she found a job and place of her own. No, she didn't have a job lined up, but she had a few connections and was confident something would work out. She was fluent in French because she had lived in France before, and also having studied French in college at Augustana in Rock Island. Yes, one of the Quad Cities. She spent a semester in France, studying in Rennes. Then took a semester off to travel around France, making her way around Europe during the summer before coming back to finish her undergraduate degree. Then she taught high school French for two years before going to the University of Illinois in Champaign-Urbana for her Masters in French Literature, where she met her now ex-boyfriend Patrick. He had received a fellowship to study in Paris at the Sorbonne and she went to Paris to be with him. She managed to get a job working as an assistant to writer and historian Bernard Lipton. She and Patrick were there about five months when they broke up, after which she came back to the States.

"Is he still in France?" asked Robert.

Elise nodded.

"I see."

"He married a French woman. Last I heard she was pregnant." She looked down at the grooved gray rubber floor. That was not something Elise revealed to people she had just met. But as each word had come to her mind, it had gone out of her mouth. Again, she thought, there was nothing to lose even if she did feel a bit embarrassed about rehashing her life and how it sounded much sadder than she wanted it to sound. Patrick had his whole Parisian life and what did she have? A string of temp jobs and temp boyfriends, and a lease on a studio apartment that had not been renewed.

Robert knew he had landed on a tender spot and that he ought to be sensitive, not impossible, with how he proceeded. This was not the time to say the first thing that came to his mind, like "Boy, that's gotta suck." He needed to change the subject.

"Must be nice to be able to watch all those movies like *Amélie* or *A Man and a Woman* and not have to look at the bottom of the screen to understand everything that's going on."

She was glad that he hadn't pushed for more about Patrick and pleased that he liked some of the movies that she liked.

"It took a long time to get to that point, but yes, it is nice." Elise then smiled at Robert for a little longer than he knew what was meant. Robert swallowed. Finally, she said, "Thank you."

"For what?"

"For changing the subject."

"You're welcome."

14   A FULL DAY'S WORK

Robert was about to leave his office and head out to lunch with Karen and some of the other people in the department when the phone on his desk rang. His first inclination was to let it ring and go into voicemail. But then he looked on the phone's LCD screen and saw it was his parents' number. That one of his parents was calling him in the middle of the day at the office was odd. It was probably his mother, hounding him to come to his father's birthday dinner. He was going to have to tell her one way or the other, sooner or later. So he picked up the phone.

"Hello."

"Robert?" said his mother.

"Yes."

"You're hard to get a hold of. I called your number and no one answered and when it went into voicemail it didn't identify you as the person at the desk. So I called into the operator and they said you had moved."

"I was promoted."

"A promotion? Oh my gosh! Congratulations!"

"Thank you. I'm the Manager of the QA Department now."

"When did this happen?"

"A few days ago."

"Do you have an office now? Is that why you were so hard to find?"

Robert's office, like those given to the company's decision-makers, was on the outer wall of the building, giving him a window. His was north-facing, giving him a not-so-glorious view of the old concrete building across the street. He sat on his chair that was larger and much more comfortable than the one he had before his promotion when he was tucked away in a cubicle.

Up until Monday, the office had been Perry's. The walls were bare and white, still showing the holes and scratches where Perry's framed posters had been hung. Among the things about Perry that annoyed Robert was Perry's fondness for motivational posters. He'd had a half-dozen of them in his office. Each was framed. Perry's favorite, Robert knew because Perry had on many occasions proclaimed it to be his favorite, was the one for "Success." Under a black-bordered picture of a man standing atop a mountain that overlooked a large expanse of green trees growing out of gray mountains wrapped in clouds, in white letters it read: SUCCESS: DO NOT FEAR IT. Robert had always thought the caption should have been: SUCCESS: THERE ISN'T MUCH OXYGEN AT THE TOP.

Robert hadn't yet figured out what he wanted to put on the walls. He knew it wasn't going to be any of those motivational posters he hated so much. Or a copy of Van Gogh's "Starry Night" or a Monet, or some dull anonymous abstract print done in broad-stroked pastels. He thought a poster of the famous photo of Johnny Cash giving the finger would make an excellent wall decoration, but knew it would not be appropriate for the work environment. He was management now. It was up to him to implement company policy. Not buck it.

"Yes, I have an office now. Though you could've called me on my cell."

"Sorry. You're right. I just...Things are a little strange these days. Is this a good time?"

"Yeah, it's fine."

"I need to talk to you about something."

"I haven't made up my mind yet about dinner on Sunday."

"It's not that. Though I want you to come, of course. It's something more serious."

"Uhm, okay. What?"

"It's your father. He's not feeling very well."

Robert thought his father must be having some health problems. As annoyed as he was by his father (and there were times when he had hated his father), he had always dreaded this day. He thought that his father might be having heart problems caused by all the cigarettes he smoked and the steak, pork chops, hot dogs, Italian beef sandwiches, and French fries he ate.

"Is he all right?" He sat up in his chair.

"He went to work today."

"Yeah? And? Doesn't he go to the hot dog stand every day?"

"No. Not the stand. To his job with the city."

"Aw ma, you had me worried it was his health or something." Robert sat back and opened up his web browser on the computer to look up the box score for the previous night's White Sox game.

"You don't understand. For the fourth day in a row now he's gone into the office."

"What? He finally feeling guilty about ripping off the taxpayers all these years?"

"Robert! He's been very nervous. And it's not just him. Your brothers, too. They're putting in full days at work, too."

"Wow. It's about time."

Karen stood in the open doorway to Robert's office. Robert held up an index finger. She nodded, folding her arms and leaning against the doorframe. She was still getting used to the idea of Robert as the boss. Seeing him in what was once Perry's and Lisa's office seemed weird. Karen was glad it was Robert and not her. She had no desire to be the boss. She liked her job; it provided her with enough challenges without stressing her out and she was able to spend time with her son Christopher, whom she and her partner Wendy had adopted. When it came to work, she trusted Robert in a way she had never trusted Perry and only sometimes trusted Lisa. The former because she thought him an idiot, the latter because for all their friendly exchanges an odd vibe would pop up whenever Karen used words like "my partner" or even "my wife."

"Something is wrong. Very wrong," said his mother.

"No wonder city services are so good these days," said Robert. "The City Council should go on strike more often. Maybe they should just abolish themselves altogether."

In addition to the CTA buses no longer running in packs and L trains arriving and departing with scheduled regularity, people were noticing, too, that the streets were devoid of garbage. No pieces of paper, used soft drink containers, beer cans or bottles, brown paper bags, or cigarette butts were to be found on sidewalks, easements, or lawns, or in the gutters clogging the drains. It was as if the people living in the city had suddenly discovered the numerous trash cans that were provided on so many of its streets. And those trash cans were never overflowing, getting emptied promptly by city employees.

"You think you're so funny," said Mrs. Grabowski. "Every day he leaves earlier and earlier, so he can get a parking space. He says there's not enough parking for all the workers."

"Why?"

"Something about the strike and how no one has cover from anything anymore. It all sounds so insane."

"Yeah, insane...What do you want from me? I've got someone waiting for me and a million things to do."

"I was hoping for a little sympathy. I guess I should have known better." Then she hung up.

Robert set the phone back on its cradle. His family was crazy, he thought, in the way most families were not, which is why he should have stayed in California. Why did he come back? Oh, yeah, Marcia wanted to come back, for the family and all that. And now he was receiving phone calls from his mother about his father finally not being a ghost worker at the city's Department of Transportation. The image of his father and numerous other ghost payrollees circling the parking lot, and looking for empty parking spots brought a smile to his face. He wondered if there were enough desks and chairs for all the people on the payroll, or if they literally had to play a game of musical chairs.

"Who was that?" asked Karen.

"My mother."

"Sounds like a pleasant conversation."

"It usually is."

15   A FEW IN THE KNOW

Coming home from work, Robert saw Mr. Logan, the building manager, with his two dogs, Nelson and Solomon. He was a retired policeman and widower who owned a condo in St. Petersburg, but managed the building and a few three-flats on behalf of the landlords, who were old friends from the police force.

Logan and his dogs were at the corner of Sunnyside and Bob Fosse Way. Solomon was a golden labrador. Nelson was a mutt; a mixture of black labrador and German shepherd, and what else Logan didn't know, having rescued him six years before from an animal shelter. The people of the neighborhood knew Nelson to be the better behaved of the two. Solomon would attempt to jump on every person and dog he met, all the while yelping an endless stream of barks and yowls, much to the constant anger of Ms. Porter, Robert's next-door neighbor. She owned a white Shih Tzu, one of the many little dogs in the neighborhood that was often terrorized by Solomon.

Robert checked his watch. It was a quarter after six. He figured he had just enough time to change out of his suit and into something more comfortable, and walk over to Lincoln Square to meet Elise. And he still hadn't called Janet to cancel. Even with twin two-year-old girls, Janet still kept the late hours of a musician.

"Hi, Robert," said Logan. "Beautiful day, isn't it?"

Robert braced himself, pulling up his bag and holding it in both hands. He expected Solomon's usual rush, followed by Logan's cry of, "Solomon! Solomon!...Don't worry, he's just friendly." But Solomon trotted along, then stopped to sniff at something in the grass.

"Yeah, it is," said Robert.

Mr. Logan had gray curly hair, deep-set blue eyes, and a nose that was red and bubbled with gin blossoms. He had been sober for almost 11 years. As a police officer, he had earned promotions through clout all the way up to Captain. But the night he showed up for duty drunk, and proceeded to drink at his desk from a bottle of whiskey, was his last night on the job. His colleagues could not cover up for him that time. When he was told to take early retirement or face a disciplinary hearing he was shocked. His drunken fog had kept him from seeing all the many ways his closest friends on the force had propped him up, especially since his wife Elaine had died at the age of 48 from Leukemia a few years before then. He would only begin to see those props after he had been sober for five or six months. While his drinking had clouded everything, he had used his clout within the police department as a way to insulate himself from ever having to be accountable for his drinking and the ways in which it had ravaged his life, from alienating his children to emotionally torturing his wife. He had always told himself that he was better than his father because he never physically abused Elaine. According to that measure he was surely a better husband and father. Out of all the things he had managed to make amends for, even reconciling with his children, he regretted never getting the chance to set things right with Elaine while she was alive.

"I just got back from taking these guys to the lake," said Mr. Logan, patting Nelson and Solomon on their backs. "You should see it. It's so calm. I can't remember the last time it was like that. It's really something. We just don't get days like this very often. But we've had nearly two weeks in a row like this. It's almost eerie how every day has been so beautiful."

Robert nodded toward the dogs. "I bet these guys had a good time."

"Oh yeah. They love to run around out there. The exercise is good for 'em. Oh, before I forget, Robert. I need to speak to you in private about something."

"What's up?" asked Robert.

"I can't tell you here." He led the dogs toward their building.

"I'm not being evicted or anything, right? The building's not going condo is it?"

He shook his head. "No. Nothing like that. Something else. Come on." He motioned for Robert to follow.

Robert followed, wishing Mr. Logan would tell him whatever news he had right away, because there was no such thing as a short conversation with him. Robert didn't have a whole lot of time before he was supposed to meet Elise. Maybe if he made it quick, didn't let himself get sidetracked, it would be okay. But if it was something related to the building why wouldn't a letter be sent to everyone? Since Logan wanted to speak to him in private, that meant it was something related to only a few in the know and he would be better off knowing sooner rather than later.

16   CHICAGOESE

John Logan's two-bedroom apartment was on the top floor in the back right corner of the U-shaped building.

"Come on in," said Mr. Logan, as he opened the door for Robert.

Robert saw the usual mess on the coffee table; papers of different sizes, shapes (some ripped, some not), and colors, with handwritten notes on them. Then there were two neat stacks of white typewritten pages. On top of the stack at one corner of the table was a pair of black-rimmed reading glasses. Robert hoped the conversation would stick close to the reason Mr. Logan had wanted to see him in the first place, which hopefully had nothing to do with the mess on the table.

"Thanks," said Robert. "What's going on? What's so important you couldn't tell me outside?"

Mr. Logan pointed to the table. "I've been cataloging our language."

"Besides that."

"Don't neglect your culture, Robert."

"I'm not neglecting anything."

Mr. Logan went around the coffee table and sat in the armchair. "Chicagoese, Robert," he said as if it was a light reprimand.

Robert gripped the bag strap in his right hand and shoved his left hand into his pants pocket. "It's not a language, Mr. Logan. It's a dialect. One that I'm sure some linguist in some university somewhere in these United States, maybe our very own state of Illinois, has accounted for."

"Ah, but have they created a modified alphabet or specific spellings for the very purpose of symbolically representing our language? I think not."

"I'm sure there are plenty of professional linguists."

Mr. Logan scrunched up his nose. "Professionals. What do they know? They'll doctor it all up and explain it so that only five other people can understand it. And the rest of us will be out of luck."

"That's not how it works," said Robert.

"Take the word *three*," said Mr. Logan, reaching out to grab his reading glasses and putting them on. "No one here says *thh-ree*. We say *tree*. We don't do the *th* sound. We say *doze*, as in *doze two over by dere*."

"Sounds great, Mr. Logan." Robert rubbed his forehead, frustrated that Mr. Logan had not told him what was going on outside and saved him this aggravation.

"And did I tell you, Robert, that I applied for a grant from the National Endowment for the Humanities?"

"No."

Mr. Logan sat back and folded his hands, resting them on his stomach. "I've applied for a grant from the National Endowment for the Humanities. They got a program for supporting dying languages. I should hear from them any day now. I bet once I get that, more people will take notice. Especially these ignorant newscasters we got."

Mr. Logan had written numerous letters to the local TV and radio news stations asking for newscasts to be done completely in Chicagoese. He was known derisively and humorously amongst the producers and reporters as "Logan the Linguist."

"They're educated," said Robert. "So they talk the way educated people are supposed to talk."

"People like you forget how you're supposed to talk. You've become ashamed of who you are."

"I talk how an intelligent person is supposed to talk. That's nothing to be ashamed of."

"According to whose rules? Far as I'm concerned, college is corrupting our kids, like you. A good Chicagoan like you should be speaking proper Chicagoese."

"It's just an uneducated way of talking. A way, I should point out, that only white people talk. Blacks and Hispanics don't—"

"The mayor talks Chicagoese."

"But that doesn't make it right!"

"According to who?"

Robert threw his left hand up in the air. "Everyone."

"Who's everyone?"

"Everyone that knows how to talk correctly."

"Yes, people who don't talk like us. What if we were the majority? Then everyone would be talking like us. We would be the ones makin' the rules about what's the right way and wrong way to say and spell things. Right now, we're being oppressed."

"Dammit! There's just no talking to you about this."

"If it's not a language then what does the following sentence mean?"

"Oh, come on."

"Listen, Robert: *Jeet yet?*"

Robert rolled his eyes. "Actually, I'm running late for dinner. I'm meeting someone."

"See? You understand me."

"Most people in Chicago would understand that. And I'm not kidding about running late."

"But you see how that came to be? First people said, *Did you eat yet?* Then it became, *Didjya eat yet?* Then *Jeet yet?* It's our own special contraction."

"It's good we have people like you to keep track of all the changes in our language." Robert looked away from Logan and the mess on the table between them. His irritation was enlarging with every word related to Logan's quixotic cause and his own inability to extricate himself more quickly from the conversation. Being very late to a dinner for which he had offered to pay was not a classy thing to do. Through the living room picture window Robert saw the bright light outside. The weather was still wonderful, perfect for eating a meal on a restaurant sidewalk.

"Which brings me to the main reason I asked you up here to talk," said Mr. Logan.

"Finally."

"We all have to cool it for awhile on the free cable. I've been warned that a big crackdown is coming. So I've had to cut everyone off until I get the all clear from my guy."

Robert snapped his head back at him. He'd had to endure that whole goofy conversation for something Logan could have simply whispered to him out in the courtyard? "A crackdown? Shoot! What am I going to do?"

"Use your antenna."

Robert threw both hands straight up into the air. "But I can't watch Sox games on broadcast TV. They're on a cable channel."

"Sucks to be a White Sox fan. Now if you were a Cubs fan like me you could watch them on WCHI."

"Very funny...All right. I understand. Thanks for the warning, Mr. Logan."

"No problem. I'm sorry. But if even one of us gets caught, we'll all get caught."

Robert turned to go. "I understand. Any idea when we'll get the all clear for the cable?"

Mr. Logan pursed his lips. "My guess is a couple of weeks. But I can't make you any promises."

17   AN INTERESTING WAY TO PICK UP WOMEN

As soon as he was out the door, Robert checked his watch again. It was 25 minutes to seven. He ran down the stairs, across the courtyard, past the mailboxes, and up the stairs to his third-floor apartment. He opened his door and yanked off the yellow Post-it note from Mr. Logan, telling Robert he needed to talk to him at his earliest convenience. Into his bedroom he flung his suit coat which landed on the bed. It was followed by his tie, pants, white dress shirt, and socks. He put on a pair of khaki shorts, a dark blue T-shirt, and a pair of brown sandals.

Outside, Robert headed North toward Wilson. He thought that he should have gone the other way and caught an L train, but then he would have felt stupid for taking the L to go just two stops. Then he remembered he was supposed to call Janet to cancel their plans. He pulled out his cell phone and dialed her number.

Janet Fischman had been the rhythm guitarist, backup singer, and one of the principal songwriters for the band Gin Wolf. They had toured successfully after their first album was released on Spoon River Records. Their self-titled debut had received great reviews and sold over 150,000 copies, quite a lot for a band on a small independent label. The band had appeared to have hit it big only to dissolve during the recording of their first album for a major record label. They were one of a handful of bands that had signed major label contracts at the tail-end of the Chicago music gold rush in the mid-'90s. Robert had known her since he had been roommates in college with her cousin David. David had explained that Janet came from the hippie wing of his family. Her father was an art teacher and her mother taught dance. David had taken Robert with him to see her play in her first band, Bubbly Creek, at a club in Champaign.

"Hey, Janet. It's Robert."

"What's up?"

"I'm sorry, but I can't make it tonight. Something's come up."

"That's okay. What happened?"

"It's a long story. But I'm buying this woman dinner because she got all pissed off at me."

"Uh, that's a new one. Sounds like an interesting way to pick up women. I have to tell you: no guy ever tried that strategy with me."

"Like they'd get a chance to try a strategy. You'd club 'em and drag them home with you before they got the chance."

"Real funny there Robert. But it sounds like your strategy worked."

"It's not a strategy. I didn't pick her up. I'll explain later."

"Come on over Saturday night at nine or so. The girls'll be in bed by then and you can tell me and Mark all about your date."

"It's not a date!"

"Whatever you say."

18   IT WASN'T A DATE

Elise was waiting with her arms folded in front of the entrance to Café Selmarie. The restaurant was near the middle of the two-block strip of Lincoln Avenue that was known as the heart of the Lincoln Square neighborhood, so named for the statue of President Abraham Lincoln at its north end at the intersection with Lawrence Avenue. Next to the restaurant was a small park-like area with a gazebo between Lincoln Avenue where Giddings once intersected but now dead-ended. In the park, three middle school-aged boys were going back and forth on the cement, attempting to flip their skateboards under their feet. Elise hadn't seen a successful attempt yet. She half-wished she still smoked because it would give her something to do while she waited. Smoking was always a great time-killer. Then she wouldn't have to stand there with nothing to do but wonder if Robert was going to show up. It was a nice gesture but such a silly thing to do; take her out to dinner to make up for starting an infuriating argument. He couldn't possibly be trying to seduce her. After getting off of work, she had stopped at her apartment and re-applied her lipstick, but had not bothered to reapply her mascara or retouch her hair. It wasn't a date. If he showed up, she was not going to seduce him. She did not want to seduce him. Not that a nice little fling before leaving the country would be a bad thing. What was he after? Or was he as nice as he had seemed? Someone who watched *Amélie* and *A Man and a Woman* couldn't be all bad. Of course, her ex, Patrick, had liked those movies, too, and look at what kind of cheating, self-absorbed jerk he was.

Elise looked around the corner into the square. One of the skateboarders flipped his board then successfully landed on it. He raised his arms in celebration. Only three tables on the sidewalk next to the café were empty. What if the conversation went dull? Small price to pay for a free dinner. If he didn't come soon though, there weren't going to be any open tables outside.

She looked back down Lincoln Avenue and saw Robert walking fast, almost at a jog. He waved to Elise and she waved back.

As soon as he reached her, he said, "I'm sorry I'm late. I got stuck in an argument with the building manager at my apartment."

She smiled. "You get into a lot of arguments."

Robert let out a snort. "That might actually be true. But this guy wants the TV news to be done in Chicagoese, okay? He thinks it should be an officially recognized language and taught in the schools. I had to at least attempt to get it through his thick old head that he's totally misguided."

"You talk that way to the guy who could leave you without heat or a working refrigerator?"

"Chicagoese is not a language!" Robert threw his arms out.

"I agree with you," said Elise as she began to laugh.

"What's so funny?"

"You. You really don't think much before you speak."

"A point had to be made."

"So you're this way with everyone?"

A bashful grin formed on Robert's face. "For the most part."

She let out another giggle.

"Are you hungry?" he asked.

"Yes."

"Then let's eat."

"Which do you prefer? Inside or outside?"

"Outside. Looks like we might get one of the last tables," said Robert with an upward nod at the tables.

19   WHY IT WAS CALLED THE CITY OF LIGHTS

Elise dabbed her mouth with her napkin and sat back. She reached for her cup of coffee and said, before taking a sip, "That was a delicious meal."

"I'm glad you think so."

"Oh, I know so." Using her fork, she scraped up the remaining crumbs of her flourless chocolate cake and put them in her mouth. She savored the richness of the chocolate as she savored the same quality of the conversation so far. Prompted by her, Robert had filled Elise in on his own history throughout the meal. After he and his girlfriend Maggie graduated from the University of Illinois in 1993, they moved to the Bay Area. She landed a job in the Marketing Department of Hewlett-Packard, he in the QA Department of Sun Microsystems. They broke up a few months after the move. It was a few years later that he met Marcia through a friend of a friend. She was fresh out of Stanford law school and working in the District Attorney's office in San Francisco. They had bonded fast, knowing a lot of the same area of the Northwest side of Chicago where they had both grown up, he being from Jefferson Park and she being from the suburb of Elmwood Park. They went to Europe to celebrate being together for a year, spending roughly five days each in London and Paris, with a few days in Prague and Berlin. Everyone thought they would come back engaged. They didn't. Marcia always said she eventually wanted to come back to Chicago to be near her family. Meanwhile, Robert worked at a couple of Internet start-ups during the dot-com boom. They were living in San Francisco. Then they were engaged. Then the boom went bust.

Watching all that money and those stock options thrown around at large numbers of people who put in crushing amounts of frenetic hours was for most people, including Robert, nothing more than some very good (and occasionally amazing) experience. It had not yielded any major financial rewards. Nothing even remotely close to the catapulting gains so storied and dreamed for.

Marcia and Robert had moved back to Chicago for the wedding and to settle. He got a job at Fourth National and she with the Federal Government. Robert had not wanted to come back to Chicago. But when he got back he saw just how much the city had changed for the better. They lived well again for a short while. But they did not work out.

Elise had decided to honor his own sensitivity about Patrick by not probing any further about Marcia. It was only fair. Besides, she understood what it was to follow a love only to have it turn on you. She set her empty fork on her empty dessert plate.

Robert looked down at his own empty dessert plate. "You know, I have a confession to make. I do like Paris and I am in fact a bit envious of what you're doing. It takes a lot of guts to up and leave your own country for another." He brought his eyes up to hers. "One of the things I wanted to do when I was there was to see why it was called the City of Lights."

Elise sat up a little. One of the things she had enjoyed the most about living in Paris was going to the Eiffel Tower at night to look at the city. The lights emerged from the deep, wide boulevards. Then came the lights from the narrow side streets, splintering, turning, and criss-crossing to create a series of jagged random-looking paths. To her it was one of the best ways to see Paris, to see the loose order of that old elegant city. Patrick had only gone with her once, the first time, and then never again. She had taken in that view at least a half-dozen times by herself.

Robert rested his elbows on the table. "Marcia and I had spent the entire day at the Louvre and both of us were tired. After dinner Marcia just wanted to stay in. She wasn't too keen on going out at all or even to the Eiffel Tower because we'd gone there the day before. But anyway, I wanted to see what the city looked like at night from the Eiffel Tower. So I did." In his mind, Robert saw the lights, brighter than in any other city to which he had been, each representing a life, a possibility, a path to take. At 27 there seemed to be countless paths still to take. A few he should've taken. There were fewer now.

Elise's lips were parted. While Robert was lost in thought, she was still with expectation at Robert's impression of the view she cherished.

"And what did you think?" she asked just above a whisper.

"Beautiful," he said, not letting go of the image inside his head.

"It was my favorite way to see the city."

"I think it's mine, too. If I ever get the chance to go back to Paris, that's one of the things I'd like to do again."

Elise felt light-headed, like she might faint. Here she was less than two weeks away from leaving the country and now she meets a guy who could carry on a lively conversation, was smart, sensitive (well, capable of it, when he wasn't starting arguments), and appreciative of Paris in the same way she was.

Robert thought Elise's face looked pained. He hoped it wasn't anything she had eaten. Then he would feel real bad. Here he had taken her out to dinner as a way to make things up to her, and then she had gotten sick from the meal. Real nice.

"Are you okay?" he asked.

"Yes. I'm fine. It's just been a long day."

"Then we should go." Robert called the waitress over and paid the check.

20   BUT THE TIMING WAS ALL WRONG

"You walking or taking the L?" asked Robert when they stepped outside the restaurant.

"Walking," said Elise, hoping he would walk with her. Her light-headedness had changed to giddiness, causing her to wonder if she was being seduced. Highly unlikely if not downright impossible. He could not possibly have known the view of Paris he had liked so much was the one she loved the most.

"Which way? I can walk you back to your place, if you want."

"Sure. If it's not too far out of your way. I live on Wolcott, just off Montrose."

Robert didn't want to come off pushy, as if he was trying to jump her bones. He had not had any significant relationships with any women since the dissolution of his engagement to Marcia. There had not been any women as fascinating and intelligent as Elise. Since she was leaving this would in all likelihood be the only evening he spent with her. And other than the possibility of a chance meeting on the L, this would most likely be the last time he saw her. He did not want to do or say anything that could crack the zamboni-smooth ice their conversation was blissfully skating on.

"That's not out of my way at all," he said. "I'm over on Bob Fosse Way."

"Do people break out in sexy dance on your street?"

He chuckled. "No. Fosse's boyhood home is there."

"Is the gin cold and the piano hot?"

"There's no hall with a nightly brawl or all that jazz. It's usually pretty quiet."

Robert offered Elise his arm. She took it and they headed down Lincoln Avenue, passing the Huettenbar tavern and the Degerberg Martial Arts Academy.

Elise could hear the clicks of a handful of numbers on a long combination lock falling into place to open and let loose all the passions, fears, secrets, drives, and loyalty only revealed and given to a special few. Love came down to just such a combination of personalities, luck, and timing. Unfortunately, if it was love, which it probably wasn't because no one fell in love over a single dinner, the timing was all wrong.

They came to the end of the block. A car turned in front of them and they crossed, going under the L tracks near the Western Avenue stop.

"Can I ask you something?" she said.

"Sure," he said.

"Did you ever really believe you would get rich while you were working at one of those Silicon Valley start-ups?"

"No. Both of the start-ups I worked for had good ideas, but they weren't the kind that cause a real, to borrow an overused phrase from that era, *paradigm shift*. Plus, they weren't the most well-managed companies. People in that era seemed to collectively forget just how hard it is to start and run a business. But it was fun while it lasted."

"The whole dot-com boom seems ages ago."

"Because no one's expecting large sums of money to fall into their laps so they can sell something, no matter how crazy, on or for the Internet."

"But 9/11 feels like yesterday."

"Everyone in this country is bracing to get hit again."

On the other side of the street was the Davis Theater. They walked in silence until Wilson Avenue, where Elise indicated they should turn left.

21 SO...

They were focused on the touch of Elise's hand on Robert's arm and their easy pace. Both were trying to figure out the answer to the question: What next? This was by far the best first date they could remember having in a long time. But it wasn't supposed to be a date. No, it wasn't a date. It was a make-up dinner. A gesture of goodwill from Robert to Elise. Nothing more.

They eventually passed the closed Ravenswood Hospital complex. A sign announced that condos were coming soon. Robert frowned at the sign. The company Derek worked for, CLT Development, was one of the partners in the redevelopment of the defunct hospital. He had offered to give Robert a large break on the price for one of the units. Robert had turned it down because he said he wasn't interested in anything too permanent.

At Wolcott they turned right. Elise unconsciously squeezed Robert's arm. Should she invite him up? No. He was too nice to fling with. She didn't want to be attached to him or anyone else for that matter. She was leaving. If not for good, at least for a very long while. But those clicks...She wanted to see him again, but what pretext could she use? She had better think of something quick. There was now less than a block and a half to her apartment.

Robert had no idea how he could ask to see her again without it being a date, or seeming to take her out on a date. She could not possibly be interested in any kind of relationship, platonic or otherwise, with any guy. She had plans that had been long in the making. If she wanted them to be interrupted, she would interrupt them herself.

After Sunnyside, Elise could see her building easily. Due to the Asian Long Horn Beetle infestation, there were only low stumps where the trees had once stood. On those hot, humid days in July, the only shade available on the entire block came from the hot brick buildings themselves. She thought about the dinner party her friend Jen and her fiancé Jay were having Saturday night to celebrate their engagement. She could ask Robert to come with. But that might be awkward for him. He'll only know her and no one else. That might not be the best situation for him. Of course, it might be a good test for him. See how he does with her friends. See what Jen thinks. But there was no point in testing him. There was nothing to test for. She wasn't serious about him. And he wasn't serious about her. He couldn't be.

She had been up front and honest about her plans. He had to know nothing could come of the two of them.

"Here's my place," she said, letting go of his arm and pointing to her building. They stopped in front of the black metal gate near the sidewalk.

Robert thought it looked a lot like the one in front of his apartment building. Then he wondered if the alderman had persuaded the landlords in the ward to buy from the same fence supplier, promising that the recommended supplier always provided code-compliant fencing. A fence company that just so happened to be run by a friend or relative of the alderman. Robert knew who to ask to find out but didn't want to know. These internal speculations (figuring out the angle of corruption) were a habit that he had managed to tone down since returning to Chicago.

"All right."

She clasped both hands around the handle of her purse. "Well, thank you. I had a wonderful time. That was the best make-it-up-to-you meal I've ever had."

"You're welcome. I enjoyed myself quite a bit tonight."

"I have to say, after our argument I never thought I would have this much fun with you. I never thought it was possible to have any fun with you."

"I don't blame you for thinking that. I'm just glad I could make it up to you."

"You more than did."

Robert looked up at her building, to its windows, wondering which one was hers. "So..."

Elise looked back at her building then back to Robert. "So..."

Robert smiled at Elise and said, "I guess I should say *bon voyage* and best of luck in your new life across the Atlantic." He held out his hand.

Elise looked at Robert's hand. This was it. Her last chance. She took his hand and they shook.

"Good night," she said.

"Good night," he said.

Elise walked to the door and went inside.

22   A FLIMSY EXCUSE

Robert waited on the sidewalk until he saw Elise enter the inner door of the building before he walked away. He strolled back up Wolcott and turned right on Sunnyside. He remembered again that cool night at the top of the Eiffel Tower. He had been alone as someone who was alone. Everyone else had been paired or in a small group. All those possibilities spread before him. He couldn't remember now what they were. But he remembered vividly one he should have taken. Later, he would have to reckon with the criticism Marcia had hurled at him and that was echoed repeatedly by friends and family: how could someone who was known for speaking up so often on so many things, often to his own detriment, not have opened his mouth sooner about something so important as not wanting to get married to her? Marcia had told him she felt betrayed, that their relationship had been an illusion like the mirage of wealth available for everyone working in Silicon Valley. He didn't have an answer then and he didn't have an answer as he walked under the L tracks.

He came to the Southbound stretch of Ravenswood, on the West side of the Metra train tracks. (The Metra tracks were lined on each side by Ravenswood street; northbound on the east and southbound on the west.) Most of the street was brick. Robert wondered once they got done renovating every building in the neighborhood, would they rip up all that old brick and replace it with asphalt? How old was it? 100 years? Or would they just pave over it, covering up a distinctive, though imperfect, feature of the neighborhood? He paused for a moment to examine the bricks. Whatever mortar had been used to keep them in place appeared to have slowly disintegrated, creating thick gaps between the fat red bricks that were worn round and smooth. It made for a bumpy car ride.

Robert crossed the brick street and walked under the low-set Metra train tracks. He noticed the sidewalk under the tracks was severely cracked. Weeds were popping up in a few places. On the corner of the Northbound stretch of Ravenswood, the building that had been the home of Joanne's, a breakfast spot Robert had frequented, was covered in scaffolding. There were rumors that an art gallery and restaurant were going to occupy the renovated building. There were rumors, too, that the Zephyr, a restaurant and ice cream parlor a block North up on Wilson, was being forced out by the landlords of the property in which it resided. Robert thought that many of the good things about the neighborhood were leaving or had left, including La Ville Venteuse and Elise. He wished he had met her sooner. One meal could not make a person fall in love, he was sure. But it was a much stronger tug than most. If he got another chance to spend more time with her, how would he feel? Would this little tug grow into something more? Oh, please, how could his mind jump to such conclusions?

"Hey!" he heard a familiar female voice shout from behind him.

Robert turned around. A woman was jogging toward him. She was under the train tracks so he couldn't see who it was at first. As she emerged from the shadow of the tracks into the light of the street lamps, he saw that it was Elise. Robert took a few steps toward her.

"Robert!" she said, wondering what in God's name was possessing her to run toward Robert and use a flimsy excuse to see him again. An excuse he would probably think was lame, and then reject, thus killing this potential relationship once and for all so she could leave for Paris without any entanglements.

"Hey," he said.

"I've got this thing to go to Saturday night. Would you mind coming along?"

Robert didn't care what it was. He said, "Yes."

"It's a dinner party. It should be a lot of fun. I just don't want to be the only one uncoupled. I know it sounds stupid. But I can promise you it'll be a very good meal. My friend Jen is an excellent cook."

Robert was nodding. "Sure, I'll go," he said, knowing he would have to cancel with Janet again.

"Great. I really appreciate it. It's not a date. I hope that doesn't bother you. You understand? I just don't want to lead you on about anything. But you're really nice and I had such a good time tonight."

"Oh, no. I understand. You've got plans and I don't want to upset them."

"Wonderful. Can you come by my place around seven? We can take the L or catch a cab to the party."

"Yeah. That sounds good."

As Elise walked away, she thought life was far too short not to at least take a harder look at the possibility in front of her.

Robert watched her disappear on the other side of the tracks, the tug in his chest feeling a little bit stronger.

23   A LITTLE RAIN

The rain started slow before midnight. A few drops with every passing minute until it became steady. It lasted for a few hours, dropping an inch of water before stopping. There were no gusts of wind, nor was there any thunder or lightning. Just the first steady rain in nearly two weeks. Enough to water plants starting to wilt and grass starting to get brown at the edges, and wash away the accumulated dust and dirt on the streets and sidewalks.

24   IT'S NOT TOO LATE TO CHANGE YOUR MIND

Elise was sitting behind the reception desk Friday morning deleting old email messages from her work account. She had made this a routine part of her day during the previous weeks. She didn't care about maxing out the space on her account. It was a way to pass the time and get rid of unimportant messages; HR bulletins, mass emails that didn't apply to her, and job requests older than a few months. She had just arranged for a taxi cab to pick up one of the firm's attorneys at 11 that morning and take him to O'Hare airport. Once she had finished deleting another batch of messages, she looked to see if Jen was online. If not, she was going to send her an email. She hadn't yet told Jen that she had invited Robert to come along to the dinner party. She knew Jen wouldn't mind. If Jen and their friends liked Robert, she was going to get grief from Jen. One nice evening out was not reason enough to drop everything. If he made an ass out of himself at Jen's then it would be that much easier to drop him and leave. Not that she could even drop him. You had to be holding on to something first in order to be able to drop it.

Seeing that Jen was online, she started typing a message to her.

Elise: is it okay if I bring a friend with me tomorrow night?
Jen: sure
Jen: don't want to be a 5th wheel?
Elise: exactly
Jen: who?
Elise: robert
Jen: who's that?
Elise: the guy who took me out last night
Jen: it went that well? :o
Elise: no
Jen: I don't understand

Elise: just **friends**, nothing more
Jen: of course ;)
Elise: I'm serious!
Elise: details to follow
Jen: I believe U

"Bonjour, Elise," said Paul Laurent. His bespectacled figure was standing in front of the desk. Elise was a bit startled, not having noticed him until he spoke.

"Bonjour, Monsieur Laurent," she said. Then she typed "brb" to Jen.

"You know, it is not too late to change your mind," he said with an encouraging smile.

"The job?"

He put his left hand on the desk, his right holding his briefcase. "I spoke with my friend over at the French school last night. They still have an opening there. I could arrange an interview for you if you like."

"Really." She curled in her lips. What if she took the interview and then got the job? Then what?

"It is up to you," he said. "But don't think too much longer. They need to fill the position as soon as possible. Classes start at the end of this month."

"I'm sorry. I can't."

His smile flattened. "I understand. But if you change your mind in the next day or so, please do not hesitate to contact me."

Laurent went off to his meeting. Elise watched him walk down the long corridor and around a corner, wondering why Chicago was suddenly trying to make it hard for her to leave. Within a week she had met a nice guy and had a prospect for a real job that would enable her to use her skills and talents. Life was not fair.

25 NOT SO WINDY CITY

Some of the many people who doubt the efficacy of the Chicago City Council strike of 2003 say that it could not have been the cause of so many unexpected bountiful occurrences. These doubters often cite the disappearance of the wind in Chicago during that period of time. They point out, as most Chicagoans know, that August is the least windy month of the year in the city. It also happens to be the month when the mayor and all members of the City Council leave for their vacations.

Chicagoans do not believe this is a coincidence.

Others say it is remarkable that the wind stayed absent with so many Chicago politicians holding so many press conferences during the strike.

26 HOW THE BATTLE BETWEEN THE MAYOR AND THE CITY COUNCIL SETTLED INTO A ROUTINE

On his lunch break, Robert took a cab up to Washington Square Park. He wanted to see for himself the spectacle of Chicago aldermen talking non-stop.

The striking aldermen had claimed Washington Square Park as their base of operations since the Monday following the strike declaration. "Bughouse Square" was the formerly common nickname for Washington Square Park when it had served as a public free speech zone during the first half of the 20th century, hosting discourses, debates, and rants of all kinds, all day, every day.

A few days after the 31 striking aldermen had settled into Bughouse Square, Mayor Nash tried to have them removed from the park. He claimed that what they were doing was a demonstration on city land requiring a permit. All demonstrations on city land required a permit from the Park District. Since the aldermen didn't have a permit, the mayor reasoned, they had no right to be there in the park. They were squatters. Removing the aldermen and their supporters would require the efforts of Park District employees and many members of the Police Department, many of whom owed their jobs or promotions to not just the mayor but also to the striking aldermen. Not to mention the fact they were public servants. Did public servants need a permit to hold press conferences on city-owned land? A columnist for *The Chicago Tribune* asked Mayor Nash if he would use bulldozers to remove the aldermen. After all, the mayor had once sent a man with a bulldozer in the middle of the night to destroy the runway on the lakefront airport known as Meigs Field. He had done this so he could spike the legal battle between the pilots and the Park District and turn the small airport into a park. The mayor accused the columnist of making jokes about a very serious situation.

Two days after Mayor Nash first mentioned it, the demonstration permit argument was dropped. It was rumored that some of the mayor's closest aides had informed him that evicting or arresting the aldermen would be a big public debacle for everyone, especially him, because it would force people to sympathize with the aldermen.

With the permit argument becoming a non-issue, the ebb and flow of the battle between the striking aldermen and the mayor quickly settled into a routine. The striking aldermen held press conferences every morning to respond to whatever attacks the mayor and his supporters had launched against them the night before. The mayor held a press conference at City Hall in the early afternoon to respond to attacks made by the aldermen. The aldermen then sent out press releases and held another press conference in the late afternoon to respond to attacks made by the mayor. In the evening, the mayor sent out press releases and responded to attacks made by the aldermen. The next morning, the cycle began again. For news organizations and bloggers, it was a bonanza. Members of the media had begun to joke amongst themselves that the City Council strike wasn't so much a strike as it was one big endless press conference.

Political pundits, editorial writers, and cartoonists for the city's daily and alternative weekly newspapers had no uniform opinion of the strike. While the editorial boards of the dailies sympathized with the striking alderman that the mayor could often be dictatorial, they argued that a strike was neither a proper or civilized means of making their voices heard. That only the vigorous exercise of democracy within the council's chamber would serve the cause of the people of the city of Chicago. The alternative weeklies were dubious of the motives of the striking aldermen, but were glad that finally someone was sticking it to the so-called "Imperial Mayor." One cartoon printed in the pages of *The Chicago Sun-Times* that found itself clipped to refrigerators and emailed to friends showed Aldermen Otter and Campbell smiling broadly while a coterie of aides placed fake halos on top of their heads and glued angel wings onto their backs. Mayor Nash was in the background with smoke coming out of his ears, fists shaking, mouth wide open, his own halo bent and falling off his head, with a bubble caption of, "You'll never get away with this!"

When Robert arrived at Bughouse Square, he saw that a stage with a podium had been set up at the north end of the park. Alderman William (Bill) Campbell was at the podium. He was the alderman who represented the ward that comprised the Gold Coast and Streeterville neighborhoods, and a portion of the Loop business district. Standing behind him were at least a dozen other aldermen, including John Wisniewski, the man to whom Robert's father had pledged his loyalty. Camera crews were parked on Walton, but not between the podium and the Newberry Library. (The aldermen had wanted to make sure the library was in the shot every time one of them spoke onstage, giving more dignity to the scene. Few aldermen had actually been inside the Newberry Library.) In front of the stage, fenced off from the rest of the park, was a place for cameras and other members of the media. Behind the media, a few hundred people stood listening. Robert only caught the tail end of Campbell's speech.

"It's about giving everyone in this city a voice in how it's run, a well-deserved voice," Campbell was saying. "People work hard and pay taxes. And for that they deserve a true voice. That's why we're here, every day, listening, holding a vigil until the mayor understands that some serious changes are going to be made to how the government works on behalf of the people. It's not supposed to work just for the mayor. It's supposed to work for the people, you!"

There were loud cheers from the crowd and lots of clapping behind him by the other aldermen.

Robert had seen a lot of crazy things in Chicago politics. As the cheering died down, Robert muttered to himself, "What's next?" Aldermen going on strike was not something he or anyone else, including the striking aldermen themselves, had foreseen.

27   SWITCHING STATUES

Alderman Bill Campbell was not known for being an unruly radical. Far from it. He was known for his prudent management in overseeing the construction of numerous high-rise office buildings, hotels, and luxury apartments and condominiums in his ward. In the process he had gained much praise from business and civic leaders and his constituents. The ward had continued to be a clean and well-maintained wealthy enclave of the city, or as he had once put it in a council meeting, "the high-falutin' part of town." He was also well-known for proposing bills to alleviate nuisances. Once, after receiving complaints from residents that some store and restaurant signs adorning the buildings on the Magnificent Mile were too garish, he successfully ushered through an ordinance that limited the size of signs and the amount of wattage they could emit when lighted. He once proposed a ban on the use of skateboards on city sidewalks located in most of the downtown area, saying the skateboarders were a hazard to pedestrians. That ordinance was sent to the Rules Committee, a committee whose sole purpose was to provide a convenient place for unpopular proposals to die. The committee's chairman, Alderman Anthony Soldiamori, used his infamous, gold-inlaid, black Louisville Slugger to bludgeon proposals to death. When a mylar balloon from a children's birthday party held in Lake Shore Park drifted into some power lines and cut power to over 1000 residents of his ward and several businesses along with the Museum of Contemporary Art, Campbell demanded that sales of mylar balloons be banned in the city. That proposal was sent to the Rules Committee. He had also introduced an ordinance banning all cell phone usage while sitting in restaurants, saying there was nothing more rude or annoying than someone talking loudly on a cell phone at the table next to you. That proposal was also sent to the Rules Committee.

What had long unnerved Alderman Campbell (and what he believed to be a serious problem) was the fact that the large statue of Abraham Lincoln (not to be confused with the smaller one in Lincoln Square) was located in Grant Park while the statue of Ulysses S. Grant was located in Lincoln Park. No one had ever explained this apparent inconsistency. It made more sense to Campbell for the statues of two of the state's greatest heroes to be in the parks that were named for them. To rectify this problem, Alderman Campbell had proposed that a study be undertaken to determine the costs and ramifications of switching the statues in the two lakefront parks. He had believed, since there was little harm in studying the matter, that his proposal would be easily approved.

Mayor Nash had thought it a ridiculous waste of money to study what he considered to be a non-problem. So he had Alderman Campbell's proposal sent to the Rules Committee. This had infuriated Alderman Campbell, who could not understand why the mayor was involving himself in such a small matter when the council allowed the mayor's administration wide latitude in awarding large no-bid contracts to companies to perform work for the city. Unfortunately for Mayor Nash, Alderman Soldiamori had been indicted a few months before and was awaiting trial on charges of corruption and tax evasion. With the Committee Chairman unavailable to wield his bat, Campbell's statue proposal had passed out of committee to the council floor for debate that Friday morning.

Alderman Campbell read the proposal into the record and stated his reasons for the need of the study. Then he took a step back from the microphone, removed his black-rimmed reading glasses, tucked them into the inside pocket of his gray suit coat, and slowly seated himself on his chair.

Mayor Nash was seated at his bench above the council floor, facing the 49 aldermen in attendance. They were seated at their microphoned desks in concentric semicircular rows that emanated out from the mayor's bench. He raised his gavel and smacked it down, giving a flat-mouthed nod to an ally. Alderman Ray Salazar, who represented the Pilsen neighborhood, knew the mayor hadn't even wanted Campbell's statue-switching proposal to be debated in the first place. From his seat he nodded his assent to the mayor. Then the mayor said, "The chair opens the floor for debate on the statue-switching ordinance. Am I the only one who thinks it would be easier if we just switched park names instead of statues?" His chuckles were joined by the laughter and smiles of a number of aldermen.

Alderman Campbell threw up his arms and slumped down further into his chair.

Louise Ahern, the alderman from Lincoln Park, indicated she wished to speak. Since graduating from the University of

Illinois at Chicago, she had worked in real estate and had eventually become the President of the Lincoln Park Neighborhood Chamber of Commerce. She had served her ward for eight years while elevating her real estate business to higher levels of success.

"The Chair recognizes Alderman Ahern," said the mayor.

"I object to a name change," said Alderman Ahern. "It would mean a name change for the entire Lincoln Park neighborhood, the Lincoln Park Zoo, the Lincoln Park Chamber of Commerce, and not to mention the street Lincoln Park West that borders the park and runs through a significant part of the neighborhood. I should also point out that there is a statue of Lincoln in Lincoln Park. It's called, 'Standing Lincoln' and we, the council, designated it as a landmark."

Alderman Campbell quickly rose to his feet and shouted into his microphone, "That's the whole purpose of doing a study! To find out the consequences of moving the statues. Or maybe we just need to have a Grant statue built for Grant Park. And for the record, I am not in favor of renaming the parks."

"You're out of order, Alderman Campbell!" said the mayor. Alderman Campbell sat back down.

Alderman Carl Otter indicated he wished to speak.

"The Chair recognizes Alderman Otter," said the mayor.

Alderman Carl Otter represented the South Shore neighborhood. As a child, he had run numbers for the neighborhood Policy Wheel out of his father's barbershop near 42nd and Indiana, getting to know the people who ran it, the people who bet on it, the cops who looked the other way, and the politicians who made sure the cops looked the other way. He had seen it thrive and then wither after the Outift moved in and took over the Policy Wheel. He later worked as a precinct captain, then as a campaign organizer, then as a council staff member for long-time machine Alderman Edward Cartwright. When Cartwright retired, he named Otter as his successor, putting all of his support behind him. For three decades ever since, he had served his ward, through blizzards, the first woman mayor, the first black mayor, the Council Wars, heat waves, and a few challenges from reformers (including an ex-Black Panther). Along the way his brother Charles had become a department head in the County Forest Preserve and a large number of their family members, extended family members, and friends had gotten jobs in city and county government departments. Through the years though, Alderman Otter had become less and less satisfied with the shrinking size of the city contract pie his friends and family had been receiving. But until his fellow aldermen were willing to take the same steps as he, there was nothing to be done except provoke Mayor Nash into an argument.

Alderman Otter stood up to his microphone and buttoned the top button of his navy blue suit coat. He cleared his throat and said, "If we are going to study the parks, we should study ways to improve the parks and lakefront on the South Side. I and my constituents are tired of having something as insignificant as tree-planters dropped here and there on a main street like Irving Park Road or some parts of State Street near the Loop. There's a lot more that needs to be done in my ward and on the South Side."

Mayor Nash's face turned red as he held his breath and pounded his gavel repeatedly. He had been counting on the passage that morning of his proposal for resurfacing a large portion of South Halsted in his childhood neighborhood of Bridgeport with the addition of tree planters in the median. He thought of himself as the Tree-Planting Mayor, doing his best to help the city live up to its official motto: Urbs en horto (City in a Garden). "I demand to know how anyone, especially an elected servant of the people, could think that there's something insignificant about planting trees to enhance the beauty of the fine city of Chicago. Not to mention showing disrespect for the hours of hard work put in by the dedicated workers who put up the planters and take care of the flowers and trees inside them. Are those insignificant?"

Denice Jefferson, the alderman representing Hyde Park, was no ally of Alderman Otter. She had often criticized him for settling for the financial well-being of his family and friends at the expense of pushing for needed services and improvements in his own ward. His response to her criticisms was similar to that often made by other aldermen when their stewardship was criticized: "Mind your own ward." She wasn't sure what Alderman Otter had hoped to gain by picking an argument with the mayor, but it was one she felt was worth taking up herself this time. "Yes," she said to the mayor, "Compared to the sad state of the streets out of site of downtown and all the gentrified neighborhoods on the North Side, the Near West Side and the South Loop. When is Midway Plaisance going to get its long-overdue facelift? In case you all forgot, it's the birthplace of the original Monsters of the Midway, the University of Chicago Maroons. And don't even get me started on the sad state of the Olmstead-designed Jackson and Washington Parks."

Alderman Salazar stood up to speak. He was one of the 18 alderman who had been appointed to the council by the mayor to fill a vacancy. His vacancy had been provided like the other 17: his predecessor had been convicted in Federal Court on charges of corruption and tax evasion. "I can't understand how the council can fight about the park system. I grew up in the city and as a child I used to play in the parks all the time, baseball, football, and basketball. As an adult now, I've taken my kids over to Grant Park and the beautiful Museum Campus, and you wouldn't believe how much they enjoy it. I've traveled all over the world and I know first-hand how important the parks are to the city and how much Chicagoans appreciate them."

This brought on emotional testimonials lasting nearly 40 minutes from the other mayor-appointed aldermen on what the parks meant to them, their families, and their constituents, in this, the greatest, most beautiful city in the world, with the greatest, most beautiful park system of any city in the world.

28   OUT OF ORDER

After the last panegyric to the city park system had been delivered, Alderman Otter said, "No one is saying that our citizens do not appreciate what they have."

"No one is criticizing the parks," exclaimed an exasperated Alderman Campbell. "Everyone loves the parks. I just want to see if a minor correction can be made. That's all!"

Mayor Nash pounded his gavel. "How long's it going to take to reject this statue-switching thing? What's next, Alderman Campbell? You going to try to ban chewing gum? It gets stuck under school desks and too many people step on it in the summer and get it all over their shoes. It's a very serious problem. Maybe we should look into that?"

"I object to your tone," said Alderman Campbell.

"Then propose something worth the time and effort of this council that doesn't waste the taxpayers' money."

"Maybe we should look into all those no-bid contracts your office approves, the ones that are the source of countless investigations by the press and the Feds right now."

There were howls and cheers from several members of the council. Within the previous year and a half, over a dozen city employees had been convicted in relation to what was called the "Hired Trucking Scandal." It had been found that roughly $40 million every year had been spent by the city's Department of Transportation to hire trucks that sat idle. The private companies (some Outfit-owned) receiving the contracts had allegedly paid bribes to various city officials for the privilege of gaining those contracts. Some had even been contributors to the mayor's campaign during the previous election. It had also been alleged that Alderman Soldiamori had steered some of those contracts to companies in exchange for official (and unofficial) campaign contributions. This larger scandal had busted through a previously bricked-up window into the relationships between a handful of city departments and private contractors, resulting in more Federal investigations that promised more indictments.

The mayor shouted, "The Gentleman from the Gold Coast is out of order!"

"I demand to be recognized. I am not out of order. I am not done speaking about this proposal," said Alderman Campbell.

"Debate is closed."

"No, it is not!"

"Debate is closed! The Chair no longer recognizes you! You are out of order!"

"I am not done talking and I demand–"

"You know as well as anyone in this chamber–"

"I am going to continue–"

"If you're going to rant on and on, disregarding the rules of this chamber, then you ought to take it outside to the street."

Alderman Campbell slapped his desk. "I'm not ranting! I demand that the Chair recognize me."

Mayor Nash nodded to one of his staff in the control booth up behind the aldermen. The alert staff member turned off the microphone at Alderman Campbell's desk.

"This chamber is for civilized debate," said Mayor Nash. "The old Bughouse Square is for ranters like you."

Alderman Campbell continued, "In my three decades serving my ward and the Democratic party I have never been treated so disrespectfully by any sitting mayor." He noticed that his voice was no longer heard through the speaker system. No one in the council chamber could hear him clearly except those seated nearest to him. He couldn't believe it! No one could silence him. He had a right, a duty, as the elected alderman for his ward, for the people he served. He was elected to speak and he was going to do it whether the mayor liked it or not. Microphone or not. So, despite his arthritic right knee, he performed a "mell;" he climbed on top of his desk and stood, held his notes high over his head, and demanded to be recognized, just as Alderman Richard Mell had famously done during the raucous council session that took place on the death of the late Mayor Harold Washington in order to name his successor. Alderman Campbell wavered a little from the effort due to the stiffness in his left knee.

"You are way out of order!" shouted the mayor. "Sergeant-at-Arms, place Alderman Campbell into his seat. If he won't sit, then escort him from council chambers."

Alderman Otter, who had been on the opposing side of the Council Wars during Harold Washington's administration all those years ago against Alderman Campbell, saw that his opportunity had arrived. Never had the microphone of a Democratic alderman been turned off. So he climbed onto his desk and stood. He was followed by Alderman Jefferson. They were followed by three, then one or two, then five, until 31 aldermen were standing on their desks.

Alderman Campbell looked around at his melling colleagues, his mouth nearly wide-open. He wondered what could possibly motivate them to mell like him. Most of his colleagues who were melling had laughed at his statue-switching proposal, ridiculed his skateboard and mylar balloon bans, and groaned at his attempt to make dinner at a restaurant more peaceful.

The only aldermen who didn't mell were Alderman Salazar and the other mayor-appointed 17. Those 18 knew that if they wanted to remain in office they would have to obey the first rule of the political appointee: "Thou shalt not follow any leaders other than your patron." The 18 remained stiffly seated, only turning their slack-jawed heads back and forth from their melling colleagues to the mayor, anticipating a great crash of some sort. Not once during the mayor's reign had the council defied him, until now. Would the mayor use his gavel to club the insubordinate aldermen? Or perhaps smote each of them with a thunderbolt?

Mayor Nash had risen to his feet, shaking his fists, his entire deep red face curled in before fully expanding in an instant to shout, "You are all out of order! You're acting like a bunch of spoiled children. Not the way elected officials who claim to serve the people should act! You should all be ashamed of yourselves! Get down from your desks! Get down!"

Alderman Otter waved his right index finger in the air and shouted, "I say we no longer conduct the mayor's business planting trees, or whatever it is he wants, until he treats us with the respect each and every one of us standing aldermen deserve. Everyone who demands their respect on behalf of the people of Chicago, follow me." He hurried down off his desk in the front row, walked to the center aisle, turned, urging his colleagues with his swooping arms, then strode up the aisle and out of the council chamber, followed by every alderman who had melled. Soon afterwards, Alderman Otter said Bughouse Square was the perfect place to set up shop, that way they could be closer to the people. Nevermind that each alderman had an office in their respective ward.

29   "WE'RE ON STRIKE FOR THE PEOPLE"

"We're on strike for the people!" Alderman William "Bill" Campbell declared shortly after the strike had begun. Campbell was standing in the hallway outside the council chamber in a crowd with other aldermen and some of their aides. They were surrounded by members of the press corps.

"What does that mean?" asked a print reporter.

"We're on strike on behalf of the people of the city," Campbell replied.

"So by not working you're going to be helping the people?"

"Yes. We're not going back to work until Mayor Nash understands we were elected to do the work of the people. Not the mayor."

And so began the Great City Council Strike of 2003.

30 ONE MORE DAY TO DECIDE

Robert came away from the spectacle in Bughouse Square bemused and bewildered, thinking that if Alderman Wisniewski was on strike then his father must know the real reasons for all of the heated rhetoric and theatrics of holding press conferences in Bughouse Square. In that moment he caught sight of his father, not far from the stage, off to the side. Asking his father now would satisfy his curiosity, but could he do it without an argument breaking out between them? He didn't have time for that. He still needed to get something to eat before heading back to the office.

Robert walked out of the park, going South down Clark Street. Since he was up in River North anyway, he figured he would stop down at the Portillo's on Ontario for an Italian beef sandwich and fries.

As he ate by himself at a small table, he was torn between his aversion to his father and the likely prospect of an argument occurring at the birthday dinner, and satisfying his curiosity and his obligation as a son. Maybe he could get Elise to go with him and provide cover. Not likely. That was too much to ask of her. He liked her. He didn't want to subject her to his family. He could not decide now. He would push it off. He still had one more day to decide.

31   SPECIAL

Robert entered his office with his lemonade from lunch in hand and shut the door behind him. He needed to call Janet and cancel their plans for Saturday night. He knew she was going to give him a hard time about it, and rightfully so. Janet would be around for awhile, at least until her band went out on tour. And then back in Chicago after the tour was over. In a few weeks Elise would be gone, probably for good, or for at least a number of years. The choice was clear.

Robert came around his desk, took a sip through the straw in the styrofoam cup, and set the drink on his desk, the ice rattling together. He picked up the phone and dialed Janet's number.

"Hey, Janet, it's Robert."

"So, how was your date?"

"It wasn't a date. But whatever it was, it was quite nice."

"Huh, a nice non-date. So, you coming by tomorrow?"

"That's what I wanted to talk to you about."

"You're canceling?"

Robert winced. "I'm sorry. But Elise asked me to go to a dinner party with her."

"Sounds serious."

"It's not. How about Sunday?"

"Can't. We're doing some final remixing on a few songs left off the album. They might end up on an EP or as B-sides. And of course there are rehearsals...How about...Crap! I'm booked all next week until the show Saturday. And then I'm on tour."

"Sorry."

"This new girlfriend of yours—"

"She's not my girlfriend. I swear."

"Uh-huh." She did not sound convinced by Robert's sworn assertion.

"How are Mark and the girls?"

"They're all good. The girls are driving me crazy. But what else is new? Hey, nice try changing the subject. This is so unlike you, Robert. She must be special."

"There's nothing special. There's nothing going on. She's moving to France at the end of the month."

"You can tell me all about it at the show. I expect details. Better yet, you should bring along your girlfriend."

"She's not my girlfriend!"

32   THE INSIDE OF ELISE'S APARTMENT

Saturday evening, Elise showered and put on a halter sun dress whose skirt came to just below her knees. The dress was light blue with a pink-, yellow-, and lavender-flowered print. She washed her face and re-applied her makeup, opting for a redder shade of lipstick than she would normally wear to work. Then she dabbed her wrists and neck with some perfume. She told herself she wanted to look good for her friends, not Robert. Besides, she was wearing comfortable underwear, not any of her sexy underwear.

While she dabbed her lips with a tissue, her buzzer rang. She dropped the tissue into the trash bin and ran out of the bathroom to the door. She pushed the TALK button on the intercom and said, "Who is it?"

"It's Robert," said his muffled tinny voice through the speaker.

"I'll be down in a minute."

She grabbed her purse from on top of the dresser and held it, thinking she should have buzzed Robert in. Why had her first instinct been to not invite him in? Good thing it was a warm evening. Why leave him standing out on the sidewalk? That was rude. He was going to think she was a bitch or something. Of course, if nothing was going to happen between them, then there was no point in him ever seeing the inside of her second floor studio apartment. Not that there was anything interesting to see. It was all temporary. Most of it was going to be donated to the Salvation Army or the Brown Elephant, the rest put into storage until she could arrange for it to be shipped to France. Elise's three-shelf bookcase was jammed with her collection of French books: Zola, Voltaire, Moliere, Balzac, de Beauvoir, Sartre, Camus, Cixous, Malraux, and Duras. Her handful of English-language books included Hemingway's *A Moveable Feast* and *The Sun Also Rises*, a worn four-year-old *Lonely Planet* guide to Europe, Toni Morrison's *Beloved* and Kafka's *The Trial*. She had spent the afternoon cleaning the apartment just in case Robert came up to see it, even doing a few loads of laundry to eliminate the usual pile of clothes next to her overflowing hamper. She also made sure her vibrators were tucked away in her dresser under her socks.

Elise went to her window and looked below at Robert. He was standing outside the gate looking down the block toward Montrose Avenue, holding what looked like a bottle of wine in one hand. He was wearing a light-blue, short-sleeve collared shirt and tan shorts. He had thought to bring wine. She had forgotten to think of something to bring. Rude again. She yanked herself around, across the room, and out her door, careful on the steps in her low, yellow, sandal heels. At the bottom of the stairs, she stopped and caught her breath before pushing open the door.

When Elise walked through the gate, she said, "You're so thoughtful. I completely forgot."

"You mean the wine?"

"Yes. What kind is it?"

He turned the label toward her. "A pinot noir."

She leaned in slightly to get a better look at the label on the green bottle. It was from the Russian River Valley in California. "Looks good. Shall we go?"

"You lead the way."

33   GOOD WINE

Robert and Elise rode the L to the Belmont stop, and walked a block and a half up Seminary. Like most people living in the Lakeview neighborhood, Jennifer and Jay did not have a view of the lake from their building. Their four-story building had been apartment units until a developer had bought it in the '90s, rehabbed it, and converted it to condominiums.

Inside the condo, Elise introduced Robert to Jay and Jen, and to their friends Adam and Sarah. Jen thanked Robert for the wine, saying it would go perfect with the main dish of seared tuna.

Jay, who was a software developer for an insurance company in the Loop, talked a bit of shop with Robert before Jen opened a bottle of wine and passed out glasses to everyone. Adam then offered a toast to the newly-engaged couple. The six took a drink, with Jay and Jen thanking everyone.

As they all munched on spanakopita, Elise observed Robert amuse the others with a few stories of working for dot-coms. One story involved the Friday morning his carpool buddy was laid off. Unfortunately for Robert, it was the day his carpool buddy had driven them to work, leaving Robert scrambling to find someone who could give him a ride home that evening.

When Sarah asked how the two knew each other, Robert and Elise looked at each other for a moment and exchanged smirks. Then Robert told them how he had met Elise in front of La Ville Venteuse, how they argued (Jay, Jen, Sarah, and Adam all laughing at Robert's characterization of moving to Paris as unoriginal), and how Robert thought he at least ought to try to make it up to Elise since he had pissed her off so much. To which Jen had said it didn't take that much to get Elise all fired up.

Before bringing out the tuna, Jay opened Robert's bottle of wine and poured it into the glasses. Elise liked the wine, confirming her belief that Robert had the kind of tastes she generally admired in a guy.

"Is it as good as a French Pinot Noir?" asked Jen, as if it couldn't be within the realm of possibility for Elise to like something American as much as she liked something French.

"It's quite good, I must say," said Elise.

"See? You can get good wine here in Chicago. Just like you can in Paris."

"I know."

"We've been trying to convince her to stay," Jen said to Robert.

"And you think good wine is enough?" he asked.

"Not really. But we were hoping."

"Actually, California wines now set the standard for the world."

Elise turned to Robert. "That is pure blasphemy! How can you say such a thing?"

"It's the truth."

"Get out of here. You are so full of it."

"France has excellent wine. But the pace is set by California. And then there's New Zealand, Australia, Chile, and of course Spain and Italy, too...France is no longer the only big-time player on the block."

"Stop now," she said holding up her nearly-full glass. "Or you're going to be wearing this wine."

"You would waste good wine on me?"

"Okay, no. But I might just jab you with my fork." She set down her glass and picked up her fork, aiming at Robert.

"Hey!" Robert held up his fork as if to joust. Elise and Robert were grinning, shoulders hunched up with their tiny weapons aimed at the other. Their eyes holding each others' bright gaze.

"We've never had a fork fight at one of our dinner parties," said Jay.

"You two make quite a pair," said Jen.

Elise and Robert pulled their eyes from each other and down to the table. Then they put down their forks and retook their glasses to take a drink, careful to avoid the amused looks from the other four.

After everyone had eaten their slices of blueberry pie, Jen pulled Elise aside in the kitchen, under the ruse that she needed some help cleaning up, and told her she liked Robert, that he was a really good guy, that it was clear Elise and Robert had a certain chemistry. To which Elise insisted that nothing could come of it. Jen dropped her shoulders, grunted, and left the kitchen.

Jen thought it was about time Elise found someone. Why was she hell-bent on going through with this move to France with so little defined? She was going to throw away a chance at a job that would be perfect for her (teaching at a French immersion school), wrecking her first shot at a decent relationship (Robert) since getting deported from France, all with no guarantees she could even get back into the country because she had been deported. Unless you had a trust fund, most people didn't just jump to another country for awhile. What was the point of moving? As much as she wanted to, Jen saw no way to stop Elise.

"What time is it?" asked Jay. He, Adam, and Robert were standing in the living area, while the women were still seated at the dining table.

"It's about nine-thirty," said Adam.

"I've got to check something." He grabbed a remote control off the top of the TV and turned the TV on.

"Why did you turn on the TV?" asked Jen.

"To catch the baseball scores."

"Couldn't it wait until after our guests leave?"

"It'll be quick. I just want to get a rough idea on how some of my guys are doing."

"You got a fantasy baseball team?" said Robert.

"Yeah."

"You can check all that online, can't you?"

He nodded his head toward the dining area. "Jen gets real pissed when I do that with company around. So I promised her no Fantasy Sports online when we have guests. She says it's rude to leave the guests unattended."

34   THOSE KINDS OF CONNECTIONS

On the WCHI evening news Mayor Nash was seen in his press room in City Hall red-faced, spurting, "This is an outrage!...It's an outrage. I think it's an outrage and the fine citizens of Chicago think it's an outrage. Never have the public servants of this fine city held its citizens hostage. Hostage!...Now all of a sudden they say they're working, that they weren't before. If they weren't working before, then how do we know what they're doing now? What do they mean? Do the aldermen even know? Maybe you guys ought to ask them that! The people of Chicago deserve better than this."

Mayor Nash's voice was known as a "textbook example" of the Chicago sound. When he was agitated, like he was every day during the council strike, his voice became even higher-pitched through his nose. The reason for the nasal quality in the voice of many Chicagoans according to John Logan's theory (which he backed up with numerous pieces of anecdotal evidence) was that Chicagoans loved to do two things: talk and eat. Since they were not willing to sacrifice one in the service of the other, they did both at the same time, forcing their voices to come out of their noses. This would also explain why Chicago always ended up on so many magazine lists of the 10 Fattest Cities.

"Boy, he sounds real pissed off," said Adam.

"Can you believe that!" exclaimed Jennifer. "This whole strike-thing is crazy."

"The Chicago City Council has never been known to be any sort of deliberative body," said Adam.

"I really could not care less," said Elise. She turned to Jen and asked, "Can I have some more tea?"

Jen said, "sure," and poured some from the pot into Elise's cup.

"The soon-to-be-an-expatriate is leaving at just the right time," said Jay.

"The council wants something. Everything else is theater," said Robert finishing off his tea.

"What do they want?" asked Jen.

Robert leaned with his hand on the arm of the tan sofa. "As far as I can tell, the three ringleaders want more power. More say over contracts, specifically. Campbell can only go so far. His strings are pulled by his Committeeman Leary, the former President of the County Board, and all the real estate developers. So maybe Leary is in on this whole thing. I doubt it. It's not his way. And Otter, he just goes the way the winds blow, meanwhile getting whatever he can for himself. Which doesn't make him any different than the rest of them. He's just a little more astute about when to raise his sails. And Jefferson? She plays the squeaky-clean independent alderman role pretty well for her Hyde Park ward, but she ain't that clean. Just try to build something in her ward and you'll see, as a friend of mine who works in real estate found out. He was told he had to 'visit her at church,' which is a nice way of saying 'give me money.'" Robert realized he had opened his mouth a bit too much for his own usual comfort around people he had only just met. He glanced at Elise, who squinted her eyes as if trying to read some fine print tattooed onto Robert's forehead. He had avoided Chicago political talk the other night, not wanting to have to discuss his family. "I dunno," he continued. "That's my best guess anyway."

"You sound more like a reporter or a political scientist," said Jen.

"I know a few things," said Robert.

"How do you know so much?" Elise asked. She set her tea cup on the table, folded her arms, and sat back in her chair. She was wondering how all that Chicago political knowledge had never come up in their conversation the night before. Then she remembered they had talked a lot about their lives (where they had grown up, college, and post-college) but not so much about their families other than the basic facts (parents alive/dead, married/divorced, number of siblings, etc.).

"My father has a job with the city and a role in ward politics."

"Doing what?"

Robert set his empty tea cup onto a coaster on the coffee table. He thought he might be talking too much. But then he thought Elise was going to leave town and he would never see her or her friends again. So what difference did it make if they knew his father and brothers were machine hacks? Or anything else that he was embarrassed about for that matter? What did he have to lose? Nothing.

"He's a superintendent with the Transportation Department. Not that the title matters. One of my brothers works for the Water Department and my other brother works for the Forest Preserve."

"I imagine those kinds of connections can come in handy," said Adam.

"Yeah. And then they own your ass," said Robert, thinking of the saying: Those who use the machine will be used by it.

"But still—"

Robert's face was resolute. "It's not worth it. Trust me on this one."

Adam and Jay nodded. Jen and Sarah pursed their lips and raised their eyebrows.

Elise tilted her head to one side, still keeping her eyes focused on Robert. "Well, looks like we have a political expert in our midst. Maybe you missed your calling. Maybe you should've been a campaign organizer or a political scientist."

Robert laughed. "Maybe."

"I'm serious. All this knowledge you could put to some good use. Reform? Ever hear of it?"

"Oh, yes. In the form of curses from the mouths of my father and his friends."

"Sounds like you have quite a family."

"Yes. They're not as interesting as living in Paris, though."

"As unoriginal as it is," said Elise.

35   HOW ELISE WAS KICKED OUT OF FRANCE

"Just remember to try to not get yourself deported this time," said Jay.

Robert gave Elise a confused look. Elise's eyes went as wide and as round as they could go. Jen began laughing. Sarah and Adam smiled.

"You didn't tell him?" said Jen to Elise. Elise shook her head. Jen continued, "Well, of course you wouldn't. Especially since you just met him."

"Tell me what?" said Robert.

"It's not that big of a deal," said Elise.

"Ha! Oh yes, it is," said Jen. "Should I tell him? Or do you want to?" Jen thought this little reminder might jiggle something sensible in Elise's brain.

Elise gave a sigh, resigned to the impending embarrassment. "Go ahead and tell him. You get a bigger kick out of this story than I do."

"But it's kind of funny."

"In some ways, yes. In other ways, no."

"We don't have to tell it."

"No, I'm sure you've already piqued his interest. So go ahead and tell him."

"Okay," said Jen. She proceeded to explain that while still in Paris, Elise wanted Patrick to know that he had betrayed her and that she was not going to let him take for himself the Parisian life they had planned together. Patrick did give Elise the courtesy of telling her that the woman he was leaving her for was the woman with whom he had been seeing behind Elise's back for two months. Patrick and Sandrine were soon engaged, with Patrick dropping his plans for a Philosophy Phd in favor of a job with Sandrine's father at the printing business he owned.

Elise made an anonymous claim to French immigration authorities that Patrick and Sandrine's engagement was a sham. This subjected Patrick and Sandrine to a thorough and drawn-out investigation of their relationship by immigration officials. So when she had heard through their mutual friends (who had suspected Elise of being responsible for Patrick's immigration trouble) that Patrick might be deported, legitimate job or not, legitimate marriage or not, she sent Patrick an email.

The next time you decide to crush someone's dreams and betray them, maybe you'll think twice. When you're on that plane heading back to the states, remember this: We'll always have Paris.

The investigation, to Elise's disappointment, ultimately vindicated the soon-to-be-married couple. Shortly thereafter, Elise found herself in trouble with the immigration authorities. What she hadn't counted on was her own sans-papier status. Her job as Harold Lipton's personal assistant was under-the-table. Lipton and his partner Evan Grant were helping to get a *carte de séjour* so she could work in France legally. If she was ever found out, he could also be in trouble.

Elise was stopped outside Lipton's apartment building on Ile de la Cité one morning by immigration authorities. They had already spoken to Monseiur Lipton and they were willing to overlook his role in the young American woman's sans-papier status. Afterall, he had contributed much to expanding the appeal of French culture to the English-speaking world thanks to his numerous books of history and his own memoirs of living as an ex-pat in France. If he did not raise any objections to the serious matter of her illegal residency in France and her own apparent attempts to have an ex-lover (with legal residency) deported, he would be free from prosecution. Lipton had not known about Elise's vendetta against Patrick.

So it was Elise on the plane to Boston (the closest U.S. city with an open seat on a plane) who was remembering the line, "We'll always have Paris," with tears running down her cheeks, sitting in a middle seat.

"You tried to get your ex deported?" asked Robert.

"He only had himself to blame," said Elise. Her legs and arms were folded. She smoothed the skirt of her dress, making sure it was pulled to her knees.

"Thanks for the warning. I'll know to watch my back if I make a mistake with you."

"You're forgetting that I'm the one who was deported."

"Yeah, but if you'd have kept your mouth shut, you'd probably still be there in Paris."

She looked down at the table to the spot where her place-setting was devoid of plates and utensils.

Robert regretted his words. He had often been told that he needed to learn when to keep his mouth shut. He had also been told that the one time he did keep his mouth shut, with regards to Marcia, the timing was completely wrong.

"That's not the point," said Elise. "He has my life, the one I wanted. The one I had, at least for a little while."

Nearly every day since her deportation, Elise had thought about how if only she had just kept her mouth shut she would still be in Paris. But she did not feel resentment at Patrick at that moment. Instead, she felt a crumbly morsel of sadness. She wanted to run over to Robert, reach out her arms, and give him a hug and tell him please don't ever fear her.

36   FAMILY

Outside it was dark. Robert was still marveling at the idea of Elise being deported from France. He thought about his own almost-wife Marcia, his friend Janet, and Elise, and how he had a penchant for attracting fiery women of one sort or another. As vindictive as Elise seemed over Patrick, he could understand her actions, and even admire them. He was standing next to one passionate woman, and felt wistful that he had only just gotten to know her.

"I want to thank you for coming along tonight," said Elise.

"I had a great time."

"I bet you did, finding out one of my secrets."

"That's classic. I don't think I've ever met an American who's been deported before. That's a rare thing. It's actually kind of impressive. Do you know for sure that you can get back into France? I mean, you're not on some list of people who are banned from France or anything, are you?"

"No. I was deported for over-staying my visa. Not banned. I'll be fine. There won't be any problems."

Elise was glad Robert knew the whole sordid affair with Patrick. It was a big dark secret that she thought she didn't care whether he knew because she was leaving and sure to repulse him. It had repulsed other men she had dated, the handful she had told. But then she was thinking again about her flight back to New York and what Jen had judiciously, thankfully, left out of the story. How after an hour of internal churning, she had drifted off to sleep on the plane and was woken up a few hours later to the voice of the male pilot over the P.A. system. He was telling the passengers that due to a problem in Boston, their plane was being diverted to Halifax, Nova Scotia. It was only after the plane had landed that the passengers were told of the attack on New York City in which thousands were presumed dead. Amid the gasps and words of astonishment, fear, and horror, Elise thought her problems, as monumental as they had seemed only hours before, were simply a series of nothings connected only by her.

Robert and Elise turned the corner at Belmont Avenue coming into the brightly lit street full of people and cars.

"I have to say I had a nice time despite the revelation of my own adventures with French immigration officials," said Elise. "But I also enjoyed hearing about your political family."

"Well, if you want to meet a real flesh and blood machine hack, you can come with me to my father's birthday dinner tomorrow."

"Are you asking me to go?"

"Actually, I haven't totally made up my mind whether I'm going just yet."

"I didn't realize you didn't get along with your father."

"Or my brothers. And my mother to some extent. I missed the last few of my father's birthdays. My family's a hassle on many levels, politics being one of them. I've often thought about ratting out my father to the Feds. But then they'd probably nail my brothers, too. And all of them would end up behind bars. Plus, their families would be in a heap of trouble. So I couldn't."

"You have got to be kidding me."

"No."

"You're kidding."

"I wish I was."

"What are they doing that's so illegal?"

"Countless things. For one, my father's practically a ghost payrollee. I don't think he ever goes into his office. Or if he does, it's definitely not 40 hours a week. And he does political work on city time. My brothers, too. It's small-fry stuff. But illegal nonetheless. And they're not the only ones. Getting them might lead up the chain of command."

"Okay, now I'm really curious."

"It's up to you. You can satisfy your curiosity before you leave the country and it would save me the hassle of going by myself."

With other people, especially women, Robert had been embarrassed by his family and reluctant to bring the subject of them up, let alone have them meet his family. Since Elise was leaving the country, there could be no lasting romance between them and he had nothing to lose by telling her most everything.

"Before you decide, I should warn you that one of the things my mother used to hassle me about is the *whole when are you going to find someone to settle down with* question. She might at this dinner, and start asking you questions. It depends on her mood. That I'm over 30 and still unmarried bugs her and my aunts."

"I have a similar problem. As an only child it's like my duty to create grandchildren. It's not my fault my parents put all their eggs in one basket. But then most of my cousins are married with children."

"Family," said Robert with a shake of his head.

"I'd like to go with you, just out of curiosity. If you don't mind."

"That would be great. If not, it's no big deal."

"I'd love to go."

"You say that now..."

37   GETTING BOOTED

Sunday morning, Robert forced himself to tell his mother to expect him at The Exchange for dinner later that day. He called her on her cellphone, just in case she was out running errands before Mass. During the week she worked at the restaurant and catering business his Uncle Vinny (his mother's brother) and wife Aunt Gina ran out in Norridge. Loretta Grabowski had been working at Don Carlo's since she was 18. She had started out waiting tables and helping occasionally in the kitchen. For the better part of three decades she had been doing the books and payroll. It was while waiting tables that she had met Robert's father. The story went that Dan had come in there with some friends and their dates. During the ordering of the food, Dan and Loretta had traded some friendly banter. After that, Dan couldn't take his eyes off of Loretta, much to the displeasure of his date. He excused himself at one point to use the bathroom and snuck into the kitchen to ask for her phone number. She refused, saying there was no way she was going to give her number to a guy who was out on a date with a girl already, now get the hell out of the kitchen. When the bill arrived, Dan made sure a generous tip was left for their waitress. At the end of the night, Dan dropped off his date and broke up with her on the front steps of her house. The next day he went into the restaurant by himself, saw Loretta, told her he had broken up with the girl and could he please take her out on a date some night? She said, no way. How do I know you're not lying to me? He said, good point. You just have to trust me. After a few moments, mulling it over longer than she needed to in which time sweat began to bead up on Dan's forehead, she told him that yes, she would go on a date with him. (It would not be the last time that Loretta heard the phrase, "You just have to trust me," spoken by Dan. Loretta and their sons had heard it many times, almost always in reference to some deal Dan had worked out.) A year later, when Dan got down on his right knee and proposed to her in front of her parents in her parents' living room, she had not needed to mull it over, but that did not stop her from staring at Dan blankly for a few moments until he looked as if he would cry before she smiled broadly and said, "yes." By then Dan knew she had a cruel sense of humor but it would take him years before he could tell when she was kidding about some absurd thing.

"By yourself, as usual?" said his mother. He had expected those words and the accusatory tone, as if Robert was purposely single as a way to break her heart and embarrass her to family and friends.

"No. Actually, I'm bringing a guest."

"Wow. Are you dating again? It's about time. You need to get yourself a wife. I'm not getting any younger. Neither is your father."

"We're not dating. We're just friends."

"What's her name?"

"Elise."

"Where's she from?"

"Rock Island."

"Where's that?"

"The Quad Cities."

"Oh, downstate." To Loretta Grabowski (and to many Chicagoans), anything that wasn't the city or the immediate suburbs was "downstate" even if it was straight west, like the Quad Cities or Galena on the Mississippi River.

"Yes."

"How did you meet her?"

"That's a long story. I'll tell you all at dinner."

"Just so you know, I'm very glad you're coming. Even though you waited until the last minute to tell me. I was really worried you weren't going to come. It's an important birthday. Your father does love you, you know."

"I know."

"Good. He could really use some cheering up. He's having a rough go these days."

"I bet. Working a full week must be tough on him. Now he knows what the rest of us feel like."

"Robert. It's more than that. It's hard to be him," said his mother. "Besides, you have no idea how hard he works day in and day out."

Her pained tone made Robert turn off his cynicism. "Is he okay? It's nothing serious, is it?"

"It's very serious," said his mother.

"What is it?"

"You're not going to believe this, but the city put one of those Denver boots on his SUV the other day. Right in front of the hot dog stand!"

"Aw ma, you had me worried," he said, flipping his cynicism back on. "And here you're just giving me a hard time."

"I'm not kidding."

"Right."

"Robert, I am not kidding."

"Seriously?"

"I wouldn't kid about something like this...Okay, I would. But I swear that this time I am not kidding you. He had to call your uncle Ted and have him cut the thing off so he could drive home."

"No way," he said, letting out a snort. He never thought he would see the day when his father was held accountable to the law like most people were. Maybe someone was finally trying to get rid of all the bugs that were corrupting the city's system for delivering services and enforcing the law.

"Yes. This is very serious. He's supposed to be clouting out of this sort of thing."

Friday afternoon, Robert's father had left the office early to check on his hot dog stand. He had been talking with a precinct captain in one of the booths. The precinct captain worked in the Streets and Sanitation Department and wanted to know if Dan could get his nephew a job in the Transportation Department. While they were talking, one of Dan's employees rushed over to their table and informed Dan that there was a city tow truck out in front of the restaurant and the driver was putting a Denver boot on Dan's SUV. Dan excused himself, pushed himself out of the booth, and went outside to see what was going on. He found exactly what his employee has described. His black Cadillac SUV was being booted. He threatened the man who was booting his SUV, informed him of who he was and that there would be consequences, but all to no avail. The boot was fastened and secured. The man said the Department of Revenue was cracking down on everyone who owed the city money, no exceptions.

Robert snickered but pulled the phone away to compose himself. Then he asked. "How much does he owe?"

"They say he owes over $54,000! Can you believe that? He could buy an all new SUV for that."

"Definitely." Robert pulled the phone away again and snickered some more.

"Can you believe the nerve?"

Robert could not suppress the laughter any longer and let out a long bouncy stream of it.

"It's not funny, Robert," she declared as if stating an obvious fact. Her tone only caused Robert to laugh even harder.

"I'm serious! You should not be laughing at your father. Your father has worked very hard to get where he is."

Robert worked hard to get control of his breathing again. "You're right, mom."

"You'd better not laugh at him like that this afternoon. I don't want you showing disrespect to him, not on his birthday."

"I won't. I swear. I promise."

"He's not the only who got booted. Even one of the Mayor's nieces had her Beamer booted. And one alderman, I forget who it was, had his car booted. That one's all over the news. He's one of the Mayor's allies. Oh, and a couple of the aldermen's staff members and county workers had their cars booted, too."

"About time," muttered Robert.

"What did you say?"

"Nothing."

"So what else is new?"

"Nothing other than the promotion."

"That's so wonderful! I'm so happy for you Robert. Your father's proud of you."

"Thank you. Look, I gotta go. I've got a bunch of stuff to do around the apartment. I'll see you tonight."

"Good. Remember: it's at five o'clock."

38   MATING RITUALS

Elise walked at her usual brisk pace as she headed up Bob Fosse Way, then slowed as she noticed the abundance of life on the block. She looked up at the long canopy of trees teeming with birds chirping and fluttering from branch to branch, and squirrels rustling across those same branches bounding from tree to tree. It was very unlike the block on which she lived because all of the trees had been cut down due to the Asian Long-Horn Beetle infestation. Robert's block and those blocks east of the L and Metra train tracks had been lucky, having been clear of any beetle infestation, retaining the beauty of the old trees and the life that went with them.

Crossing Sunnyside she saw the orange brick courtyard apartment building on her left just as Robert had described in his directions to her. At the black metal gate she pushed the button next to his apartment number. The courtyard was covered in shade. Along the walls were neat clusters of red and yellow pansies and low-rising rounded shrubs.

Robert buzzed Elise in through the gate and told her he would be right down. He went out the door of his apartment and locked it from behind. He thought he should have invited Elise up, but thought it silly to have her hike up three flights of stairs only to go right back down. Earlier in the afternoon, he had cleaned it, even hiding his porn DVDs. He had done it just in case she might see his apartment, even though there was no point in her seeing it because it's not like she was ever going to see it. She had no reason to. There was nothing going on between them.

At the bottom of the stairs, Robert saw that John Logan was holding the end of a green garden hose in one hand and talking to Elise. Robert closed his eyes and slumped his shoulders, thinking, crap, crap, crap, there was no telling how late they were going to be to his father's birthday dinner.

Robert pushed open the door and walked into the shaded courtyard.

Logan saw Robert and said, "Hey Robert. Don't worry. Elise and I have already introduced ourselves."

"Wonderful."

"I was gonna water the flowers and the grass when I ran into your girlfriend," said Logan.

"We're not dating," said Elise.

"Oh, I'm sorry. OK. Where you guys going?"

"To dinner with my family," said Robert. "It's my father's birthday."

Logan looked from Robert to Elise with a slightly furrowed brow, then shook his head. "You young people. I don't understand your mating rituals. It was a lot more simple in my day."

39   A CLOSED SYSTEM

"I'm sure it was," said Robert. "Hey. Any word on how long we have to keep things cool?"

Logan shook his head. "Sorry. No word yet."

"No problem."

"So, you must have a bit of clout in the first place to make this free cable thing happen?" asked Elise.

"Shhh," said both Robert and Logan.

"Sorry," she said in a whisper.

Logan pursed his lips. "You could say that."

"So, what do you know about this council strike?"

He tried not to smile, but the left corner of his mouth raised itself. "I know what everyone else knows."

"Which is?"

Mr. Logan gestured toward Robert. "As Robert here can tell you, Chicago politics is a closed system. So change can only come from the outside. All this stuff the council is threatening about reform is a lot of talk. They want more power from the mayor. He's been squeezing them pretty hard, but even they will only take so much. So they're making a big stand to see what they can get."

"But they're talking about holding hearings on a bunch of stuff," said Elise.

"Sure. They've talked about it. Notice they haven't set a date?...Don't pay attention to what they say. Pay attention to what they actually do, and remember this: you can't have change without a little heat. Learned that in high school chemistry. Nothing's burning or exploding, so nothing's really changing just yet."

"Makes sense," said Elise.

"But some things are turning the right way."

"Like what?"

"They're finally gonna spell the name of *Soldiers Field* the right way."

"It's already spelled correctly," said Robert.

"No, it's not," said Logan. "No self-respecting Chicagoan pronounces it without the 'S.' No one says *Soldier Field*. They say *Soldiers Field*."

"Which is incorrect! It's *Soldier Field!*"

"They didn't name it correctly to begin with. Who ever heard of a field for one soldier? Which soldier is the field named after? That don't make any sense."

"I don't have time to argue this with you. We're going to be late to dinner."

"Mark my words: the Park District is going to fix this one right."

"Bye, Mr. Logan."

"Bye, Robert. It was nice meeting you, Elise. Robert, tell your father I wish him a happy birthday. There's not many left like him."

Robert took a big breath and looked warily around the courtyard. "Oh, don't you worry. There are plenty like him. They continue to breed."

Robert and Elise went through the gate and out to the sidewalk.

As soon as they had crossed Sunnyside, Elise said, "Now I understand why you were late the other night."

"He's a real nice guy, but he's a bit crazy on the Chicagoese thing."

"And how was he getting you free cable?"

"I don't know. And I don't want to know. All I do know is that I paid him 400 dollars in cash, got a box, hooked it up to the cable outlet in the wall of my apartment, and that was the end of it. I've been enjoying all the channels ever since."

"How long?"

"Almost three years."

"My God! That's so cool."

"It was cool while it lasted. Now I might have to call our friendly neighborhood cable company and sign up like everyone else."

40   THE EXCHANGE

Elise and Robert stood outside the entrance to The Exchange. The Workingman's Exchange restaurant and bar was opened on Rush Street in the Spring of 1915 on the first floor of a brick three-flat. In the coming decades, the restaurant would expand to the second and third floors. The third floor served as a banquet hall. During Prohibition, the restaurant had served as a neutral meeting site for gangland leaders. Originally owned by Cassius McDonald, it was now owned by two of his grandsons, the twins William and Thomas McDonald. They were in their seventies, with William continuing the family's successful real estate and restaurant businesses, and Thomas one of the city's most prominent criminal defense attorneys as a partner in the firm of Accardo, Humphries, and Ricca. William's only daughter

Carol ran the restaurant on a day-to-day basis. It had been at her urging that the name was shortened to simply "The Exchange" in 1989. It was well-known for its delicious hearty food and for cuts of steak named after various neighborhoods in the city: Filet Mignon was known as the Gold Coast Cut, New York Strip as the Streeterville Cut, Rib Eye as the Loop Cut, London Broil as the Lakeview Cut, and the Porterhouse as the Bridgeport Cut.

"You can still back out," said Robert. "It's not too late."

"I'm in," said Elise, feeling a little nervous. Her lips were dry like they were at the beginning of a job interview. She thought that Robert's family would be treating this as a kind of interview for the position of Robert's girlfriend, even though she didn't want to have any interest in being his girlfriend. The morning she had packed up most of her books, leaving a few to be read until she was settled in Paris. Before she had walked to Robert's she packed the last of her cold weather clothes, leaving out a brown leather coat and two sweaters, again to tide her over until she found her own place. So she reasoned, even if she passed the interview, she was not able to accept the position.

As Robert had explained to her on the L ride down, Dan Grabowski had started working for the Department of Streets and Sanitation at the age of 18. Back then it was common practice for some workers to go in on Friday to collect their paychecks and then pay their bosses x-amount of dollars for each day of the week that they had missed. He retired after 30 years but shortly thereafter was given a desk job as some sort of inspector for the Department of Transportation, the department under investigation for the Hired Trucking scandal. Dan had assured his family that he had nothing to do with what the Feds were after. "Trust me on this one," he said. Not that it mattered much that he had a city job. He seemed to spend more time running his hot dog stand, the one he had owned for nearly 25 years, than he did at his job for the city.

"Okay," said Robert. "Then I should warn you that my mother might take one look at you and say you need some meat on those bones. She says the same thing to me. She just about freaked the first time I came home to visit for the holidays from San Francisco."

"Why?"

"I'd lost weight. The son of a Polish-American father and an Italian-American mother isn't supposed to be so lean. I used to be nice and husky like my father and brothers. But living out there in California, and exercising and eating sushi, fish, more veggies, and no hot dogs or Italian beef sandwiches, I lost weight. I've kept it off since."

"You keep warning me about your mother. I thought your father was the one who you always get into it with."

"It's not often that she sees me with a woman. So she might get all wound up."

Inside the restaurant Robert told the maitre'd that they were part of the Grabowski party. She led Robert and Elise away from the bar, past many tables overflowing with food around which were many people, and up the stairs to a long table near the back of the second floor. Elise thought the dimly-lit restaurant looked its reputation as a domain of men. The tables and chairs were made of the same dark wood. The walls were paneled a few shades lighter. There were no pictures or mirrors on the walls. The exceptions were hung in the bar, and they consisted of pictures of celebrities who had eaten at the restaurant (like Frank Sinatra, and actors Gary Sinise, Russell Crowe, and Sylvester Stallone). There were a handful of children in the restaurant and a number of couples. The rest were men wearing suits with open collars. She suspected (rightfully so) that the handful of families was an aberration. That during the week this old restaurant at the heart of the Viagra Triangle was all business; powerful men and women met to discuss and make deals. Friday and Saturday nights the place was filled with couples dining alone, or in groups, and Viagra-eligible men adorned with young, beautiful women.

41   MEET THE GRABOWSKIS

Elise stayed close to Robert. When they arrived at the white tablecloth-covered table, a large man with thinning gray hair was seated at the head of it. He was laughing at a little girl who was seated further down using a straw to blow bubbles in her glass of milk. A man and a woman sitting next to the girl were frowning at her. The woman finally said, "Okay, that's enough."

The man at the head of the table noticed his youngest son. Robert waved and walked over to him. They shook hands. Dan thanked Robert for coming and Robert wished his father a happy birthday. Then Robert went to his mother, who was sitting to Dan's left, and gave her a kiss on the cheek and a hug. On the table between Dan and Loretta was an ashtray on which were set two smoldering cigarettes.

Robert introduced Elise to his parents and then to the rest of his family. Next to Mrs. Grabowski was the oldest grandchild, Daniel, who was ten and the son of Anthony, the eldest brother, and his wife Denice. Next to Daniel was his sister, seven-year-old Alice, then their mother Denice, and then their father Anthony at the end of the table. To Dan's right was his other daughter-in-law Angela, his middle son Michael, and their three-year-old daughter Katie, the one who had been giggling and blowing bubbles in her milk. It was Angela and Michael who had not been very happy about the milk bubbles and grandpa's encouragement at their making. (Robert and his brothers saw it was yet another example of the kind of behavior his father had never tolerated from them but now encouraged in his grandchildren.) Angela was five months pregnant but barely showing it.

Robert sat at the end of the table directly across from his brother Anthony. Elise sat in-between Robert and Katie. Of the three brothers, Elise thought Robert looked most like his father, with the same rounded face, thick hands, and hair color that must have matched at some point. Mr.

Grabowski's face was clean-shaven, though both of Robert's brothers wore goatees. His brothers had more of the barrel-chested shape of their father, his lighter skin, and their mother's black hair. When the elder Grabowski spoke, she thought Mr. Logan would be proud of the accent.

"I hear you got a promotion, Robert, so I guess congratulations is in order," said Dan. The family all congratulated Robert, raising their glasses. Anthony clinked his glass with Robert. Robert thanked them all.

"I tell you what, though," continued Dan. "It's put up or shut up time for you, my son. You can't just point out what's wrong with things. You gotta fix'em. Remember this: no one can rule without shedding blood. Every ruler has blood on their hands."

"Please. I'm managing a QA Department," said Robert.

"Whatever you say. I keep forgetting: you know everything."

"I learned it all from you."

"How can that be? You don't listen to me. You've never listened to me."

"Oh, yes I have. It's nearly impossible to get a word in when you're in the room."

"Gimme a break. It's the other way around. Almost no one can get in a word edgewise with you."

"You're doing pretty well right now."

Elise couldn't suppress a chuckle. Dan was about to reply, his mouth half-open, when the waiter arrived and asked if everyone was ready to order. Dan ordered the Bridgeport Cut. Robert ordered the Gold Coast Cut. Elise ordered the grilled salmon.

42   GETTING OUT IN TIME

Once the waiter left the table, Dan took a drag off his cigarette. He was pleased that Robert had come to his birthday dinner, and curious about the new woman. He did not want to disown Robert, though he had come close many times. How could he not think that when Robert was always telling him, his own father, that what he did and how he did it was wrong? What kind of son did that to his own flesh and blood? He dodged a bullet to the heart when Robert broke off the engagement with Marcia, and for that Dan was grateful.

Dan set his cigarette back down on the ashtray and asked for everyone's attention at the table. "I've got a few things to say to you all. First, I want to thank everyone for coming. This is exactly how I wanted to spend my birthday; having a very nice dinner with my family. Second, the other reason I'm glad you're all here is because you are the people I want to know before anyone else when I tell you what I'm about to tell you. After talking it over for some time with Loretta, I've decided to retire at the end of this year, completely. I've worked long enough. I'm going to retire from the city, sell the hot dog stand, and spend more time doing things I really enjoy, like being with my wonderful grandkids and going down to Florida."

"You're retiring for good?" said Anthony.

"Yes, I'm retiring for good this time. I already promised Loretta. I won't be coming out of retirement again."

Everyone at the table voiced words of congratulations and support. Loretta held her husband's hand and started to tear up. On Robert's face, Elise saw moderate surprise. Her own father would be sixty in four more years. He could have retired at 55, but instead opted to teach a few years more. He was a biology teacher at Rock Island High School. He loved being a teacher. He was proud of the letters and emails he had received through the years from former students thanking him for what he had taught them. He loved it when she was a teacher for those two years. He would be ecstatic for her if she took that job teaching in the French immersion school.

"From the looks of things, I'm getting out in time," said Dan. "First, they start investigating the department I work for, then they make me work a full week, and then my car gets booted. I can't remember the last time I worked a full week. Nothing's normal anymore. The whole regular way of doing things has been corrupted thanks to this strike business."

"You ain't kidding," said Anthony.

"You got that right," said Michael.

"Hang in there," said Loretta. "Soon, none of it will matter."

"I know, I know," said Dan. His head was bowed down, as if in contemplation of his plight. He pulled Loretta's hand to his mouth and gave it a kiss on the back.

Birthday or not, Robert could not tolerate even the idea of his father as some kind of martyr. He knew he shouldn't say what he was thinking. But the display of entitlement at the table was exasperating in its misappropriated sympathy.

"Sucks to actually have to earn a living like everyone else, huh dad?" said Robert.

"Here we go again," said Dan.

Michael groaned before grabbing for the glass of beer in front of him. His wife Angela pushed her chair back and said, "Time to take a restroom break."

Denice stood and said, "Yes, indeed." The two mothers ushered their children out of their seats, with Daniel saying, "Why do I have to go potty now?"

"Because we should use the potty before we eat."

"Okay," he said, sounding resigned to the fact that he would have to go to the restroom even though he didn't want to.

"You can come, too, if you want," said Angela to Elise. "It might be awhile."

Elise knew she was being given a chance to escape. She looked at Robert who gave her a shrug, and then grinned. "I'll stay," she said.

"Suit yourself," said Angela.

43   THINGS THAT ARE AGAINST THE LAW

Once Angela, Denice, and the children had left the table, Anthony said, "For once, Robert, could you just let it go?"

"For once, Anthony, would you quit sticking up for the wrong thing?" said Robert. "Oh, wait, I'm sorry. You can't because you're in the same racket."

"Hey, I work my tail off."

"Some of us work eight or ten hours a day, not eight or ten hours a week."

"Oh, don't give me that. You're just jealous because Michael and I have gotten sweet jobs and you're still busting your tail for a faceless corporation."

Robert laughed. "That's a good one. I am so not jealous of you two."

Dan turned to Elise and said, "Mr. Straight-as-an-Arrow over here ain't afraid to cut a few corners himself. Did he tell you about his free cable?"

"Actually, he did," said Elise. "And he doesn't get it anymore."

"It wasn't quite free," said Robert.

"So what happened? You start feeling guilty?" said Dan.

"No. I was told we had to cool it for a bit. There's supposed to be a big clampdown on pirate cable."

"The fear of getting caught cheating."

"Cheating a monopoly is one thing," said Robert. "Cheating the public is another."

"Sometimes you sound just like an attorney. If I told you once, I told you a hundred times: you missed your calling.

You shoulda gone to law school like your almost-wife. You coulda made a killing."

"No thanks."

"That's okay. I don't care if you get free cable. It's never bothered me. There's lots of things that are against the law, but that don't mean they're illegal."

Elise looked at Loretta. The face on Robert's mother remained serious but impassive. She periodically took a drag off her cigarette, appearing to be interested in the outcome of the argument without claim to a stake. Elise, whose head had been whipping from Robert to Anthony, then to Robert and Dan, with each line delivered across the table, couldn't understand how Mrs. Grabowski could just sit there and hear what was being said and not try to intervene. Why didn't she say anything? What kind of mother was she? She's the one who had pushed Robert to come. Why did she do that if she knew that this would be the outcome?

Loretta glanced at Elise, then back to Robert. She thought Elise was pretty, not as pretty as Marcia, who, let's face it, was quite a looker. Robert would probably never top her when it came to that. Good thing she had Anthony and Michael or she wouldn't have any grandchildren. The most embarrassing day of her life had been there in the church with the whole family when Robert left Marcia standing there. There had been plenty of arguments at meals between her husband and sons, and Robert and Marcia. For once she wanted the entire family to sit down for a meal and not have an argument. She would never admit to Robert that she thought he was right. Loretta had wished that Dan had stayed retired, quit when he was ahead. They had enough to retire on. Could have sold the house and the hot dog stand, and gone down to their place in Tampa. No more jobs. No more snow. No more worries that the clout would run out. No matter how often she asked, Dan had assured her he was fine, the Federal investigation at the Department of Transportation would not touch him. She was relieved when he had told her he wanted to retire, for good this time.

"There's lots of strange things going on," said Michael. "There was a big truce announced yesterday between all the street gangs."

"See how long that lasts," said Anthony.

An historic truce had been reached on Saturday between all the street gangs from all over the city. It had been in the works for months, thanks to the efforts and encouragement of a number of clergy from many different faiths and non-profit community groups that help gang members transition out of gang life. As one gang member put it, "Violence is bad for business." Mayor Nash applauded the gang leaders for putting down their guns, and thanked the clergymen for their hard work. (He also said that if gang members can work together, then surely the striking aldermen could come back to City Hall.) The hope was that the truce would stop the bloodshed and allow members to leave the gangs and build healthy, productive lives. Due to gang-related violence, the murder rate in the city that year had been on a record-setting pace. Since the council strike, there hadn't been a single homicide-related death in the city.

"And to top off everything," said Dan, taking a drag off his cigarette, "that almost-wife of yours, Robert, is trying to ruin what good that's left about public service in this city."

"As far as I'm concerned, she's doing the right thing," said Robert.

"What's this about your almost-wife?" Elise asked Robert.

"Marcia, my ex-fiancé, is a federal prosecutor. She's one of the people who are on the Soldiamori case, the alderman who was indicted for bribery, racketeering, and tax evasion."

44 HOW ROBERT LOST A FIANCÉ AND GAINED AN ALMOST-WIFE

"Wow. I didn't know that," said Elise. "But what I meant was, why do they call her your *almost-wife*?"

The eyes of Robert's family shifted from Robert down to their plates and laps, and then to one another with sly smiles and smirks. Anthony and Michael laughed with the gleeful anticipation of siblings who can't wait to hear how their brother explains himself out of an uncomfortable situation.

"Hey, I'm not saying another word," said Dan. "I'm not trying to make my son look bad. Besides, in the end, he did the right thing."

"He shoulda done it sooner," said Loretta, lighting another cigarette. "And saved people a lot of trouble, money, and anguish."

"What did you do?" asked Elise. "I thought you said you broke off the engagement?"

"He did," said Loretta. Dan was nodding and making no attempt to hide the grin on his face.

"He left her at the altar, literally," said Anthony.

"No!" Elise turned to Robert.

Robert took a large, long breath and closed his eyes. "Yes. I did."

"Wow."

Everyone was in the church, St. Vincent Ferrer. The best man, Martin Lee, and the groomsmen, Derek Jaeger, Robert's brothers, and Marcia's two brothers, were all standing on the altar with Robert. On the other side were the maid of honor, Marcia's sister Laura, her other sister Michelle, and her cousins Gina, Christine, Angela, and Deanna. Robert's face looked as white as freshly-fallen snow. He had been throwing up all morning. Derek and Martin kept telling everyone it was a combination of nerves and a hangover (though Robert had not gotten drunk the night before at the quite tame bachelor party). As Mr. Bartolozzi presented his daughter Marcia to Robert, Robert's knees were trembling. Mr. Bartolozzi held out his hand which was holding his daughter's hand. Robert didn't reach out to take it. This went on for what seemed to the Priest, the wedding party, and all in attendance as an eternity. Martin whispered, "Dude, take her hand." But Robert's hand stayed at his sides, his knees still rattling, and every component of his face arranged to show only one emotion: fear. Mr. Bartolozzi, who at first looked confused, was starting to look pissed when it was apparent that Robert was not going to take Marcia's hand. Then suddenly, Robert turned and ran into the back room from where the groomsmen had emerged and out an emergency exit. He got into his Saturn coupe and drove on North Avenue toward the city, but not to the condo he and Marcia shared in Wicker Park. As soon as the car was in the city, Robert used his cell phone to call Martin. He was still standing on the altar with everyone else. The groomsmen looked dumbfounded, with the exception of Marcia's brothers who were conferring with each other and looked as if they were getting ready to break Robert's legs, even though neither of them had been in a fistfight since grade school. The bridal party looked astounded. Marcia was crying into her father's shoulder. The attendees were all whispering and chattering. When Martin's phone rang, the entire church became quiet. Martin, who had met Robert when they were hired at Sun Microsystems at the same time, was the one who had to inform everyone that the wedding was off. Then he handed the phone to Derek, saying Robert wanted to talk to him. Robert wanted to stay with Derek and his wife Sherry at their place in the South Loop for the time being. To which Derek said it was okay.

"You know how when you hear crazy wedding stories," said Anthony, "you never think you're actually going to witness one. But there I was standing up there with the wedding party thinking, Holy cow! My brother just left his wife-to-be at the altar!"

In his dating adventures since he had left Marcia at the altar, Robert had made the mistake of telling a couple of women about it, not being evasive about the issue. His candor had been rewarded with appalled looks and unreturned phone calls. He didn't think he was a bad person. Wasn't it better to not get married to someone you didn't love instead of going through with it and ending up divorced? Apparently, no. So he always avoided the details of the broken engagement until he could get a sense of how the woman might take it. Which meant that he had completely stopped telling the story.

45 FROM EACH ACCORDING TO HIS ABILITY TO EACH ACCORDING TO HIS CLOUT

"Good thing I didn't count on my family to help me make a good impression today," said Robert.

"No, you're ashamed of us," said Dan.

"Dan! Settle down!" hissed Loretta.

Dan looked momentarily chastened, but then furrowed his brow. "It's the truth. I'm tired of pretending otherwise. I'm tired of do-gooders ruining a good thing. I'm tired of working my tail off for these politicians and now they tell me they can't help me when I need them the most. That all the clout I've earned is on hold. All these years I've been rounding up votes by knocking on doors, doling out favors, getting people jobs, covering for people, making phone calls, delivering signs, walking precincts, and they tell me they can't fix it anymore! The whole point of doing all that was not to be one of those suckers who paid parking tickets and got stuck dealing with all the countless other daily BS-type things of living in the city."

Dan's voice was at a level short of booming. Diners at other tables were turning their heads in Dan's direction.

"I am just plain tired!" he said. "I want to retire, sell the house and the hot dog stand, and sit in the sun down in

Florida. And once we're down there, Robert, you won't have to worry about me anymore."

Loretta put her right hand on Dan's shoulder. Elise grabbed Robert's hand under the table.

If his father was going to try to turn his birthday celebration into a pity party, then Robert was going to spoil it. His father had been spoiling things for the average person in the city for years. No way was Robert going to let him try to get sympathy for his supposed plight.

"Oh, boo-friggin'-hoo," said Robert. "You've been living on the borrowed efforts of other people for years. Now the bill is coming due. Everyone has to pay sooner or later."

Dan let his fingertips rest on the edge of the table, looking down at them. "It's my birthday and this isn't how I want to spend it. Maybe you shouldn't have come. Your mother said you should come...We're a family...It sure would have been a lot more peaceful without you."

Robert nodded. He pulled his hand away from Elise, then took his wallet out of one of the front pockets of his khaki slacks and counted out five twenties and set them on his plate. He turned to Elise and said, "You ready?"

She swallowed and nodded, putting her hand on his arm.

46   IF HE HAD STAYED IN CALIFORNIA

Outside the restaurant Robert felt his stomach grumble. "Sorry about that. I shouldn't have asked you to come."

"That's okay," said Elise.

"Hell, I shouldn't have come in the first place."

"Are you okay?" She had a hand on his shoulder.

"Yeah. I'll be fine," he said with a frown. "Typical. I don't know why I bother. It's times like this that I think I should have stayed in California. No family and the weather is a lot more mild." He put his hands in his pockets. He thought that if he had stayed in California and broken off the engagement to Marcia, his life would have proceeded a lot more smoothly the past few years.

"If you'd stayed in California, we wouldn't have ever met," said Elise, trying to make it sound matter-of-factly. She did not want to sound as sad as she felt at the idea of never meeting Robert. She didn't want him thinking that was how she felt.

Robert was worried that he had insulted her. He felt bummed out about the idea of never meeting her.

"True," he said. "And you wouldn't have had to sit through that argument."

"I got to see where you get your mouth from."

"Yeah. But we didn't even get to eat. Let me fix that."

Robert hailed a cab and told the driver to go to Miller's Pub down on Wabash. The cab pulled away from the curb.

"Usually we at least get to the appetizers," said Robert. "Sometimes the main course. I haven't completed a meal with my family in years."

"You're joking," she said.

"No, I swear, that's the truth. This one's pretty extreme with no food at all."

"Oh, you're putting me on."

Robert grinned. "I am. But that's not the first time I didn't even get to the appetizers."

47   MEET ROBERT'S ALMOST-WIFE

The maitre'd at Miller's Pub told them that there would be a wait of approximately 15 minutes. So Robert and Elise sat in Veeck's Corner, the area of the bar named for the beloved, deceased, former owner of the White Sox, Bill Veeck. They both ordered a beer and when the bartender set the drinks in front of them, Elise insisted on buying the round. Robert thanked her but said that dinner was still on him.

"You haven't told me much about Marcia. You ran away from her!" Elise's eyes were wide with astonishment.

"It was not one of my better moments," said Robert, his eyes darting from Elise, to his beer, then around the restaurant. He was surprised that she hadn't seemed revolted by his run from the altar. Great, he finally meets a woman who's not freaked out by that and she's leaving the country.

"Why did you do that? Why did you wait until the last minute to call it off?"

"We were a steady and secure thing." He bit his bottom lip. "I did love her. But I stopped loving her at some point. Real love. It was only when I was waiting in the back of the church with my groomsmen that I knew that all the puking I'd done that morning was not a good sign. I dry-heaved a few times before walking out onto the altar. Anyway, to marry her would have been worse. So I got out of there, hopped into my car, and drove away to Derek's. I knew he'd take me in. I stayed with him for a month. Then I got a place of my own, the one I'm living in now, as a matter of fact."

"She must have been devastated."

"Marcia's the kind of person who won't let you see her weak. She tends to get angry and seethe. She was furious. She threatened to kill me. So did her father. So did her entire family...The red flag to me should have been when she said she wanted a Catholic wedding, even though she knew I wanted nothing to do with the Catholic church. In college, once I was living on my own, I stopped even being a Chreaster."

"Me, too. But a lot of people still get married in a Catholic church out of tradition."

"Tradition's fine as long as you believe in the tradition."

"Or you do what my parents did: chuck the Catholic church, have a hippie wedding, then later become Episcopalians."

"Your parents were hippies?"

"You'd never know it now just by looking at them. But there are photos to prove it. They exchanged Claddagh rings, barefoot, on a bluff overlooking the Mississippi River."

Robert was smiling at the idea of Elise being raised by such parents. He didn't know why. Maybe it was the image of the long-haired hetero couple barefoot on the grass with the wide river below, surrounded by friends on a sunny day that seemed so appealing. The idea of being inside a church made him feel as if being jammed tightly during rush hour during a heatwave in an L car with the air conditioning broken. There was something free about creating their own marriage ceremony.

"Enough about religion," said Robert. "She also talked about moving back to Elmwood Park to be close to her family. I wanted to live downtown or up in Lakeview. We compromised on Wicker Park. These days she works for the U.S. Attorney's office here in Chicago as a Federal Prosecutor. She's also a Republican, which was another reason my family wasn't too keen on her. She's very good at what she does. Very tenacious and focused."

Just then, Robert saw Marcia walking by the maitre'd. She had light olive skin and black hair that was chin-length. A tall man was walking behind her with very erect posture. Marcia paused to let people clear a path for her and her companion to pass through on their way out of the restaurant.

Marcia glanced to her left and saw Robert. She stopped. She could not pass up this opportunity. She hadn't seen her former fiancé in nearly two years. She had to say hello, ask how he was doing, and tell him her good news. As far as she knew, he was still unmarried and living alone. There was a time when she would have run across the room and attacked him with whatever physical object was available. She did not feel like attacking him, but there was still an anger in her stomach at the sight of him, like smoldering gray coals that at a touch disintegrate.

Robert turned his head away and took a drink from his beer. "And she's here," he said.

"Who?"

"Marcia. This ought to be good. You've met my family. Now meet my ex."

The thought of Marcia coming over to speak with him and Elise made his shoulder muscles feel as if quick-setting concrete was being poured onto them. He glanced in Marcia's direction. She was closer now, weaving between people who were waiting for a table. She would be there in a moment. The concrete had set.

"Hello, Robert," said Marcia glancing at Elise and then bringing the full force of her attention back toward Robert.

"Hello, Marcia," said Robert.

Marcia nodded her head at Elise. "Who's this? Another potential victim of yours?"

"Glad to see you've maintained that sweet disposition of yours," he said.

She put a hand to her hips. "Good to see you've maintained your sense of civility."

"Marcia, I'd like you to meet Elise. She's just a friend. "

"Then she's lucky. Hi Elise, I'm Marcia. Nice to meet you."

"Nice to meet you, too," said Elise.

Robert set his beer down on the bar. The figurative concrete was making his shoulders sore. "I don't want to fight with you, Marcia. I told you before that I was sorry. Many, many, many times. And I still mean it."

Marcia stepped closer to Robert. "I don't want to fight either. Though I can't say the same for my family. You should continue to avoid Elmwood Park."

"I have made it a point to do so."

"Smart. So what brings you two here?"

"Aborted dinner with my family. I owe her a dinner out," said Robert.

"Where did the argument take place this time?"

"The Exchange."

"The Den of Corruption itself. Wow, Robert. Were you trying to get on your father's good side?"

"It's his 60th birthday. So I figured I'd indulge him. Unfortunately, Elise here had a ringside seat for the match."

"Some advice, Elise: if you're going to stick around, get used to the fireworks between Robert and everyone else in his immediate family. I have to admit that in this regard, Robert is almost always on the right side of those arguments."

"We're not that way," said Elise. "I'm not even staying in Chicago. I'm moving to France at the end of the month."

"Wow. That's quite a move. Good for you."

"So what's new with you, Marcia?" asked Robert.

"I'm engaged." She held out her left hand to show off a one-karat diamond ring.

"Congratulations," said Elise.

"Congratulations," said Robert. "Who is he?"

"A tax attorney at Keane, Bloom, and Giles. He's standing over there." Marcia turned and waved to the tall man by the entrance. He waved back. "We'd only been dating for about four months when he proposed, last week as a matter of fact. But we both knew it was right."

"That's really great, Marcia" said Robert. "I'm happy for the two of you."

"Thank you," said Marcia.

Marcia and Robert both sighed. Robert no longer felt the concrete weight on his shoulders. He was thinking that he should have had the sense to let go of Marcia sooner, for their sake, but mostly for her. He was talented at finding bugs, the errors in software, and reporting them clearly and diligently. What he had done to Marcia (and himself) was the defining example of how he was unwilling to find and confront the errors in his own reasoning, reasoning used to shield himself from taking risks. He had to stop these self-delusions.

Elise watched them, and measured the silence between them, and thought the two needed to resolve something without an audience.

"If you'll excuse me," said Elise, "I need to use the Ladies' Room." She slid off the barstool.

"It's back over there," said Robert, pointing toward the sign for the Restrooms.

"Thanks."

48   YOU NEVER LOOKED AT ME THAT WAY

Robert watched Elise move along the bar, and weave between the tables, dispirited that she had to witness him fighting with his family and then had to meet Marcia. In one day, she had now seen most everything having to do with the worst about him. Good thing he wasn't trying to impress her.

"She is different, isn't she?" said Marcia.

"What do you mean?" he asked.

Marcia gave Robert a crimped smile. "You never looked at me that way."

Robert couldn't raise his face away from his beer to look at Marcia. He thought she must be projecting something onto him. Of course he didn't look at Elise the same way. They were friends. Not lovers. What guy who saw her and knew her wit and sense of humor, and many other talents, wouldn't be attracted to her? Not to mention being a real trooper to attempt to sit down to dinner with his screwy family, witness an argument, have the meal cut short and, afterwards, not only not be angry about it but be concerned about him. So what guy wouldn't feel honored to have Elise as his girlfriend?

"It's okay," said Marcia. "Because I can see the way you are with her: unguarded. That's not how you ever were with me. It's like you feared me more than you loved me."

Robert took a drink from his beer and curled in his lips.

"That's right," she said. "You didn't love me. You respected me, but not enough to tell me you didn't love me. I hope that you have enough respect for her to tell her how you really feel."

"I haven't trusted myself since I left you at the altar," he said.

"You knew how you really felt all along. You just didn't say anything. I still don't understand how you kept it to yourself. I don't know what you were afraid of. It goes without saying that sooner would have been better."

Robert had known long before the engagement that he did not want to marry Marcia. It was more than doubt that had filled him the morning after he had given her the ring. It was knowledge that he had made a mistake. But they had been together so long, living together. They seemed to work together as a couple should in order to get married and stay married. But the sparkling warmth of love had faded leaving only their habits and expectations as a couple. Marriage, after so long a coupling, had seemed to be the next logical step. The knowledge that the engagement was a mistake only deepened with the fights they had. She wanted a large number in the wedding party. He wanted fewer. He wanted to hold the reception at the restaurant owned by his uncle (who had offered to close it for the night). She said it wasn't big enough. She wanted the wedding to take place in the Catholic church in which she had been Baptized, made her first Communion, and had her Confirmation. Robert had suggested they hold the ceremony in Lincoln Park with a Justice of the Peace. Robert didn't want chicken for any of the meals at the reception, saying he was tired of eating chicken at weddings. She said beef was too expensive. Robert said if we cut the invite list, we'll be able to afford beef for everyone. He lost nearly every argument. She even accused him at one point of trying to sabotage the wedding. Looking back, Robert realized he had lost most of the arguments over the wedding arrangements because he hadn't cared.

"I know," he said, finally meeting her look. "I've gone over it many times. I deluded myself, thinking that staying with you was the safe and logical option. When really, it was a cop-out to being honest with you."

"I have a confession to make. You probably won't believe this, but what you did was one of the best things that ever happened to me."

"What?"

"We would not have been happy together."

"We would have been miserable."

"The divorce would have been nasty."

"I would've been hosed. You know all the good lawyers."

They laughed. Robert couldn't remember the last time he had laughed so carefree with Marcia like that. It felt good.

Then Marcia composed herself and took a long deep breath. "Don't hold back with her, Robert. Be honest with her."

Robert saw Elise coming back towards them. "She's leaving the country."

Marcia glanced in the direction Robert was looking. "Don't cop out. For her sake and yours."

"It's not that simple."

"It is that simple."

Elise returned to her seat next to Robert.

"Well," said Marcia. "I suppose I should leave you two to eat in peace. You've already had one loud dinner. If I stick around, I might stir up some more trouble," she said with a smirk.

"It was good to meet you," said Elise.

"It was good to meet you," said Marcia.

"Marcia, it was good seeing you," said Robert

"It was good seeing you, too, Robert."

Marcia looked at Robert with what could only be construed as concern. Robert wondered if it was appropriate to hug, if that's what they should do. He hadn't so much as brushed against her since the day he ran out of the church.

49   NOT SO ALLURING

Marcia glanced at Elise. Elise was looking at Robert. She looked back at Robert and lowered her voice so that only Robert and Elise could hear her. "Robert, I want you to know something. But the only thing I can say about it is that very soon the net is going to be cast wider."

"More indictments?"

"Yes." She tried to read his face, to see if he understood what she was trying to tell him.

"That's good news for you. It'll be great for your career."

"But very bad news for a lot of other people. Cases are being built against even some of the so-called 'small-fries.'"

Robert kept holding onto her gaze, wondering what she was implying,...and then he knew. He had often wondered how he would feel at that moment, when his father, or even his own brothers, were caught. In his more angry moments he had hoped they would rot in jail. He nodded. Through the years, whenever Robert had thought out loud of tipping off the Feds about his father and brothers, Marcia had told him numerous times that he should. To which he would ask her how come none of the Outfit's family members in her hometown of Elmwood Park or nearby Melrose Park had ever ratted out their own? She said it wasn't a fair comparison because mob informants ended up dead, with their bodies placed somewhere in a public place. When Robert had informed his father that his new girlfriend Marcia was a prosecutor, his father had said, "Thank God she's over there in California and not here in Chicago." He knew his father had only been half-joking.

"I understand," he said.

"Take care of yourself, Robert," said Marcia.

"Thank you. I will. You, too."

Marcia rejoined her fiancé. Robert held onto his beer.

"I guess my father's time is up."

"How do you feel?" asked Elise.

"Pity."

In his twenties, Robert had often fantasized about his father going to prison for all of his corruption. Then he could say his father was in prison, which would give him a dark, alluring edge of hurt in the minds of sympathetic beautiful women who would have sex with him because of such an unique allure. Who would suspect a QA tester of having a convict for a father or brother? Besides, there was nothing sexy or cool about being a QA tester. The programmers who made the software and managed the computer networks were the cool geeks. The CIOs, CFOs, and CEOs were the stars. The marketing and sales people had the sexy jobs and all the good seats to Golden State Warriors games when Michael Jordan was in town. Testing software for bugs was a clearly defined job with little room for ambiguity. Software either performed the functions for which it was designed or it didn't. He had no worries that the Feds would be knocking down his door and playing recorded conversations of him talking about fixing parking tickets or being a ghost payrollee or giving someone kickbacks on a contract or fixing the results of a hiring exam in favor of one person over another. He had a level of security in his life his father believed he had for himself and his family, a belief that would soon be destroyed. Having a convict for a father did not sound alluring anymore.

"It's really going to suck for my mother. He'll lose his pension and who knows what else...He might be able to take a plea."

"I'm sorry," said Elise.

"Glad I'm a QA tester. Glad I don't need to face off in a courtroom against Marcia."

"Oh, can I just tell you? I don't think I'd ever be that gracious with Patrick, my ex. Ever. I'm surprised she didn't hit you."

"Me, too."

"She's a better woman than me."

"No, she's not." He took a drink. "She's a lawyer."

"She did do a nice thing for you."

"Telling me? I'm not so sure. Knowing what's to come is not exactly comforting. She wasn't supposed to do that. She could get in a lot of trouble."

50   THE HEAVIEST PIECE OF ART IN THE CITY

When they had finished eating dinner, Robert and Elise decided to take a walk. They took Adams east to Michigan Avenue, where they headed north at a leisurely pace, side-by-side up to Millenium Park. Barefoot children were running in the shallow water from the Crown Fountain. The fountain consisted of two high blocks that faced each other, with water cascading down into an inch-deep pool in-between. Faces of all races and ethnicities were projected onto the blocks, with a periodic stream of water shooting out of the point where the mouths were. Parents aimed cameras and video cameras at their children in the hopes of capturing the fun before all the usable sunlight was gone. Both Robert and Elise thought this would be a great place to take their kids someday and watch them have fun in the water and gaze at the ever-changing faces on the two fountain walls.

The couple made their way toward the shiniest object in the city: the art installation properly titled, "Cloud Gate," but due to its shape it was known widely by Chicagoans as "The Bean." Two guys straddling their mountain bikes were looking at the ginormous stainless steel thing. They were in their early twenties and wore black bike shorts and blue bike jerseys. They had ridden along the lakefront path from Wrigleyville down to the Museum Campus and had decided to take a side journey on their way back through Millenium Park to see the Bean. The sun had already gone down behind the wall of buildings along Michigan Avenue, and with it the stunning shine on the smooth sculpture itself was starting to fade.

"Doesn't look like no gate to me," said the first bicyclist.

"Doesn't look like any gate I've ever seen," said the second.

"You can't open it. You can't walk through it. It doesn't look like it leads anywhere."

"You can see the clouds reflecting off of it."

"But there aren't any clouds in the sky today."

"If there were you could probably see them reflected off of it."

"Probably."

They both looked at each other and shrugged.

"Well, I'm done," said the first.

"Me, too," said the second.

They remounted their bikes.

"Last one back has to buy the first two rounds at Hi-Tops tonight," said the second.

"Bet!" said the first and they were pedaling off on their race.

Robert and Elise watched the two men on their bikes go around the sculpture and bound down the steps on the other side.

"Behold: The Bean!" said Robert extending his right arm in the direction of the sculpture. "The Heaviest Piece of Art in the City."

"Give me a break," said Elise.

"I, of course, mean 'heavy' in both the literal and metaphysical senses." He let out a snort.

Elise shook her head with a smirk while taking a few steps from Robert toward the underside of the art, all the while looking up and down it's reflective curves. It was the first time she had seen the Bean up close other than in photos.

Robert saw parts of her bent, turned, and stretched on the surface of the art, bathed in the orange-tinged light of sunset.

"It is big," she said. "Much bigger than I thought it would be. It really is quite huge."

Robert nodded. "The photos don't do it justice."

"Didn't this whole park cost like double or triple what it was supposed to cost?" she asked.

The city's original estimate to build Millenium Park was $150 million. The eventual cost, like so many public works projects in Chicago, was much more. In this case, the total cost was over $450 million.

"Yes," said Robert. "But the thing is, no one in, say, 20 or 30 years will remember or care. They'll have this beautiful park and that's all that will matter to the vast majority of people."

"I know. But it's frustrating, all this corruption."

"You're telling me."

"Do you want to keep walking?"

"Yes," he said.

51   HOW THEY SAID GOODBYE

They continued walking north on Michigan Avenue. There were plenty of people walking in both directions on the sidewalk. Most of the people coming from the Magnificent Mile held shopping bags.

As they stepped onto the Michigan Avenue bridge, the lights underneath flickered and illuminated, bouncing off the cool ripples of the Chicago River. Then the lights under the bridge at Wabash flickered and illuminated. Then the lights under the State Street bridge, and then the next bridge that crossed the river turned on, and so on, each in their turn, westward, to the split where the North and South branches meet, and then around, following the Southern branch.

Elise knew that she could love Robert, if she was staying. She wasn't, so what he knew about her and what she knew about him didn't matter. If she was staying, she could see herself taking more walks like this with him, going to movies and restaurants with him, and spending the night with him, and even taking a weekend trip to Rock Island to have him meet her parents. Yes, she wanted her parents to meet Robert. They would like and welcome him. But she was not going to stay in Chicago.

They stepped off the bridge and neared the white Wrigley Building, the floodlights illuminating it from the riverside. Robert remarked in his mind that here they were taking a casual stroll up Michigan Avenue while not even talking and they were content. He didn't want to say a word and risk puncturing the red balloon that seemed to be carrying them along so lightly.

They were silent as they looked at the lights in the trees twinkling down the median and on either side of the Mag Mile. They were silent as they looked at the tantalizing store display windows. They were silent as they watched the people of all ages bustling up and down the sidewalks. They were silent as they looked at the old Water Tower. They were silent, too, in the cab, each with a relaxed smile all the way to Elise's building. Their hands remained inches from each other, resting on the back seat in the dark.

The cab came to a stop. Elise opened the door, turning on the light above the back seat. The bright light felt more like a slap than a welcome dose of visibility.

"So this is goodbye, I guess," she said, sliding a little toward the open door, the seat creaking under her.

"Yes, this is," he said.

She could invite him to stay the night. But it would make everything so very complicated. She had spent nearly two years planning and saving for Paris. And it was not like he could come with her. She would be toying with him, she told herself, by asking him to stay with no real prospect of a relationship. It was not fair that with only a few weeks before she was to leave that she met Robert. It was not fair that she would have to put her life on hold for Robert. It was not fair that Robert could not come with her to Paris. Life was not fair.

Robert could see that Elise looked a little sad and unsure. Robert wanted her to stay in the cab, ride with him down Lake Shore Drive to gaze at the skyline and then back, and invite him up. He thought that if he asked her, based on that look in her face, that she would say yes. But it would be selfish, he told himself, to tell her he wanted her to stay, dump his feelings on her, and try to put a kink in her plans. He could invite Elise to go with him to see Janet's band. Inviting her might be a lot easier than explaining to Janet how he didn't invite the woman who caused him to cancel plans he had made with her twice in a row. Or maybe it was easier to just let Elise get out of the cab and go on with her life, a life that was headed to the other side of the Atlantic ocean.

"I had a great time today," she said.

"You're being nice. Thank you."

"No. I mean it. I had a wonderful time with you."

"I'm glad. I had a wonderful time with you."

"Oh, I should give you some money for the cab." She reached inside her bag for her wallet.

"No, no, no," said Robert. "Save your money for Paris. You're going to need it."

"You sure?"

"Positive...Send me a postcard or shoot me an email when you get there."

"I will."

"Goodnight."

"Goodnight." She got out of the cab and leaned down to look at Robert, holding the cab door in her right hand. Then she shut the door.

With every breath Robert took he felt a little more empty, watching her walk through the gate and into the building. As Elise stepped inside, she wiped a tear from her left eye.

52 THE WIND RETURNS

Robert and Elise were laying in their beds. Through the open windows of their apartments, they heard the wind blow for an instant. It filled the air with the loud rustle of the collective shaking of every leaf on every tree in the city. The noise startled them. Then, as the wind slowed and came to a stop, every leaf became still and Robert and Elise were left alone with themselves. It was awhile before they could finally give in to sleep.

53 ROBERT'S DAYDREAM

I really enjoy spending time with you, Elise, he would say.
I'm glad, because I feel the same way, she would say.
I want to go with you to Paris.
Now that I've met you, I don't want to leave Chicago without you.
If I asked you to let me go with you, would you say "yes?"
Yes.
Would you let me go with you?
I never thought you would ask! Yes, Robert. Of course, yes.
And they would embrace and kiss...

Robert became aware that he was sitting at the end of the long table in the Wright Conference Room Monday afternoon, alone. His heart had stopped beating with the force of a jackhammer like it had at the start of the meeting. He heard a copy machine out in the hall churning multiple copies, and then he noticed that a slender white man with glasses was standing just inside the doorway to the conference room and looked as if he was waiting for a reply.

"What?" asked Robert.

"I asked if this room is still being used."

It was the third time that day that someone had repeated a question or sentence to Robert. The two previous times, once with Karen and once with Frank Bertuzzi, they had asked Robert if he had heard what they had just said to him. He would say yes, shoving Elise's pretty pixie image or the sharp sparkle of her voice out of his mind. Then he would attempt to reconstruct the missed statement from the context of the conversation, concentrating hard on what was being said, cursing himself for getting fixated on an unattainable goal (Elise) while there were plenty of attainable goals (work) in front of him. What was he thinking? Why was he so fixated on a woman who was leaving the country? He should stop this. No good could come of thinking about her. She was a distraction. She was out of his life and would soon be out of the country. So what if she had invited him to a dinner party? So what if she had been willing to go along with him on Sunday for his father's birthday?

"Oh. No," said Robert. "I was just leaving."

Robert stood quickly and grabbed his notes off the same table in the same room from which he had launched his tirade against Perry that had the unforeseen effect of giving him Perry's job. It had been nearly a week since Robert had been introduced as the new department manager. Despite his worries that he might some day have to give one or more of his former workers a poor performance review, or discipline or fire them, the transition from co-worker to boss had been smooth. Derek had warned Robert to expect a chill to fall between him and his workers because being the boss meant being a boss and all that goes with it. So far, Karen and the other workers still chatted and joked easily with him. He thought his first full meeting as the department manager had gone well. On the day he was introduced as the boss, he held a short perfunctory meeting where he told everyone to keep working on their projects, that he would be meeting with each of them individually, and holding a formal department meeting once he had a handle on things. He spent the rest of the week meeting with each person in the department, discussing their work load, their problems, what things they were happy with, and their ideas for improvement. At that first meeting he had told his workers that no one was to be laid off, but that the department had a lot of work to do in repairing the damage caused by Perry. So if they didn't make themselves useful to the company, the company would get rid of them. It was that simple. He reiterated what he had said in his individual meetings with them: if any of them had any ideas for improvement, he was all ears.

When Robert announced he was discussing with HR the possibility of instituting a flex-schedule, allowing them to come in late and leave late or come in early and leave early, a handful of his workers actually clapped. He wasn't sure whether HR would allow it. Rose Santos had told him she wasn't against the idea of a flexible schedule, but that it had to be something other departments would also be able to implement. Robert liked the idea and wanted to see just how much power he really had to run his department. When Robert told his workers that he was having Karen research automated testing tools there were "thank you's" from more than half of the staff. In fact, he had simply asked Karen to update the report that she and he had written months ago for Perry. Perry had dismissed the idea, saying it was too costly. Robert had reviewed Karen's updates and sent the report to the CIO, Ted Allen. Robert had even announced the shuffling of priorities and the re-allocation of people to different projects to no complaints.

With such a leadership change remarkable for its lack of malice or negativity, Robert didn't understand what was so hard about being honest with the people who worked for you. Or why Perry had earned so much contempt both inside and outside the department. Being a manager wasn't that hard.

In the hall Robert took out his cell phone and looked at the screen. He had set it to vibrate before the meeting and it had started shaking on his belt clip shortly after he began the meeting. There was one message. He dialed into his voicemail and listened. "Don't forget," said Janet, "to invite that Mystery Woman of yours to the show this Saturday. No, you don't get off that easy. I want to meet the woman who got you to cancel plans with me not once, but twice in one week."

Robert shut the phone and stuck it back into his belt clip. He couldn't just call or email Elise and invite her. He had already said his final goodbye to her. That was it. Their flirtation or dalliance or whatever you wanted to call it was over. Why did no one understand that? He would not call Janet back now to explain. He would deal with her later. Right now he had a meeting with Ted Allen.

54 THERE IS NO SUCH THING AS "CODE FREEZE"

Ted's office was on the 10th floor. It occupied the northeast corner. His desk was filled with papers stacked around his PC monitor, a stack of full paper trays, and two 5 x 7 brown picture frames, the contents of which Robert couldn't see as they were facing Ted and not him. On one wall was an abstract painting in yellows, peaches, and greens, with soft, square edges bleeding from one color to another. Robert thought it looked inoffensive in the way most abstract office art was inoffensive in its lack of meaning.

"I asked you in here, Robert, because I wanted to see how you were doing so far," said Ted. He was thinking about preserving his own job in the merged company and the battles in which he was involved regarding who was to be moved or laid off. The reorganization would happen soon. Ted intended to protect his resources as much as possible. Promoting Robert had been a way to keep the QA Department intact. If it had remained headless, then it would have been easier to shift over to the domain of BMC's QA Department, not to mention folding the entire department and hiring an outside firm to do QA. No, there were talented people in QA with a lot of institutional knowledge, the kind of knowledge that just could not be replicated through outsourcing. The department simply needed to be managed well. If Robert couldn't do it...

"So, how are things going?" asked Ted.

"I think well, so far," said Robert. "I'm just finally getting a full grasp on all the projects we currently have plus the ones coming down the pike. And there are some others that might come our way. I had lunch with Frank last week. He says he wants a better working relationship with our department. I wanted to talk to him about some of the chronic issues between our departments and how they can be resolved."

Robert had tried to be as direct with Frank as he could without being confrontational, saying that he knew that in the minds of programmers there was no such thing as "code freeze." They kept working and slipped in changes and fixes whenever they wanted, regardless of whether the code for a particular version of software was supposed to remain untouched and deemed complete. If each complete version was actually an unofficial work-in-progress, Robert and his people had no reliable way of tracking a bug through successive versions, and therefore no way of being confident that a problem was isolated to a particular version. Robert knew that it was an acute problem with only two particular programmers (Bill Morrison and Craig Miller) in Frank's department, but he wanted Frank to understand the difficulty his QA workers faced. And he wanted it to stop. It also made them look bad when bugs were reported, but the fixes had already been slipped in by one programmer with another programmer (who doesn't realize the bug has been surreptitiously fixed in their version of the build) unable to reproduce the bugs. Frank had complained that QA reported too many bugs that either weren't bugs or did not exist. What he hadn't figured out, but that Robert was trying to make clear to him, was that the "non-existent bugs" problem was isolated to projects with those two programmers.

Frank said to Robert that he understood how the integrity of each software build had to be maintained, but that he wanted more accurate bug reports. They were under tight deadlines. Time spent attempting to fix non-existent bugs was time wasted. Robert said he saw no reason that couldn't be done.

"That's good." Ted looked out the window to his left, with the glass glimmering from the building across Lasalle. "You've been given quite an opportunity."

"I know."

"It's good that you know that, and it's important that you do the most with it. Because you never know when an opportunity to change your career or your life for the better is going to come along. They don't come along very often, let alone second chances."

Robert could not help but think of Elise. He could send her an email or call her. The worst thing she could say was "no," right? What would be the harm? No, she might actually say "yes" and then he might actually tell her how he really felt, thus putting his disappointment at her leaving onto her. He couldn't ask her to stay. That was downright unreasonable. Sure he hadn't told Marcia how he had really felt until it was almost too late. But that was a completely different set of circumstances. Here he was trying to spare Elise's feelings and not attempt to ruin her long-thought-out plans to move to Paris. You didn't just tell someone they should cancel their two-year-old plan to move to another country. He was thinking of Elise, whereas with Marcia he was thinking of himself. Yeah, that's it. By freezing their relationship as it was and not saying anything, he was doing Elise a favor.

"Is there anything else?" said Ted.

Robert adjusted his position in the chair so that he was sitting up straighter. "Actually, the report I sent you about purchasing some automated testing tools?"

"Oh, yes, yes. I'm anxious to read that. Anything that will save the company money is always welcome."

55   CRACKDOWNS

Derek had season tickets for the White Sox at Sox Park. Sox fans, like Derek and Robert, did not refer to the baseball stadium using its official name, "U.S. Cellular Field." Instead, they used "Sox Park," which was shorter and easily conveyed the place where the White Sox played their home games. When he wasn't entertaining business partners or family, Derek often invited Robert to come along. The seats were located in the first row behind the White Sox dugout.

Derek was talking on his Blackberry phone when Robert came down the aisle. This did not surprise Robert. He was used to entering a place where Derek was already present and engaged in a conversation over the phone. Derek did not give his undivided attention for long periods of time to anyone except his wife Sherry, on occasion. For their fishing trip up to Door County, Sherry wouldn't let Derek take his phone with him. She had told him she wanted him to "unplug, unwind, and relax." His father-in-law, who owned the company Derek worked for, told him, "when you go on vacation, you should *go on vacation*. Besides, the company will still be here when you get back." Derek spent much of the trip waiting for the phone he didn't have to ring. Robert and Mike had brought their phones and anytime theirs would ring, they would say, "It sure is nice to have my phone and be able to stay in touch with friends and family." Derek would grunt and attempt to focus his attention on whatever he happened to be doing; eating, driving, or watching TV.

Robert sat next to Derek, with his beer, bratwurst, and fries, and began to eat. The two had met while freshman at Weber High School, two of the few White Sox fans in that

North Side school, and had been friends ever since. Derek had dropped out of Loyola University in Chicago after his second year. He had been majoring in business, and after his sophomore year he landed an internship at a real estate development firm. He told Robert that he had seen his ticket to a Gold Coast condo and a Latin school education for his future children. By the age of 29, he was a millionaire and engaged to Sherry.

Derek closed his cell phone and looked Robert up and down. "If you're going to wear a suit, why don't you wear one for me? I can make you a hell of a lot more money," he said.

Derek believed quite strongly that Robert was wasting his time as a QA tester. He believed that once Robert got a taste of real estate development, he would like it as much as he did. He didn't understand how Robert could be content to sit in front of a computer all day finding things that were wrong with computer software.

"You want me to help you make a lot more money," said Robert.

"Ha. Would I benefit? Of course. But your knowledge and skills are withering. Don't you want to be truly appreciated? Have the true worth of yourself compensated? And build something lasting in the city that can be seen, felt, and lived in?"

"It is tempting."

"Look, it sounds like you're finally getting your due there at the bank. But my offer still stands. There's probably just about nothing I couldn't get built here if I really wanted to do it. But even I can't get free cable. Yet, somehow, you can."

"That's a special case."

"But it's you who's got it."

"Not anymore. My guy's been told to cool it for awhile. Apparently, there's some big crackdown."

"You're telling me. There are crackdowns on everything these days. This afternoon, one of my guys calls me up from the job site at the Windsor Condo tower. They poured the sidewalk in front and the city inspector came out there. He checks the concrete and says everything looks good. Meets city standards, etc. Great. Nothing unusual. But here's where it gets funny. He pulls my guy aside and says the assurance fee won't be necessary. Since when does that happen? I've never heard of such a thing."

"The Assurance Fee?" Robert took another bite from his bratwurst. He thought it funny how Derek couldn't just come out and say "bribe."

"Yeah. He gets a little something for every square foot of concrete we pour for sidewalks. Every contractor figures it into the bid. Every developer figures it into the total cost. I was like, you're kidding me, right? And my guy tells me he can't believe it either. But that's not all. If it was just that one thing then I'd chalk it up to a fluke. But then last week, one of my other guys came back to me with the briefcase of money he was supposed to deliver. The guy who was supposed to take it from him told him there was nothing to be done. Now, I don't know how I'm supposed to get those bungalows re-zoned out on the Northwest side so I can build three-flat condos. There are some strange things going on in this city. Wish I knew what it was. But it's crimping the styles of a lot of people."

"Why are you telling me this?"

"Because I want to know what you think. I mean, what does your old man think?"

"His Cadillac SUV got booted last week."

"Whoa!"

"For what he owes the city in unpaid parking tickets he could buy a new SUV. He's livid."

"So what's his take?"

Robert was not going to tell Derek about what Marcia had hinted to him about his father. The secret was only safe with him and Elise. He trusted Derek, but he knew if he told Derek, that Derek would tell his wife, and she could possibly tell her father, who could possibly tell his already testy friends and business partners (the vast majority of Derek's and his father-in-law's friends were business associates), and the secret would no longer be a secret.

"He thinks it's all BS. That they're getting out of hand letting the do-gooders do their good."

"Between Soldiamori and Campbell, things were running pretty smooth all over. And then the council goes on strike and everything gets thrown up in the air. Soldiamori agreeing to cooperate with the Feds is really going to hurt a lot of people. There's a whole lot of hell that's going to break loose. And your almost-wife is to blame. It's a good thing you didn't marry Marcia. I'd have to stop talking to you." Derek grinned and took a drink from his beer.

At 10 o'clock that morning the media were in the press room of the C. Everett Dirksen Federal building. Indicted Alderman Frank Soldiamori, the Chair of the Council's Rules Committee, stood behind a podium with over a dozen microphones on it. At 68 years of age, he stooped a little in his shiny gray suit. His black-rimmed glasses always seemed to be on the verge of slipping off the tip of his nose whenever he spoke in front of a microphone. He was flanked by his attorney Caleb Grimm on his left side, and U.S. Attorney Jonathan Hynes and Federal prosecutor Marcia Bartolozzi on his right. The alderman's trial was scheduled to start in less than a month. In a statement which Alderman Soldiamori read aloud, he said, "I have decided to end the pain and suffering this long investigation, and the inevitable trial, is causing my family. It has also disrupted my service to my constituents of the First Ward and come at great cost to the taxpayers of this fine city. Yes, I am guilty, guilty of abusing my power as an alderman. I want to take this time to apologize to my family, my friends, and the good citizens of Chicago, whose trust I have broken. I also want to take this time to declare my intention to cooperate with the Federal government's *Don't Make Waves* investigation. That's all I have to say at this time. Thank you."

There was a momentary silence amongst the members of the local media. If it had been April First, they might have thought it was some kind of joke. But no. Here was one of the most powerful aldermen in the city council, the one thought to be too slick to ever get caught at anything, the one who had always been suspected but never indicted until late the year before, the one the political reporters and commentators believed was going to walk, suddenly admitting his guilt and willingness to cooperate with Federal investigators. The reporters wanted to ask questions, but Soldiamori and his attorney refused to take any. Hynes and Bartolozzi said they couldn't comment on any of the testimony that Soldiamori was offering because it might affect ongoing investigations. So the reporters scattered, rushing over to Bughouse Square and City Hall to ask the striking council members, and the mayor and his allies, what they thought. Few would agree to say anything more than that it was a sad day in Chicago. The few who would say more argued that Soldiamori had been framed and railroaded by an overly-aggressive U.S. Attorney office.

The reporters were grateful (especially those for TV) for the strike, and for all the events related to it. Without any murders in the city, TV reporters were left scrounging for other bits of news and having to do research. In the case of a murder, usually a gang-related, drive-by shooting, the TV reporters could simply show up with a camera crew on the front lawn of the home of the deceased's family and allow the family to have their grief and sorrow broadcast all over the Chicago area. Thankfully, the council and the mayor only required them to show up with a camera. Otherwise, they would be stuck filling airtime by mentioning once again how no one was murdered in the city, how much safer residents felt because of the lack of murders, and how the police were happy but extremely wary and worried that the lull in killing was the calm before a big storm.

Robert had read about the press conference online during his lunch break. He wondered if it was possible for his father to have anything to do with whatever it was Soldiamori had been doing. He didn't think so, though. Based on what Robert knew of his father, his father's activities were confined to the ward that included the Jefferson Park neighborhood in which he resided and in which Robert had been raised, making it highly unlikely that Soldiamori's problems were related to Robert's father. Most likely, his father would be caught in a widening investigation into the Hired Trucking scandal in the city's Department of Transportation. To this day Robert didn't understand why his father had come out of retirement. Maybe if he had remained in retirement he wouldn't be one of the next to be indicted. Between his father's coming indictment and Elise, keeping his mind concentrated on work had been a challenge. He thought it was a good thing that being the QA Department manager had been easy so far.

56   THE DEPARTMENT'S LAST RESORT

"I still can't believe I was promoted," said Robert.

"Would you quit selling yourself short?" said Derek.

"Huh?"

"Did you ever stop and think about why they promoted you? Or why I want you to work for me? It's not all the clout stuff that you know your way around. Shoot, I could train most anybody to do that. It's because you're smart, you learn fast, you've got good judgment, and, most of all, I trust you. And obviously, other people see your talents, too. Got me?"

"Yeah."

"Good. Now, let's watch some baseball."

Derek's phone rang. He pulled it out and looked at the screen. "Excuse me. I gotta take this call."

Derek explained to an architect how much he absolutely loved the floor plans the architect's firm had designed for a proposed condominium tower, but that they needed to squeeze one more unit onto each floor to make the development more profitable. As the conversation went on, Robert turned his attention to the field down below. It was the first inning and the New York Yankees were batting. Mark Buehrle was on the mound for the White Sox. His first pitch was hit for a pop-up to second baseman Tadahito Iguchi. His second pitch was grounded out to third baseman Joe Crede. His third pitch was a fly-out to outfielder Jermaine Dye. Robert had never seen the side retired on three pitches, let alone against the New York Yankees. The crowd was roaring as the White Sox returned to the dugout and the Yankees took the field.

Derek hung up his phone, looked at the field and said, "Damn, that was quick."

"Buehrle is fast, but no one's this fast," said Robert.

"You know you're the department's last resort, right?"

"Where did that come from?"

"It's just my read on the situation. So the guy who originally hired you—"

"Woman."

"Woman. So the woman who hired you leaves after you've been there what? Six months?"

"She said she was burnt out, wanted a new challenge. She's a consultant now."

"Right. Burnt out from what? Bucking management? Banging heads with the head of Software Development? Uh-huh. So they bring in your friend Perry who makes a bad situation worse. And given the opportunity, they fire him. Looks like management is itching to cut back on your department, or turn everything over to the QA Department of the bank you guys just merged with, or outsource entirely. Someone probably figured that if you're bold enough to challenge Perry out in the open, you might be the one to turn the department around. Or you might be the guy to run it into the ground. Either way, someone figures you're the right guy for the situation."

"It's not going to be like that. Everything's going very smoothly."

"That's good. You're getting a honeymoon period. But I wouldn't be your friend if I didn't tell you my read on the situation: you are the department's last resort. If you don't turn it around, I'd say your department is history."

Robert remembered Lisa Timoshenko's frustrations with her inability to make the case for the department's necessity, constantly getting into disagreements with Frank Bertuzzi. Frank complained that the QA Department never caught enough bugs. Lisa countered that her department found plenty of bugs, but that Frank's department didn't fix them. And they would go round and round, with the two frequently in meetings with Ted Allen's predecessor, John Long, as he attempted to mediate between Lisa and Frank, who argued over turnaround times on bug reports, and what was a "bug" and what was "by design."

When Perry was brought in, it was as if a fresh lake breeze had suddenly been allowed to pass through the permanently shut windows of the Fourth National Bank Tower. He had energy, plenty of smiles, and compliments for everyone, including himself. "Wait 'til you see what I'm going to do with this department!" "I'm going to shake things up!" "You'll find no bigger cheerleader on your behalf in this company than me!" By the third month of Perry's reign, the doubt made itself felt inside Robert like the taste of raw onion three hours after having eaten a hot dog with everything: rottingly unpleasant.

"I have to tell you though, you can't believe how smooth things are right now," he said.

"Things don't stay smooth," said Derek. "You know that. Bumps and full-blown roadblocks have a way of appearing in whatever smooth path you set. Half my job is lining up all the necessary pieces. The other half is keeping everything in line." He took a bite of his hot dog and drank a bit from his cup of beer. The Yankees were on the field and Scott

Podsednik was up at the plate. Podsednik hit the first pitch from Mike Mussina into left-center field for a base hit.

57   WHAT IF?

"How'd your father's birthday dinner go?" asked Derek. "Did you make it to the dessert this time?" Robert told him that he and Elise didn't even get to the appetizers and how they later ran into Marcia.

"Now that's a rough day."

"It wasn't so bad."

"What did Elise think?"

"She took it all pretty well."

"What's going on? She your new girlfriend or what?"

Robert shook his head. "No, no, no, nothing like that."

"Then why bother? You do want to get married and settle down someday, right?"

"Yeah. Of course I do."

"Then what gives?"

The count for White Sox Second Baseman Tadhito Iguchi was at 2-0. Mussina threw to first base. Podsednik, who hadn't taken his usual big lead, was back in time. Safe.

"There's nothing between us," said Robert with a drink of his beer. "We said our goodbyes last night."

"Not even a little fun?"

"I told you, we're not like that."

"I'm not saying bang her and leave her."

Iguchi took the next pitch for a ball; 3-0 was the count.

"We're just friends," said Robert. "We're barely even that."

"You must like her, though, a lot."

"It doesn't matter."

Iguchi fouled off the next pitch. Derek and Robert watched the ball fly into the stands about eleven rows behind them.

"Sure it matters." Derek set his beer onto the top of the dugout.

"I'm not going to try to woo someone who's leaving town."

"You could always visit her in Paris. You're in management now. You've got the money to do it."

"Look, nothing's going to come of it. Can we just watch the game?"

Derek took a bite of his hotdog. He chewed, watching the field. After he swallowed, he dabbed his mouth with a napkin and said, "Robert, you and I have known each other a long time. But I still do not understand you when it comes to women."

Scott Podsednik ran for second base. The crowd cheered as he slid into the base. The throw from catcher Jorge Posada went off the glove of Shortstop Derek Jeter and into center field. Podsenik ran to third base standing up. The crowd was roaring.

"You've got nothing to lose. Call her up and offer to take her out again. It can't be any worse than the non-dinner you had yesterday."

Robert couldn't hold back his laugh.

"See?" said Derek. "I'm just trying to help you out. You won't know until you try. If she tells you 'no,' then you can get on with your life and you're not left sitting around wondering 'what if?' If she says 'yes,' then hey, who knows? You guys could live Happily Ever After."

The next pitch from Mussina was a fastball down the heart of the plate, which Iguchi hit deep over the center field fence. The fireworks flew up behind the scoreboard, popping high in the sky. The crowd was on its feet. Derek was clapping and whistling. Robert was clapping, thinking that Mussina must have been rattled by the stolen base to offer up such a fat pitch to Iguchi. No, you never did really know what could happen until you tried.

58   ELISE'S DAYDREAM

I love spending time with you, Robert, she would say.
I love spending time with you, too, he would say.
Now that I've met you, I don't want to go to Paris.
I don't want you to go to Paris.
If you asked me to stay here with you, I'd say "yes."
Elise, would you stay here in Chicago with me?
Yes, with you, yes.
And they would embrace and kiss...

Elise became aware that Jen, who was standing next to her, was saying something. It was Tuesday evening. They were in one of the stores on Jewelers' Row on Wabash in the Loop. Jen had wanted to look at wedding bands and get Elise's opinion on them. They met after work and browsed a few of the stores. Jen had made a point of having Jay purchase her diamond engagement ring from one of the shops on Jeweler's Row. The prices were better than at any of the big jewelry stores in the malls. Plus, her parents had purchased their wedding rings from a place on Jeweler's Row.

"What did you say?" asked Elise. She had been gazing at a case filled with gold and silver Claddagh rings. Her parents wore gold Claddagh rings on their left hands. When they were dating, her mother had told her father that she didn't want money wasted on a rock. Elise's parents had met at Illinois State University in 1968. Her father graduated in '69, the year before her mother did. He found a teaching job in Rock Island and they continued to date long distance. At first, her mother had thought the distance would be too much, funny even though it was only about two and half hours by car. But Linda Connor missed Donnie Callahan. As her father put it, with his usual touch of silliness, "I was a streaking comet that was pulled into orbit around your mother." Elise and her mother would both roll their eyes whenever he said it. "I managed to tame the city slicker," is what her mother would say, Donnie having grown up in Gage Park on the southwest side of Chicago. The love between the two had stuck. They were engaged in the winter of 1970, and married after Linda's graduation in July of that year. Elise had a Claddagh ring, one she rarely wore, and had thought of Robert and being able to wear it on her right hand with the heart pointing towards her body, and then her mind had daydreamed the same conversation that she had already daydreamed a number of times the last two days.

"You were going to tell me about what happened after meeting Robert's ex-fiancé Sunday," said Jen. "Hello! I want complete details. I've been waiting two full days for the report on this date of yours."

"We're not dating. How many times do I have to tell you?"

"He took you to meet his family. That's not a man who thinks lightly of you. He's trying to impress you."

"Or he's trying to scare me off."

They laughed.

"So what else happened?"

"We had a nice dinner at Miller's Pub. I even ate the ribs. He said they were good, and he was right."

"Messy?"

"Of course. But he didn't care and I didn't care. Then we took a nice walk on Michigan Avenue all the way up the Mag Mile, and then took a cab home, which he insisted on paying for, telling me to save my money for Paris."

"That's it? No kiss!"

"Yes. That was it."

59   LIFE WITH ROBERT

Elise had held back on one detail: the warning from Marcia to Robert about his father's impending indictment. She knew that it must have weighed on Robert, no matter how much he hated how his father conducted his life. Poor Robert. She wanted to call or email him and see how he was doing. It's not like she could call him up and ask, "Has your father been arrested yet?" That would be crass. And if she called him, though she surely wouldn't, having said goodbye already, she didn't ever want him to think of her as crass. When she had gone to Augustana right there in-town, she lived on campus. Her parents had given her no restrictions on what subject in which to earn a degree. Unlike Robert who had had to make the case for his course of study, even though it seemed eminently practical to her. What that must've been like at the age of 19, to have to justify yourself and your life choices to a father constantly? She could see that Robert had managed to not be overly insecure, probably because he had at some point written off his father and his father's sense of judgment. Who could blame him? Robert was about to be vindicated about his father's criminal behavior. Or maybe Robert had worked through all his anxieties in therapy. He hadn't mentioned being in therapy. But he had lived in California, where everyone seemed to go into therapy like everyone else in the country went to get their hair cut.

"He sounds like a gentleman. You should call him. Life's too short."

Elise kept her eyes down at the glass counter full of Claddagh rings and clasped her empty fingers together.

"Life is too short. That's why I'm moving to Paris."

"You've already lived in Paris. You've lived in France twice. You've done it."

Elise turned away from the counter and headed for the door. "I don't want to pass up this opportunity I've created for myself."

"You haven't really dated anyone since Patrick. You even had a job practically given to you!"

"That job is now filled by someone else. Besides, there will be plenty of men and jobs in Paris." She pushed open the door to the sidewalk.

Earlier in the day Elise had contacted Paul Laurent to ask him about the position at the French school. She had been daydreaming a conversation with Robert when Carol had brought her back to the reality of the Tinker, Evers, & Chance reception desk by asking her to pick up the call on line four. After she routed the call she thought in that moment that if she got the job teaching at the French immersion school she would stay and be with Robert, and it sounded wonderful; going to restaurants, movies, the theater, teaching him to speak French, taking a trip with him to Paris, the Loire Valley, and maybe even Provence.

She called Paul. He didn't answer his cell phone, so she left a message on his voicemail asking whether the position at the school had been filled. She left her message a little before 10:30 in the morning. She continued to imagine her life with Robert until Carol asked her if her phone call to Paul Laurent meant she was interested in staying in Chicago.

Elise told herself not to claw out Carol's eyes. Only a few more days, and she would no longer have to sit next to this woman and listen to her chatter or deal with inappropriate questions like the one she had just asked.

"I'm not sure," said Elise.

"Hmmph," said Carol

"What's that supposed to mean?" asked Elise.

"That doesn't sound too clear to me. If you've already decided to leave, then why would you bother with a permanent job?"

"Because I'm simply curious."

"Curious about a job you won't be taking?"

"It's none of your business."

Carol took out some scrap paper and started making a grocery list. "O-kay."

Elise glared at Carol. Carol was an attractive woman of 39, who had always been friendly to Elise. Elise had not seen the point in getting to know Carol too well since the job was temporary.

For lunch Elise had brought a salad and some leftover minestrone soup, and had eaten it quickly, unable to occupy herself with anything other than waiting for Paul to return her call. She decided to go outside and take a walk around the block. She knew the building where Robert worked. So she walked down Lasalle, hoping to bump into him. She didn't bump into Robert after circling the Fourth National Bank Tower once, and returned to her office. When her phone rang and she heard Paul's voice, her heart bounced inside her chest. But he informed her that he had just gotten off the phone with the school's principal and that the position had indeed been filled, but only just the day before.

"You sound disappointed," he said.

"Oh, it's no big deal. I just thought, you know, it's really stupid of me to turn down an opportunity to at least interview for that job."

"Would you have taken the job?"

"I might have. I don't know." As the words left her mouth Elise knew it was the wrong answer. A dumb, wishy-washy, answer. How is it she messed that up? There was no sound on the line for a few moments, not even some background noise. She glanced over at Carol. By her tone and speed, Elise was sure Carol was talking to someone she knew, most likely one of her sisters or daughters. She seemed oblivious to Elise and what Elise was discussing. At least she hoped so. She didn't want to follow the current awkward conversation with an uncomfortable conversation regarding what her first conversation had been about.

"It was probably for the best then that you did not interview for the job," said Paul.

"You're right," said Elise. "I'm sorry to bother you. I don't know what I was thinking."

"Best of luck in Paris."

"Thank you." She had tried to sound happy and excited, but the words had come out flat and perfunctory.

60   LETTING THINGS GO

As Elise and Jen came to the stairs that led up to the Madison L station overhead, Elise thought that maybe she was breaking, that her very desire to go to Paris was waning. But even if that were true, and she wasn't willing to believe it true, it simply couldn't be. The one-way plane ticket had been bought. The apartment lease had not been renewed. There was no going back now.

"All right, whatever you say. You know best," said Jen. She had tried to not sound so sarcastic. She had been trying to not tell Elise what a bad idea she thought the whole thing was. There were times when it was better to lie to your friends if you wanted to keep them as your friends. Like when they were marrying someone who was horrible for them. You could not tell them what you thought. You would lose the friend even if you turned out to be right. It had happened to one of her high school friends, Kelly. Kelly had gone to Northern Illinois University and joined the Sigma Sigma Sigma sorority. A sorority sister Kelly had been close with had gotten engaged to a complete jerk, and Kelly had told this young woman so. The young woman stopped speaking to Kelly. Even after getting a divorce from the guy four years later, she still wouldn't speak to Kelly. This was one of those life decisions where it was best to be quiet and support her friend, no matter how hard that was.

"What is with you?" asked Elise. "It's like all of a sudden you think my big move is a bad idea."

"I never said it was a bad idea. I just don't think it's something you have to do. I told you that before, long ago, but you probably weren't listening, all caught up in your constant dreaming of living in Paris again."

"But it's never been on my terms."

"You met Patrick, the Sartre scholar, and went with him to Paris. He cheated on you. He got engaged. If you'd have left it at that—"

"No one knows better than me what would have happened had I let things go."

"You still haven't let things go."

Patrick had told her something very close to that early on in Paris, when their relationship was still working (though not necessarily well). They had been in their one-room furnished apartment on Rue de Malte for a month. It was a mostly residential street close to the Oberkampf metro station. But then a World Gym moved in across the street from their building.

"That's the most ridiculous thing I've seen so far," she said. "You can't even get away from American culture anymore."

"They built a replica of Paris in Las Vegas," said Patrick, "and there's also a version of France in Epcot Center in Florida. The re-creation is more authentic than the real thing. If you read Beaudrillard it all makes sense."

"But why did it have to open across the street from our apartment?"

"Elise, why do you let these things bother you? It's as if you think they're personally out to get you. You're in Paris! We're around the corner from Rue Voltaire. There's no Twain or Melville Avenue in New York or D.C. Think about it! They revere writers and intellectuals here."

"And our monthly-subscription-style gyms."

"Let it go."

Every day upon leaving their building, she would see that blue and gold sign and think how utterly ludicrous it was. She had lots of time to walk around the neighborhood, sit at a café, and read a book. Because of that, Patrick had expected her to do more around the apartment; to cook, clean, do laundry. She felt as if he had only brought her along to keep house for him, and order in restaurants for him, or interact with the shopkeepers for him. His French wasn't bad. But he wasn't confident, never having lived in a foreign country before. He was there to study, he said. So study more French by hiring a tutor, she said. Then he told her to get a job, that if she wasn't going to take care of the place, she needed to do something and not loaf around.

The World Gym was just one more thing ruining her Parisian dream. Once she had gotten the job with Professor Lipton, she began to enjoy Paris more, and everything between her and Patrick had seemed to be moving along nicely. With his one-on-one lessons, Patrick quickly became more confident in his French-speaking abilities...And then Patrick revealed to Elise that he had been cheating on her with the friend of his French tutor. He moved out of the apartment shortly thereafter. For a few weeks she would sit alone in the apartment listening to the radio, or sit alone at the brasserie down the street, sipping coffee, munching on chocolate croissants, and staring vacantly behind dark sunglasses at the people passing by. She felt abandoned. And then it hit her that she was "stranded" in Paris. There were much worse predicaments in which to be. She soon got into contact with people she had known during her first trip abroad, made new friends, and made it her mission to visit every single Literary Landmark in the city: from Balzac's house to the cafés that the likes of Hemingway and Picasso had frequented. Then she heard about Patrick and Sandrine's engagement, and her fury was inflamed.

Elise and Jen waited on the platform, boarded the train, and rode the L together all without speaking. Before Jen stepped out of the train at her stop, they said curt goodbyes to each other. Elise didn't understand how Jen could do this to her. She needed her support, not her criticism. Robert was a nice guy, a really nice guy. Nothing more. Okay, he was a smart, considerate, and funny guy, the kind of guy that she could settle down with in Chicago, of all places, share a home, and have kids. How was that different than any other guy she had met? Sure she couldn't think of any other guys off the top of her head. Sure she had spent the morning fantasizing about life with him. But that wasn't the point. She would have stayed had she interviewed for that job and gotten it. But it was all wishful thinking now.

61   A CONTENT LIFE

When Elise exited the Montrose L station and began her walk towards her apartment, she saw that the door to La Ville Venteuse was propped open. She hurried to the shop. All the tables and chairs had been removed. One of the two pastry display counters had been removed. From inside she could hear the sounds of clanging and men talking.

Elise went inside, her steps echoing across the dark wooden floors and off the bare cream-colored walls. She cautiously peaked into the kitchen and saw Monsieur Dusable talking with two men she had never seen before. Around them were numerous cardboard boxes, stacked on the floor and on the stainless steel tables and counters. It was the first time she had seen Dusable in street clothes. To her it looked strangely inappropriate.

She said, "Bonjour, Monsieur Dusable."

Dusable turned with a startled look, which quickly transformed to joy as he saw Elise. "Ah, bonjour, Elise!"

Their conversation continued in French. The first time Elise had seen Marc Dusable, she had been sitting at a small table next to the window of the shop. She was by herself drinking coffee and eating blueberry cheesecake, while reading Simone De Beauvoir's *The Mandarins*, when she saw this paunchy middle-aged man in a white chef's smock and hat amble from the back room to the front of the counters. He had a cigarette dangling from his mouth as he looked over the contents of the display counters. Dusable was from a small town in Northern France called Fler, that was now filling up with British retirees, attracted by France's health care system, small-town life, and easy access to the ferries to England. In Fler a number of British retiree-caused car accidents had recently forced the local government to put up posters in English reminding people to drive on the right side of the road.

"Jean-Claude is out back," said Dusable. "He would love to talk to you."

"I can't believe the shop is closing. I love this place," said Elise.

"It is disappointing but also wonderful. As much as we enjoyed this, the catering business will be much better. Are you still moving to France?"

"Yes. I'm so excited."

"Then I am happy for you."

"Have you ever thought of going back?"

He shrugged. "All the time. But my wife and children are here. My wife has a good job. My children are in school. They have friends here. My wife and I have a lot of friends here. Our life is here." He said it with what Elise could only believe was contentment. Seeing how matter-of-fact he was about it, made her realize once again just how discontented she felt. She was not living in the city she wanted to live. Nor was she doing the kind of job she wanted to do. She was not living the kind of life she wanted to live. She told herself that once she landed in Paris, she would breath more easily and her path would set itself for her.

"I understand," she said.

"I wish you the best of luck in your new adventure. Let me go and get Jean-Claude."

"Thank you."

Elise went back to the front of the shop. The space no longer looked as if it was even capable of feeling cramped as it could on those mornings when there was a line from the counter to the door.

Elise heard the slap of footsteps from the back of the shop. The sound bounced across the wood floor and against the windows. Mr. Beaubien called out in French to her. She answered. As he came through the doorway, he smiled when he saw her. He was lean, just under six feet tall, and 43 years old with some gray patches in his brown hair behind the temples. They greeted each other, kissing on the cheeks.

"This is crazy," said Elise, gesturing with both arms around the empty room.

"It's for the best," said Monsieur Beaubien. "I need to devote myself full-time to the catering business and expand it. Closing this barely profitable shop will allow me to do that. Actually, it's expanding on its own. These last few weeks I can barely keep up. Without having to run back and forth between two locations, I'll have more time for my family."

Elise grabbed the shoulder strap of her purse. She thought about her parents back in Rock Island. She had said goodbye to them over two weeks ago. They had driven up for the weekend to see her before she left for France, staying with her uncle Mike (her father's brother) and aunt Vicky in Oak Lawn. All of her grandparents were dead. Her father's parents had passed away within a year of each other shortly after she graduated from college. On her mother's side of the family, she had a few aunts and uncles and cousins spread from Peoria and into Iowa and Minnesota. On her father's side, she had family living in Oak Lawn and Evergreen Park. One of her cousins, Eileen, was living with her husband in Lincoln Park. Their was a great aunt who lived in a nursing home in Tinley Park.

"How are you?" he asked. "Are you all set for your big move?"

"I'm all set."

"You obtained your *visa de long séjour*?"

Here Elise had to think whether she should lie to him. She closed her mouth and looked about the empty shop. There was nowhere to sit, nor anything to lean on. She did not in fact have a *visa de long séjour*. Which meant she would not be a legal immigrant. She was not planning to do so. She knew she would most likely not be able to obtain the proper paperwork for attaining legal residency in France because she had once been deported. Unless she had a job in hand. Which she did not have and was not likely to obtain based on the fact she had once been deported.

"Uhm. Not exactly," she said.

"Elise! What is wrong with you? What are you going to do once you get there?"

"I'll be fine. I have some job leads through a friend. Us Americans don't even need a visa to enter the country."

"Things have changed since 9/11. It's not as simple as it was to be an American going to Europe. Every country has tightened their borders, their entry process. I'm a French citizen and it's still a pain to get back into France. And it's an even bigger pain to get back into this country, my adopted home. I can't wait until I take the citizenship test in a few months...You are asking for trouble."

"I'll manage."

Beaubian sighed and closed his eyes for a few moments. "Why do you want to live in Paris so badly? What is it you hope to gain there that you cannot gain here, in your own country?"

"A Parisian life."

"And what is that?"

"Living happily in Paris. Strolling along the Seine. Going to see films. Eating fresh baguettes. Not being hurried in restaurants."

"Those things will provide you with a content life?"

"There are no places like Mariage Frère or Café de Flore here."

Beaubien blinked his downcast eyes, appearing to acknowledge the truth of Elise's statement. He furrowed his eyebrows and pushed his lips together. No, there were no centuries-old institutions in Chicago. There were few centuries-old things in the U.S. As a country it was still relatively young, full of opportunities, still mostly unencumbered by its own history. He felt as if he was talking to his four-year-old son who was about to have a tantrum over the fact he couldn't stay outside any longer and had to come inside to get ready for bed. You could explain all you want. It wouldn't change a thing. The kid was going to be brought inside kicking and screaming.

As the silence continued Elise thought Beaubien looked perturbed. He had never before been perturbed at her. She was afraid she might have offended him somehow. But why was he now questioning her plans, plans he had known about for over a year? Today she had been at the end of so much glaring silence: Paul Laurent, Jen, and now Beaubien. It was uncomfortable, awkward, and frustrating that she'd had to suffer through these long painful silences today.

Beaubien raised his pale blue eyes to her and said, "I think you want romance more than you want Paris. And romance can happen anywhere. From the biggest chateau overlooking a sparkling river to a tin shack along a mud road."

"I'm not some naive undergrad who's going there to study for a semester or backpack through Europe."

"I know that. But I do not think you are going to Paris for good reasons. I think you are trying to prove something to that ex-boyfriend of yours. I don't think you will be happy or content in Paris."

She opened her mouth to say that he was wrong.

He held up a hand. "I hope I am wrong in what I am thinking."

62   THAT TEENAGE FEELING

Standing on the sidewalk in front of the empty storefront that was once La Ville Venteuse, Elise asked herself what the hell was going on? Why were people turning on her? First Jen, now Beaubien. She had to focus and stay focused. She would be eating fresh baguettes and buying tea from Mariage Frère. Yes, tea. She would be able to stroll along the Seine, sip coffee during an afternoon at Café de Flore, window shop, shake her head at the tourists going to Les Deux Moulins and the Moulin Rouge, linger through an evening at a restaurant without ever being hurried by the wait staff. That she had no one with whom to do those things was an idea she told herself she would quickly and easily rectify. Her friends Sophie and Marc had gotten married since she had last lived in Paris. Claude had moved to London to work in Finance and be with his English girlfriend. Julie was engaged to be married in the Spring. All this she had heard not from them, but from Catherine. Catherine was the only one of her French friends still speaking to her. Sides had been taken during those last days in Paris, and Elise had been on the losing end. Her only ally had been (and continued to be) Catherine, who had once boxed up a cheating ex's entire collection of jazz CDs, packed them into her brother's Fiat, drove them to a bridge over the Seine, and then emptied the cardboard boxes into the river. Catherine had sympathized with Elise and had believed Elise was justified in her attempt to have Patrick deported. The few English-speaking expats in their circle of friends had come to view Elise as an oddity, she knew, perhaps even crazy and mean-spirited. But she was going to show them all. Catherine, who was living with her boyfriend Jean-Yves, said Elise could crash at their place as long as she needed to, and had told her as recently as last week that she had some job leads for Elise. So yes, Elise would get to live the exotic ex-pat lifestyle that others would envy. That others expected her to live now that she had told everyone of her plans to move to Paris. *Carte de séjour* or no *carte de séjour*. Job or no job.

An L train at Montrose rumbled off, going north. People streamed out of the station, the vast majority splitting in two directions on the sidewalk, east or west, with a few jogging or walking fast across Montrose. Dozens of people were coming towards Elise. She took a few steps back in the direction of the shop, in order to get out of the way of the moving crowd.

Soon, so very soon, she would no longer be among those people in the eight-to-five grind. She would be in Paris. She closed her eyes and pictured the Seine, its wide green-gray body winding its way through Paris, a serene river split by the Île de la Cité on which both Notre Dame Cathedral and the Vert-Galant garden resided. It was also the quiet spot where Lipton's apartment was located, where she had spent so much time doing searches on the Internet, taking notes, and making trips to the biblioteque to retrieve and return books. She would be able to walk those old streets again. When she opened her eyes the crowd had disappeared like a wave crashed ashore.

Then, from her right, Elise heard the familiar pleasant voice of the Siren of Ravenswood. Her head turned in the direction of the singing and she saw her dressed in a black spaghetti strap dress, black sandals, rose-tinted sunglasses, with buds from her iPod tucked into her ears. For the first time Elise saw that she had a small marijuana leaf tattooed onto her outside left ankle. Elise did not recognize the song, but quickly guessed it was about love as the Siren sang about how she was holding out for that teenage feeling.

Elise watched the woman stroll past, her eyes focused on her pink lipstick-covered lips forming each word. The woman's voice carried through the din of cars, trucks, horns, footsteps, and chatter. A few people passing in the other direction looked at her with contempt or bafflement. She continued to sing with her eyes forward. Elise had come to admire her unabashed desire to sing. She would miss this one quirky thing about her neighborhood there in Chicago. With her eyes she followed the woman as she walked under the tracks of the L, where she stopped to turn off her iPod before entering the station. And then Elise saw him come out of the station, holding his cell phone up to his left ear.

She thought of running to Robert and throwing her arms around him and shouting, "I want to stay here with you!" feeling all tingly inside. Stop! Stop! Stop! she told herself. This is wrong. She was going to mess up her own nearly-two-years-in-the-making plans for a guy she had just met? No, no, no, and no again. The easiest thing to do was to let it all go. Right?

63   RUN

It was now twice in two weeks that Robert's mother had called him on his cell phone. The phone had rung as he was exiting the train at Montrose. Robert explained to his mother that it was hard to hear her with all the noise because he was just getting off the L. No, he wasn't trying to avoid talking to his own mother.

"You can't blame me for thinking that," she said. "You're not the most active member of our family."

"I'm also the least corrupt," he grumbled.

"What did you say?"

"Nothing, mom," he said loud and clear. He was going down the steps slowly, letting others who were in more of a hurry to go around him. "What's going on?"

"I'm sorry about Sunday," she said. "Your father's sorry, too. You know, it really hurts him how the two of you don't get along."

"I'm sure it does."

"You should go and talk to your father."

"I don't think so," said Robert.

"He's your father. Go see him at the hot dog stand tonight. He's working so Charlie can have the night off. I won't tell him you're coming. Surprise him, for me. Please."

Robert felt as if both of his brothers were standing on his chest. Talking to his father by himself in person? Could he do that? He had been hoping he would be able to wait until after the indictment to speak with him. Why did Marcia do this to him? He supposed he could try to talk to his father, just once, in the way he imagined most other fathers and sons spoke to each other; the way his friends like Derek and Martin spoke to their fathers without having to have an arms-waving, finger-pointing, shouting match.

"I dunno."

"Please. I'm asking."

"It never works out, Mom."

"Please. This time. For me."

Robert stopped at the bottom of the stairs. He might not get a chance to speak to his father before the inevitable arrest. He had no idea when it would happen, since Marcia had not indicated when. No doubt it would be very soon, within weeks in all probability.

"All right. I will."

"Thank you. I want you two to get along."

"I know."

"What an impression for that new girl of yours we must've given her on Sunday."

Robert rubbed his forehead. "She's not my girl."

"Whatever you say. I didn't even get a chance to talk to her. What does she do?"

Robert walked through the turnstiles. "She works as a receptionist at a law firm. But it's temporary. She's fluent in French, so she's moving to France."

"What's she going to do there?"

"I don't know."

"So why are you two dating if she's leaving the country?"

"We're not dating. She's just a woman I met in front of a closed pastry shop one day and now we're friends. End of story."

"Boy, you're a fountain of information."

When Robert stepped out of the station he saw that weird woman who was always singing around the neighborhood walk past him and into the station. He took a deep breath, telling himself that the onslaught of lovelife questions would be over soon, once she realized there was no information to be retrieved. Then he could hang up the phone without telling her to empty their bank accounts, get dad, and run. Where? He didn't know. But it had to be anywhere but Chicago and their place in Tampa Bay. Why? Dad's going to be arrested. How did he know? He just knew.

Robert could not say the words. He knew his mother was not innocent. She knew the clout business as well as any of its purveyors. As a restaurant owner, his uncle had to make sure he donated to the right politicians or he could find himself answering the door to an overzealous Health Inspector, and dish out free meals to those inspectors. Not to mention comping some cops' meals or heavily discounting the per-plate price when an influential politician rented out the banquet room.

"That's just how we are." He glanced to his right and saw her standing in front of the closed pastry shop. She was looking at him.

"You need a good woman," said his mother.

"So everyone tells me."

"They're right."

He waved to Elise. She waved back, took a look over her shoulder, then started walking towards him. He took a step towards her.

"It's not for lack of trying," he said.

"Okay. I need to let you go. I've got to finish making dinner."

"Okay, mom, bye."

"Love you, Robert."

"I love you, too, mom."

64   THEY MEET AGAIN

Robert tucked his cell phone away, wondering how he was going to pull off a one-on-one visit to his father, something he hadn't done in a very long time. He had always felt safer with other members of the family around even when they were all against him. With an audience, the arguments proceeded like a performance. Without anyone's impressions to live up or down to there would be no script to follow.

Elise was now standing in front of him.

"Didn't I already say goodbye to you?" he said with a grin.

"Then what are you doing talking to me?" she said, grinning back.

"I could ask the same question."

"You're the one who started the conversation."

"You were looking at me."

"You were looking at me."

"I thought you'd be far from Chicago by now."

"I've got less than a week. Five days to be exact."

"So what's new?"

"I was just talking to Monsieur Beaubien."

"Any chance he's going to re-open?"

"No, not at all. He's devoting all of his time now to the catering business. It's been far more successful than the shop itself."

"Well, that blows for me."

"I feel your pain," she said.

Robert thought that since he had bumped into her, the hell with it. Might as well see if she would be interested in hanging out with him just one more night.

"Okay," he said, "My friend Janet is going to kill me if she finds out I ran into you and didn't invite you to the concert her band is having this Saturday at the Metro. Twice I had plans to meet up with her and her husband Mark, and both times I had to cancel because of you."

"When did you cancel plans with them?"

"The night I asked you to dinner and the night of your friends' dinner party."

"You shouldn't have canceled plans."

"It's done. No big deal. By the way, you should invite your friends Jen and Jay, too, if you want. I don't know if you're into her music. But her band The Clips are great."

"What time?"

"Nine o'clock. You guys can meet me out front and we'll go in together."

"Wait. You're friends with Janet Fischman?"

"Yeah."

"How do you know her?"

"Her cousin was my roommate freshman year in college. I liked her first band Gin Wolf. Even saw them play when I lived in California. Anyway, you interested? It's no big deal if you aren't or if you can't. I know you have a ton of things to do between now and Sunday when your flight leaves."

"That sounds like a fun way to spend my last night in Chicago. So yes, I'm up for it. And I will definitely tell Jen and Jay."

"Cool. Then I'll see you Saturday."

"Great. Looking forward to it."

See, thought Robert, that was easy. She didn't even hesitate...There was definitely something there between them.

65   "SOLDIERS FIELD"

Robert was through the front gate to his building, and halfway to the entrance, when Logan called out to him from across the courtyard, "Robert! did you hear the news?"

He stopped. "No. What news?"

With Logan were his two dogs Solomon and Nelson.

"They're officially changing the name of *Soldier Field* to *Soldiers Field*. The Park District announced it today. It's long overdue."

"You're kidding me."

"No. I swear on my wife's grave. It's on the news, or check it out on the Internet. They're finally listening to me."

"To you?"

"Who do you think has been complaining to them for years that they weren't spelling it correctly?"

How ridiculous, Robert thought as he walked up the three flights of stairs to his apartment. There was no way they were adding an S to the end of *Soldier* in *Soldier Field*. What was next? The grocery store *Jewel* was going to bow to how so many people mispronounced its name and change it to *Jewels*? No way. The day they let nuts like Logan dictate spelling and grammar was the day he left town.

When Robert turned on his computer and opened up the *Chicago Tribune* web site in his browser window, there was the headline: "Soldier Field Renamed *Soldiers* Field." It was under a story titled, "Aldermen Decry Mayor's Latest Comments," and above a story titled, "Mayor Criticizes 'Do-Nothing Council.'"

The Chicago Park District announced today that it was officially changing the name of the Home of the Bears from "Soldier Field" to "Soldiers Field," said Park District Commissioner Gordon Rice.

"The name change was discussed on and off over a period of years," said the Commissioner. "We finally decided to go ahead with it. Afterall, the vast majority of Chicagoans and even Park District employees pronounce it with the S at the end. It's a better reflection of reality."

The Park District plans to have the S added in time for the Bears' first regular season home game on September 7.

Robert closed the browser window and went to his room to change out of his work clothes, thinking the city was going collectively crazy, for better and worse. California had its own trademark form of experimental crazy but nothing like this. Why did he ever let Marcia bring him back to Chicago? Family was a lot easier to deal with when you lived two thousand miles away from them...He could blow off visiting his father tonight. His father would never know. But his mother would.

66   ROBERT DEVOURS A HOTDOG

It was just after eight in the evening and the sun had already gone down when Robert parked his silver two-door Saturn in the parking lot of Dan's Dogs. Other than to the grocery store, he rarely drove his seven-year-old car. Robert had gone running, eaten an apple, and showered before heading out to meet his father. He had intended to only run three miles. But when he reached the three-mile mark, he was still feeling anxious and not very tired. So he ran for another mile as fast as he could, in the hope of working off the tension he was feeling. Now, as he stood next to his car looking at the hot dog stand, he felt tense again. As a kid, Robert had spent a lot of time there in the summer. He would ride his bike and lock it to the chain-link fence in back next to the dumpsters. During high school he worked there part-time. Sometimes he gave certain friends, like Derek, free food. His father caught him once and docked his next paycheck by $50, telling him, "This place is supporting our family. When you cheat this place, you're cheating yourself." Robert never did it again.

A few years later, shortly after Robert had graduated high school, his father had confided to him that if he had to do it over again, he would have started a different business than the hot dog stand. Something like a trucking, delivery, or cleaning service that would get large city contracts. Far more profitable and devoid of the thicket of city hiring rules. No hassle about who to hire and fire. With that kind of money he could have quit working for the city altogether.

Robert locked his car, thinking it had been at least a year since he had last eaten at his father's hot dog stand. That time he had stopped in on a Saturday night to get a strawberry milk shake, having spent the day at a cookout with Derek and Sherry at Mike Farley's house out in Buffalo Grove. Mike and his wife Jill had been married for four years and had recently bought a three-bedroom house. Jill was pregnant with their first child (a girl). Both Mike and Jill worked out in the suburbs. Like so many of the people he and Derek had known, Mike had moved to the suburbs after college. They wanted better schools, bigger yards, and freedom from the city's corruption. Robert didn't blame them. He hadn't yet made up his mind to raise any future children he might have in the city.

Robert went in through the front entrance. The smell of the place consisted of boiling hot dogs, shredded beef simmering in its own juices, burgers grilling, and French fries and onion rings frying. While living in California he had missed that smell, and places like his father's stand. There were good fast food places in California, but not like in Chicago. None in California could conjure the unique feeling that was a mixture of his youth, the people he knew, and the neighborhood itself, though the people in the Bay Area were definitely less portly than those in his hometown. He still ate his hometown's fast food, but nowhere near as often as he had before he had moved to California and back.

Robert's father was behind the counter talking with two of his workers, a young white woman of high school age and an Hispanic man in his early twenties. Robert didn't know them. It used to be that he knew all of them, the good ones (who stuck around for awhile) and the bad ones (who the elder Grabowski would either fire or make their working lives hell). There were only five people eating inside, all of them teenagers.

Richard Hellinga

"I didn't expect to see you tonight," said Dan.

"I thought I would come by," said Robert

"You hungry?"

"Oh yeah."

"What do you want?"

"A hot dog with everything."

"Sweet peppers?"

"Yeah."

Dan turned to his workers and said, "You guys hear that?"

"I'm already on it," said the young woman. She put a hot dog in a bun and began covering it with mustard, onions, tomatoes, relish, a pickle, and sweet peppers. Then she set the hot dog in a wrapper-lined red plastic basket and added a generous amount of French fries. They were freshly cut. Robert always liked those kind the best. He'd had to operate the slicer in the back room many times, cutting pounds of potatoes into long thick strips ready to be fried.

Robert and Dan sat in Dan's usual spot, the four-person booth in which he usually sat when talking to friends (social or political). It was in a corner, away from the restrooms. The laminated plastic booths had red contoured seats and yellow tables.

Robert took a bite of the hot dog. It tasted good.

"I just wanted to come by and say 'hello.' Especially after last weekend," said Robert after he swallowed that first bite.

"Oh," said his father.

Robert took another bite of the hot dog. He wanted to tell his father to pack a suitcase for himself and his mom and just leave. Fly to the Caribbean. Run. Hide. The Feds are coming for you. But as soon he swallowed, he put some French fries into his mouth. As soon as he swallowed those, he took another bite of the hot dog, and so on until every bit of the hot dog was gone and the fries, too, even the tiny crunchy ends. Not once did Robert look at the face of his father. If he had, he would have seen how perplexed Dan looked at his son devouring his food like he was starving.

"Are you getting enough to eat?" asked Dan. "If you want more, you can have more."

"No. Thank you. That was enough. I took a run after work. So I had a bit of an appetite."

"Okay."

Robert wiped his mouth with a napkin, gave a small burp, and looked at his father. He looked tired. Working full-time at his city job and now working a weekday night so one of his managers could have the night off was wearing on him. Robert did not think his father had it all that easy. He had many obligations to fulfill, some for his job with the city, many for his hot dog stand, some for the politically-connected, and above all for delivering the vote on each and every election day. The latter was the foundation upon which everything else rested. If he didn't bring in the vote for the right people, there went his ability to perform and accept political favors. His father had chosen to live that way, and now, finally, he would have to suffer the consequences.

Robert could not tell him to run. Just like he could not tip off the Feds about him. Despite his revulsion at the way his father, brothers, and thousands of people conducted their business in the city, Marcia and the Feds were doing what he could not bring himself to do; he could not rat out his own family. If courage was tipping off the Feds to their activities, then he did not have it. The brother of the Unabomber had it. And therein was the dilemma for Chicago: in a city where getting a government job was seen as a way to get ahead, and helping your family and friends to the exclusion of all others was valued so highly, clout would always prevail over merit.

"Why do you hate me?" his father asked.

"Aw, dad. I don't hate you," said Robert.

"Come on. You can tell me. I wanna know."

"I don't—"

"There's no other explanation! I mean, what else could it be?"

"Dad, can we talk about something else? Why do we only talk about the stuff we don't agree about?"

"'Cause there's a lot of it." Dan smiled.

Robert smiled back. He knew that of the three boys, he had always given his father the hardest time, that he had been the most challenging to raise. Robert was the one who always asked "why?" Robert asked why he had to go along to mass every Sunday now that he had already made his Confirmation. Robert asked why his curfew was earlier than his friends. Robert asked why he couldn't borrow the car. Robert asked why Mayor Harold Washington was so bad for the city. Robert asked why his father never worked "full-time" at his city job. His older brothers had rarely spoken to their father in the irreverent tone Robert had often used in high school. While his oldest brother Anthony had joined the Marines after high school and Michael had gone to work for the county after his graduation, Robert had insisted on going to college. Dan had been skeptical that his most argumentative and troublesome son would be successful away from home studying at a university. It was Loretta who convinced him that Robert would do well in college. She turned out to be right. Robert did not depend on his father and his father's connections for his livelihood.

"How's Elise?" asked Dan. "How does she figure into your life these days?"

"She's just a friend. She's moving to France in a few days."

"How does someone work that out?"

"She lived there before and has friends there. She wants to go back. So that's what she's doing."

"I'm not going to push you about it like your mother. Besides, you've never taken my advice when it comes to women, or anything else for that matter."

Robert had always discounted his father's clout-motivated advice. So here was a moment for him to make a peace offering.

"There's one thing I could use some advice about and that's my new job," said Robert. "You've managed people for a long time. What can you tell me?"

"Get used to justifying yourself."

"What do you mean?"

"You're in a bit of a different position than I am," he said, then gestured with both arms up and around. "Here, even though I have to follow the law about hiring, taxes, and health codes and all that, I make all the rules. I have sole authority. You, on the other hand, are in charge but you've got constraints and limits because of what the guys above you allow you to do. If I say we need new tables and seats, as long as I've got the money, I just order them and have them installed. If I want to give one of my workers a raise, like Trisha or Javier over there, who hustle their asses better than most of my people, then I just do it. If you need new computers for your people, I imagine you've got to get approval before a single dime is spent, even if your department already has money allocated in its budget for such a thing. That's how it is for me at the city. Miles of red tape 'cause it's the public's money. You've got to make the case for it, fill out the right paperwork, etc. The other thing is that you're going to have to carry out a bunch of stuff that the company and upper management want that you might not agree with or, knowing you, that you think is downright stupid. Those are the times you're going to have to keep your mouth shut and do what you're told, without question." Here Dan leaned toward Robert. "And then there's what your workers want: time off, compliments, respect, raises, and all the things they need to do their jobs. Before, all you had to do was worry about you and the job you were doing. Now, you have to make sure your people are all doing their jobs with the resources upper management allows. It's a balancing act. But I can guarantee you that there are gonna be some days you're gonna feel like you're caught in a vise. You're gonna feel like you don't get to decide nothing."

Robert nodded. He had forgotten just how intelligent and insightful his father could be. He wasn't a stupid man. He had managed to elude the law all those years. But he was about to be caught. The question Robert wanted answered was this: How was Dan Grabowski going to react once captured? By being loyal to the machine and going to prison quietly or testifying against others in exchange for a reduced sentence?

"Make sense?" said his father.

"Yeah," said Robert. "Thanks. I appreciate it."

"If you ever have any questions, you know you can always call me and ask. Bossing people around is harder than it seems...Some days I wish I'd stayed retired." He looked over at the front counter. Trisha and Javier were taking an order from a middle-aged man with glasses.

Robert wished his father had stayed retired. The man clearly had no idea what was coming.

Dan turned back to Robert. "How are things now on the job?"

"They're going well. Pretty smooth, actually. Derek warned me that things'll get bumpy soon enough. He also thinks I'm the department's last resort."

Robert explained the situation with the past two department managers, the merger, and Derek's reading of what that all meant for Robert. The elder Grabowski thought about it for a short bit, rubbing his chin with his hand.

"Derek's got a good point."

"Think so?"

"Yeah," he said with a nod, his face solemn. "You'll need to watch yourself."

"You can't be serious. You think Derek's right?"

"I do. He's a smart guy, to make the kind of money he's made."

Derek and his father couldn't both be right, thought Robert. Why would he be set up for failure? Why would anyone do that to him? To his department? No. They had to be wrong. They didn't know anything about IT or how QA was done. It was very different than real estate, running a hot dog stand, or working for the city. Everything was going so smoothly. Though he disagreed with his father's take on his promotion, this felt good to Robert. It had been at least a decade since he'd had a calm, conflict-free, meaningful conversation with his father like the one he was having now.

"So, can I ask," said Robert, "without trying to start an argument, why your SUV got booted and why you're having to spend more time at your job with the city?"

"You really want to know?"

"Yeah."

"Thanks to the strike, the rules have been suspended. That's what Wisniewski told me. There's no one to enforce them or mediate disputes because the two main factions of the system are fighting each other. It's mucking up everything. There are developers waiting for zoning changes, friends waiting for appointments to various city boards, merit promotions on hold at all the city and county departments, city contracts on hold. You name it, it's on hold right now, or worse, unprotected. So there's nothing to prevent the do-gooders from doing what they think is right. Reporting supposedly unauthorized absences, code violations, substandard job performance, all that stuff. It's created a whole lot of chaos for a lot of people. Things just aren't working the way they normally do."

"And until the strike is resolved—"

"It's not even a real strike so much as it's a job action. The mayor is a great one but he needs to share more of the pie, and not keep the council on such a short leash. He has many, many strengths, but sharing ain't one of them."

Richard Hellinga

67   WHAT ROBERT AND ELISE WOULD NEVER KNOW

In most Chicago city departments, there was always a known list (not always written down) of preferred contractors and well-regarded businesses. The former were those with whom it was acceptable to award contracts for services. The latter were those businesses exempt from inspection, including restaurants and catering companies. One such catering company was Sanchez Brothers Catering. On the Tuesday following the council walkout, an inspector from the city's Department of Health showed up on the premises of Sanchez Brothers Catering on Ashland Avenue in the Back of the Yards neighborhood. Sanchez Brothers Catering had never been the subject of a city inspection. Its owners, Jaime and Carlos Sanchez, were cousins of Alderman Ray Salazar, one of the Mayor's strongest supporters. The inspector found numerous code violations from copious amounts of rat droppings to faulty plumbing. The owners protested and threatened the inspector, but Sanchez Brothers Catering was closed until further notice. The brothers tried to use their clout, but there was nothing to be done on their behalf until they fixed all the violations. They were forced to cancel many event contracts at the last minute. This left people in charge of the events scrambling to find a caterer for their event. Frantic calls went out to caterers all over the Chicago area. At least a dozen other caterers ended up with the business Sanchez Brothers was supposed to have performed. One of them was Jean-Claude Beaubien's La Ville Venteuse Catering, gaining a dinner at the Chicago Cultural Center and a brunch at the Winter Garden of the Harold Washington Library. Beaubien decided then to close his storefront. He could not do the events and run his shop at the same time. The business decision was clear. When he closed the café and pastry shop on Sunday afternoon, he closed it for good, taping the note to the inside of the front door. When Robert and Elise arrived the following morning, they found a darkened shop and each other.

68   THE FAMILY BUSINESS

Thursday afternoon, Robert was sitting in his office examining the list of projects and attempting to evenly match them up with his department's resources. But try as he did to determine an adequate distribution of pending and current projects to people and time, he kept thinking about what Derek had said to him at the ball game about how he was the department's last resort. There were so many software projects and simply not enough people to put in the hours necessary to effectively test them all in the time demanded. A certain level of creativity with their time would be needed on his part and theirs. His main consolation was that in terms of time, his workers were ahead thanks to faster turnaround with some of the projects during the past few weeks. By now Robert had hoped to have heard from Ted Allen about his proposal for purchasing the automated testing software. He thought that would allow his department to thoroughly test all the projects more quickly. Maybe Elise had the right idea; he should quit his job and move to France. Maybe if he asked, she would let him tag along.

Years before, at the end of their two week trip, Robert had suggested to Marcia that they not go back to California and instead travel around Europe, staying in hostels. She said it was a nice thought but that they were not the kind of people who do things like that. There were careers to manage, savings to build, a first house to buy to build equity in order to buy the second, bigger, house for when the children came. Robert remarked that was probably more sensible, though there was plenty of time to do those things.

He had calculated how much money they could use for such a trip and have enough left over to cover living expenses back in the states for a few months. But Marcia could not just walk away from a DA job for a month or two or more. It was frowned upon. She would not be viewed as "dependable." He had to admit, he didn't know of any lawyers with bohemian tendencies. They didn't have time to indulge such impulses, nor the luxury of having such indulgences not be looked upon with disfavor by future potential employers. Elise was discarding all of that. Then he remembered he had followed Maggie out to California and how that relationship ended shortly thereafter, and how he had followed Marcia back to Chicago and how that ended in disaster. So following a woman across the Atlantic Ocean seemed like an even worse idea.

The phone on Robert's desk rang. The LCD screen indicated it was a call from outside the company. He picked up the receiver and said, "Good morning. This is Robert."

"Good morning, Robert," said his mother in a flat voice. "I hope I'm not interrupting anything."

"No, you're not." On his computer he minimized the spreadsheet he had been working on. Then he eased off his desk and sat back in his chair.

"It was a good thing you did the other night. You made your father very happy. I haven't seen him that happy in a long time."

"He actually had some good advice for me about my new job."

"Good. I'm glad."

"Me, too."

Robert was expecting his mother to follow-up, but she didn't. The silent second slipped into another silent second which then added another silent second and kept doing so until Robert, wondering what was wrong, said, "What else is going on?"

"It's your father."

"Is he all right?" Robert thought maybe this was really it, that he had finally been arrested. He could never tell them that he knew beforehand that his father would be arrested. Never. That he had the chance to warn them and didn't.

"No." Her voice cracked.

"What happened?"

"The FBI arrested him this morning as he was leaving the house."

"Oh, no." Robert looked at the door to his office. He felt a bit relieved that it was closed. This was not a conversation he wanted anyone else to hear. When the topic came up (rarely), he told people at the office that his father worked for the city and left it at that.

"I can't believe it."

"Why did he ever come out of retirement?"

"Because he was asked to."

His mother explained how his father had been asked to come out of retirement and work in the Department of Transportation under a trusted member of the machine. They had wanted someone who was experienced, skilled, and above all, trustworthy to handle some of the nitty-gritty details of the hiring process. (Robert translated that as "rigging the hiring process in favor of those people the machine wanted to be hired." He could hear his father justify it all, "What if you already know someone who deserves the job? Why should you have to go through all the BS of posting an ad and interviewing people? Just hire the guy. Why shouldn't it be any different than the private sector? If you want to hire a friend you just do it.") Someone higher up made the decisions. It was the job of his father and some others to make sure it all happened. He was only following orders, like he had always done. It was a sign of how much people respected him that he had been asked to do such an important job.

"Wow," said Robert. How stupid, he thought. His father had actually quit while he was ahead. And now, thanks to his inability to keep his greed under control (not that someone so used to indulging his greed could), he was headed to prison.

"But it's not just your father," said Mrs. Grabowski. "When I tried getting a hold of your brothers to tell them what happened, I ended up talking to Angela and Denice...Anthony and Michael were arrested at work." She began to cry.

"What?" Robert sat up. He had not expected that. Marcia had not given him any clue really as to who was going to be arrested. He always figured it would be his father. He had always believed that his brothers were too insignificant to bother with.

She managed to take a number of breaths so she could speak again. "Your father's lawyer says the Feds don't have a whole lot on them, that they're going to use them as leverage against your father."

"Enough to indict, though."

"Obviously...You know, we aren't stupid, Robert."

"I never said you were...Okay, I might have called dad and Michael and Anthony 'stupid' on a few occasions."

"You've called them 'stupid' and a lot of other things on a lot of occasions. You should give them a lot more credit than you do."

Nevermind, he thought, how little credit they gave him, always implying he was a sucker for working so hard at a "straight" corporate career in a field that yielded him no political power, nor garnered him special treatment. Nevermind their dismissal of him as naive whenever he told them that breaking the law wasn't a requirement for living a productive life. Nevermind their contempt for his education. Easy, he told himself, easy. Yes, he was always the one who had to control his behavior, but it was not the time to have that argument.

"How are Angela, Denice, and the kids?" he asked.

"They're about as well as can be expected. The kids haven't been told a whole lot just yet. How do you explain something like this to your children?"

The paragraph that was forming in Robert's mind was one he knew he should keep to himself. He felt bad for his nieces and nephew. But he wasn't the one in jail right now. He wasn't the one who needed to tell his kids that daddy and grandpa got caught doing bad stuff and now they're going to jail. He was the one who went to college, got a degree, and made a life for himself outside all the corrupt crap his father, Anthony, and Michael had been swimming in along with all the other corrupt idiots in that city. And somehow he was the one who was supposed to show sympathy for them? He was the one who had been treated like the family's black sheep by them and most of his aunts, uncles, and cousins. Heaven forbid anyone should point out their corrupt crap. Everyone had told him to shut up and not be so disrespectful to his own flesh and blood. He had given up counting how many times so many relatives had told him to go easy on his father. It was always him who had to play nice. It was always him who had to come to the birthday party, wedding, or whatever family event and shut up, while everyone else pretended everything was hunky-dory and said how wonderful it was that dad and Anthony and Michael had sweet jobs...They made their decisions. They did what they did. Now they had to live with the consequences...He loved his father and brothers. But he detested how they had lived their lives.

With his mother's trembling voice on the other end of the phone, all that anger was collapsing under the weight of the depression that was coming down all over Robert like sleet. Every second he was pelted by the wet ice of sadness. This was not how he thought he would feel. No vindication. No schadenfreude. No relief. Prison. He could hear the blunt clink of metal bars against concrete.

"Robert? Are you still there?" said his mother.

"Yeah. I'm here. I don't know how you explain any of it, mom. I don't want them to go to prison. I love dad, and Michael, and Anthony."

"They love you, too, you know that, right?" Her voice was cracking again.

"I do."

"I've always been happy you went to college, Robert. I'm so proud of you. I love you." This time the crying overwhelmed her.

"I love you, too, mom."

She could barely utter the word "goodbye" before hanging up.

Robert set the phone back on the cradle. His mother had been ecstatic when he had graduated from the University of Illinois and had told him then how proud she was. Hearing the words now lessened the sadness he was feeling, but only a little.

69   OPERATION: GREASY THUMBS

The arrests of the elder and younger Grabowskis were part of a wide-ranging investigation on the part of the Federal Government called "Operation: Greasy Thumbs." (It was a completely separate investigation from the one which nabbed Alderman Soldiamori, "Operation: Don't Make Waves.") Over four dozen employees of the city of Chicago and Cook County were arrested. The charges ranged from fraud, bribery, extortion, racketeering, and tax evasion. All of it was related to falsifying time sheets, changing the results of hiring exams, rigging the bidding processes for city contracts, taking and demanding kickbacks, using city and county assets for personal use or political work, and doing political work on city or county time.

Immediately after the one o'clock press conference, where Federal prosecutors announced the arrests and indictments, members of the media raced to City Hall and Bughouse Square to get the reactions of Mayor Nash, his allies, and the striking aldermen. But the mayor wasn't in his office. His allies on the council were not in their offices either. The striking aldermen never showed up at Bughouse Square. A number of people did show up to take turns at the open microphone ranting about the city's poverty, poor public schools, crime, street gangs, drug use, gun violence, and overly generous subsidies for developers, and raving about the city's beautiful parks, new buildings, clean streets, cleaner neighborhoods, and good restaurants.

The media did manage to get word from a few sources that negotiations to end the strike were underway between the mayor and the striking aldermen. But that was all. There were no press conferences, press releases, or even leaked comments. This confounded the media. Normally, all that was needed was to give a Chicago politician a microphone to talk into and they would hold forth on whatever was on their mind. This quiet was baffling.

70   SEEING GHOSTS

During a mid-afternoon lull, Elise read the story about the mass arrests of city and county employees on the web site of *The Chicago Sun-Times*. At the end of the story was a complete list of the people who were arrested, a list that consisted of people who were mostly male but spanned from white to Hispanic to black. Among those names were: Dan Grabowski, Anthony Grabowski, and Michael Grabowski. Poor Robert, she thought, the whole world could see it now. Marcia hadn't indicated that his brothers would be indicted. She should call him and see how he was doing. But discussing something like that at work didn't seem right because she didn't want Carol or anyone else to know about Robert and his family. She would call him as soon as she left the office.

Elise closed the web browser on her computer and turned her attention to her email. There was a message from her friend Catherine in Paris.

"You'll never guess who I saw today! I ran into Patrick at a brasserie. He was coming in with some other guy just as I was going out. He looked surprised to see me. We said 'Hello' and chatted a bit. He said he was just back from a wonderful vacation in Greece.

"When I told him you were returning to Paris in a few days, he looked like he'd seen a ghost. He said it was impossible. I couldn't resist laughing. He asked why you were coming back and what you were going to do. I told him not to worry, that you were not going to stalk him. He seemed scared. He kept asking why and I told him why shouldn't you come back? You spoke French, loved Paris, and had friends here. What more did you need? Until I told him you were coming back, he looked quite happy and confident.

"I can't wait to see you in a few days. We're going to have so much fun."

Yes! Elise thought, finally, the bastard had to sweat again. Being back in Paris: awesome! Making Patrick nervous: priceless! There was justice in this world.

71   WAR OF THE WORLDS

Robert spent the rest of his work day going through the motions with as much vigor as he could muster, which was not a lot. It was like mourning a death in secret. After work, Robert didn't feeling like talking to anyone or going to his apartment, so he switched off his cell phone. He decided he would get some dinner at the Zephyr, the diner up the block and around the corner from his apartment. Or maybe he would skip dinner altogether and try to eat their 10-scoop ice cream sundae known as the War of the Worlds.

Robert was one of the few people inside the restaurant there on Wilson Avenue. He had started going there in high school with his friends, lingering over generous plates of food and large milk shakes. He took a few girls there after movies on a Friday or Saturday night. In those days, the place was always packed. In the time that he lived in the Ravenswood neighborhood, he noticed the steady decline in customers. Where once on a weekend evening it was common to see teenagers, families with small children, twenty-somethings, retirees, and the occasional off-duty policeman or fireman, now the place would be half-full. The newer yuppie residents wanted something other than an old-fashioned neighborhood diner. No wonder it was rumored to be closing.

"I'll have the War of the Worlds," he said to the waitress. She was young, white, and high-school aged.

"For dinner?"

"I'm having one of those days."

"I understand."

"It's all right. I'll add an extra mile or three to my nightly run."

She smiled and took the order into the kitchen.

Robert had heard the rumors for the past few months now. Neighborhoods always changed, he thought. Places opened and closed, some faster than others. Landmarks were designated, like those for Carl Sandburg's old home a block up on Hermitage Avenue, and buildings torn down to make room for the new. Maybe he should move. With his new salary he could afford Lincoln Park or even Streeterville. When his lease was up at the end of May he could move.

When the waitress came back she set a large glass of ice water in front of him.

"Can I ask you something," he said, "Is it true? Is this place closing?"

"Look around you. See anyone in here?"

"Crap. When?"

"End of next month. Landlords want more rent. And apparently they're going to get it from someone when they turn this place into an Irish pub."

"We don't need another Irish pub. They're already everywhere."

"Well, someone thinks this neighborhood is in dire need of one, and so they're going to get one."

"Lovely."

She shrugged. "What's there to say? There isn't much to be done about it. It sucks." She left to take the orders of some other customers.

Robert hadn't tried eating a War of the Worlds since college. He was with his girlfriend Cathy. She had gone to Madonna High School and was going to DePaul at the time. That was the summer after freshman year. She told him he was crazy to eat something so big by himself, and that she would share it with him. She managed two or three scoops and Robert finished off the rest. He was bigger back then with a bigger appetite. There was no way he was going to finish the sundae. Besides, there was nothing healthy about eating a 10-scoop ice cream sundae, especially for dinner.

After putting the remains of his sundae in a to-go box (he ate five of the scoops with some of the toppings), he paid the bill, leaving the young waitress a 40% tip. As Robert was walking toward his apartment, he turned his cell phone on. There were two messages, one a voicemail and the other a text message from Derek that read, "r u ok?" Robert could never understand how it was that Derek had a full keyboard on his phone but still typed text messages as if he had only a keypad. The voicemail was from Elise, saying she had read the news about the arrests and that she was sorry for him and his family.

Robert deleted both messages and turned his phone back off. He would call them later. For now he didn't feel like talking to anyone.

72   A DEAL IS REACHED

Shortly before five o'clock Friday afternoon a joint press release was sent from the offices of Mayor Nash and Alderman Campbell, stating that the council strike was over and that a deal had been reached. No details were offered. They cited only the necessity of putting aside their differences in order to "work together to make Chicago the best city in the world."

73   HE'S ALWAYS PICKING FIGHTS

Robert arrived at the Metro with Derek and his wife Sherry a little after eight Saturday night. Elise was waiting out in front with Jen and Jay. Robert handled the introductions and then they all went into the club. No one said anything about the arrests of Robert's father and brothers, and Robert was glad of it.

Robert had made the rounds of his family earlier that day, visiting his parents first. What he had expected to see was a large confident man now reduced in size and strength. Instead, his father was proud and indignant. He started out by declaring to Robert that he didn't care what the Feds claimed, he was not guilty and neither were Anthony and Michael. He couldn't believe they were going after them, too. It was insane! When the case went to trial, it would all come out how he had done nothing wrong. He was not going to prison, and neither were Michael or Anthony.

"I don't want you to go to jail," said Robert shortly before he left.

"I'm not going to jail, Robert," said his father. "I'm not guilty."

Robert hugged his father. "I believe you."

"Thank you," his father said quietly. "It means a lot coming from you."

Michael and Anthony, however, were openly scared. They talked about their worries for their wives and kids, and their shock that their father was being taken down. Both brothers had been surprised not just that Robert had come to visit, but that he had not condemned them and had instead shown them support and affection. Robert wanted to tell a joke or two, the grim kind he and his brothers would normally say to each other in odd situations in order to cut the tension and provide comfort, but he could not think of any.

Robert came away from those visits more depressed than when his mother told him about the arrests. He got to thinking about how if convicted his father would lose his city retirement, the cost in legal fees, and where that would leave his mother. What about Michael and Anthony? Both of their wives worked full-time outside the home. Did they earn enough to support a mortgage and daycare? Probably not. What should Robert do to help his family? He didn't know.

Inside the Metro, the mostly white crowd was large but not to the point where you couldn't move. The show was open to the public, but with many of the tickets set aside for the press, industry types, and friends. At the door, people were handing out free copies of The Clips' new CD, to be released the following Tuesday, entitled, "Whatever." A handful of lucky fans were able to get free tickets by registering on the band's web site and being chosen through a lottery. The Clips would be touring the U.S. and Canada for the next three months, returning to Chicago for a handful of shows after Thanksgiving.

Janet was standing in front of the bar, surrounded by four men, only one of whom Robert recognized: Mark Schulien, her husband. Mark ran a recording studio that was located in the storefront of a former hardware store on Howard Avenue. He started Crypt Studios over a decade before with his friend Henry Grunewald in the basement of a rundown three-flat a few blocks from Loyola University.

"Let's go say 'hello,'" said Robert to Derek.

They greeted Janet and Mark, who thanked Robert, Derek, and Sherry for coming. Janet was short with dark straight hair. She was expecting to meet the woman with whom Robert was enthralled, a man she had never known to be enthralled with anyone. He didn't drop everything for Marcia like he did for this woman he claimed was leaving the country. When Robert came to see her at one of The Clips' first low-profile gigs at Thurstons, he had run from the altar only months before. She was engaged to Mark at the time. After the gig, she, Mark, and Robert had gone downstairs to the bar for a drink. Robert was still feeling pretty morose. Now he looked buoyant.

"Where's your date?" said Janet. "The one you keep blowing me off for."

"Over there." Robert waved to Elise and she waved back.

"You can see why he's fallen for her," said Derek. Sherry slapped him on the arm.

"What was that for?"

Sherry glared at Derek. "Robert has enough to deal with without you giving him a hard time. Why don't you get us some drinks."

"All right."

"Bring her over," said Janet. "I want to meet her. What's her name?"

"Elise."

"So tell me about her."

"When she was living in France, she tried to get her ex-boyfriend deported."

"I like her already," said Janet.

Robert motioned for Elise, Jen, and Jay to come closer.

Derek stepped up to the bar. "Robert, you want anything?"

"Yeah, a beer," he said. "And can you get one for Elise, too?"

"Sure."

"So how do you get a date with a woman who you met by having an argument?" asked Janet.

"In my defense, I was a little cranky that morning. My favorite pastry shop had suddenly closed up for good, so I couldn't get any coffee, and I had a headache. It was also Monday."

"What did you say to her?"

"I'm getting to that. She said she couldn't wait to get out of Chicago, that she was moving to Paris, and I said that moving to Paris wasn't very original."

"Dude, you've got to be kidding," said Mark.

"That's horrible," said Janet, who was laughing.

"I know it wasn't the nicest thing to say," said Robert, "but the fact is when I realized how pissed off she was, that she was still pissed off a few days later, I apologized and offered to make it up to her by buying her a cup of coffee. She said she had already had some but thanks anyway. So I offered to take her out to dinner, no strings attached. And she said 'yes.'"

"Where did you guys go?" asked Janet.

"Café Selmarie, up there in Lincoln Square."

"Nice choice."

"Nothing happened afterwards."

"Of course. I can't imagine she would want anything to happen, especially after you trashed what I'm supposing is her dream."

"I apologized to her! But I still maintain I was right about Paris being an unoriginal place for an American to move to."

Janet held her vodka martini to her chest and sighed. "And therein lies the problem with you, Robert."

Elise sidled up to Robert. Jen and Jay were unable to get any closer because of the crowd near the bar. Robert introduced Elise to Janet and Mark.

"We were just talking about how when Robert first met you he picked a fight with you," said Janet. "He's always picking fights."

"He is," said Elise. "But it turns out he's a really nice guy."

"I did apologize and make it up to you," said Robert to Elise. "I even introduced you to a genuine Rockstar over here."

Janet rolled her eyes and sipped her drink.

"You know, Robert," said Mark, "Out of all the guys I know, you're the one who really knows how to get under a woman's skin without even trying."

"I'll second that," said Janet.

"I'll third that," said Derek over his shoulder. He handed a beer to Robert, then to Elise.

"What?" cried Robert.

"You know you have a way," said Janet.

"I don't go out of my way to be mean or anything. It's not like I'm some sort of love'em and leave'em kind of guy."

"You were with me."

Robert gripped his cold perspiring beer bottle a little tighter. This is what Robert thought Janet would never reveal, let alone so publicly. Airing the details of his sex life was not how he had planned to spend his last night with Elise. Not that there was much to reveal. There was Cathy, then Maggie, then Tina, then the one night stand with Janet, and finally Marcia. He hadn't had sex with anyone since Marcia.

"I think it was the other way around," said Robert. "How many guys were you with on that tour?"

Mark closed his eyes and smiled. Derek and Sherry laughed. Elise's mouth hung half-open. Janet knew she had said a dumb thing, the kind of thing that made her look bad. There was a time, like on that tour, when she didn't care who knew what about her or with whom she did it. Now she cared. Having kids had done that to her. She didn't want to embarrass Robert and now it was too late. She should have kept her mouth shut.

74   JANET THE SEXY ROCKSTAR

It had happened months before Robert had met Marcia. Robert had gone up with Martin and another friend to see Janet's band Gin Wolf play at the Fillmore.

Robert had slowly pushed his way up to the front of the stage during the first few songs. When Janet saw Robert she gave him an exaggerated look of surprise. She was playing rhythm guitar and singing backup to their lead singer Tom Urge. She was wearing a white T-shirt with the sleeves cut off and a picture of the Ramones on it, red leather pants, and black Converse All-Stars. Robert still remembered because he had focused on every detail of her throughout the entire show, partially in disbelief that his college roommate's cousin was now a bona fide Rockstar and because for the first time, despite how ordinary-looking he had always thought her, he saw just how sexy she really was.

After the show the band and three-person road crew had gotten some burritos from a takeout place, then gone to the motel to eat and unwind. Which meant a small party with Glaze, the other band on the tour with Gin Wolf.

"You work with computers! Wow, a real geek," said Janet.

"Yes, I work with computers, but believe me there are plenty of people who know a lot more about them than me, and are a lot more geeky."

"But you're a cool geek. Like the guys who work in the studio."

"Glad to be one of the cool ones."

"Can I tell you how cool it is to see a familiar face? You always were the coolest of my cousin's friends."

"I couldn't miss this. This is amazing right now. This! You're a Rockstar."

She blushed and pushed him. "Oh, shut up. I am not."

"To this geek you are a Rockstar."

"Okay, I am. Hey, I noticed you lost weight. You look great."

Robert had lost just over 40 pounds since living in California.

"Thanks."

"Enough of this. Let's smoke a joint." She headed toward the door and Robert followed. In the hall Robert asked, "Where are we going?"

"Just trust me."

They entered the room next door. Janet locked the door behind them and fastened the latch.

They were sitting on the bed watching videos on MTV and had finished nearly half the joint when Janet said, "Kiss me."

And he did. They rolled their beer-soaked, pot-smoked tongues together. Robert had felt at once ecstatic to be with Janet the Sexy Rockstar and disembodied from himself, the person who was stripping off her clothes.

75 DIRTY LAUNDRY

"Janet," said Derek, "You're supposed to be helping Robert impress Elise. Not embarrass him."

"Are you saying it's embarrassing to have sex with me?" said Janet.

"Yes," said Derek.

She turned to her husband. "Is that what you think, dear?"

"Of course not," said Mark.

"The details of someone's past sex life can be left to at least the 20th date," said Derek. "Come on! This is Robert's last chance to impress her."

Sherry pinched the back of Derek's upper right arm. He yowled in pain, nearly spilling his beer. Then he said, "All right, all right."

At first, Elise was jealous. Then she quickly became very annoyed at Janet for embarrassing Robert that way. She saw that his face was reddening and that he was clutching his bottle of beer with both hands. Just because she was a Rockstar didn't give her the right to drag out all her dirty laundry at someone else's expense. So what if she slept with him? That didn't mean she had some sort of claim on him.

"I'm sorry, Robert," said Janet. "I'm sorry, Elise."

"It's all right," said Robert.

"No worries," said Elise, fixing a smile onto her face. She took a drink from her beer and thought about pouring the rest over Janet's head. But that was a surefire way to get herself thrown out and embarrass Robert even more.

Jen and Jay managed to push their way next to Elise.

"So what's going on here?" asked Jen.

"We're hanging out with a genuine Rockstar," said Elise.

76   REMEMBER THIS NAME

The music on the PA system faded out and the lights dimmed in the club.

"Oh," said Janet, "That's what I need to tell you guys about. The Wood Ravens are opening up for us. They've just been signed. They're going into the studio next month to record an album. What a voice this woman has got. Wait 'til you hear it. Gabby Tomczak. Remember that name."

The crowd started to whistle and clap as four white women took the stage, The Wood Ravens. Elise nearly dropped her beer when she saw who walked up to the microphone. It was the Siren of Ravenswood, dressed in her black Converse All Stars, a black cotton dress with white polka dots, and thin white tights.

Robert thought, hey, it's that crazy chick from the neighborhood who's always singing to herself.

Elise, Derek, Sherry, Jen, and Jay moved closer to the stage. Robert was going to follow them when Janet grabbed his arm.

"She is so into you, Robert," said Janet.

"She's moving to France," said Robert.

"Excuse me," said Janet. "She's leaving the country, when?"

"Tomorrow."

"Oh, so she has all kinds of time what with packing and a million other details, to spend an afternoon or evening with the family of a guy she just met, and hang out with you the night before she's leaving the country. Yeah, she's totally uninterested in you. She chose to spend her last night in this city, this country, with you, Robert. Hello!"

"It's out of my hands."

Robert wanted to believe there was something he could say or do to change Elise's mind, to keep her from getting on that plane tomorrow. Nothing he could think of doing or saying seemed a credible convincing gesture. The plan was set. He had to accept it.

"When I blurted out how you and I had a one night stand, did you see the look on her face? She was ready to kill me. As a woman, I can tell you Robert, you don't make that look if you don't care. She cares. And again, I'm really sorry. Us bigmouths go too far a lot of times. Please tell her I'm really sorry and that I didn't mean anything by it, okay?"

"Okay."

"All right. I've got to get ready for our set. See you later."

77   WHAT GIRLS WANT

The crowd responded warmly to the Wood Ravens during the 30-minute set of their high-energy brand of pop-punk. They ended with a ballad called "Twilight on the River" that featured Gabby accompanied by the guitarist playing her electric guitar with the distortion turned off. The crowd roared at the song's end.

Afterwards, Gabby was at the bar smoking a cigarette. As she waited for her beer, she fielded compliments from many people, including Elise and Robert.

"You guys were great," said Robert.

"Thank you," said Gabby, taking a drag off her cigarette.

The way Gabby held it, right hand aloft holding the smoldering cigarette with her other hand cupping her right elbow, made her look elegant, thought Elise. Such a contrast from the swagger she displayed onstage. She wanted to bum a cigarette off her and start smoking again.

"We've seen you singing around the neighborhood," said Elise.

She laughed. "You guys must think I'm crazy."

"No...Well, yeah, a little. Why are you always singing? Not that I mind. You're voice is wonderful to hear."

Gabby shrugged. "I just love to sing. People think nothing of talking or kissing in public. But for some reason everyone thinks you're crazy if you sing in public. Also, there's a lot of weirdos in the city. Singing keeps them away. They think I'm the crazy one."

"Well, I wish you and your band all the best," said Elise.

"Thank you." She took a drag off her cigarette.

"See you round the neighborhood," said Robert.

"See ya."

Robert and Elise headed back to where their friends were standing.

"This is fun," said Elise, touching Robert's arm. "I'm so glad you invited me to come along."

"That's good. I'm glad you could join me."

"That's so amazing about Gabby. I never knew her name. I never knew she had a band."

"I never knew she wasn't a total whack job."

Without thought, Elise slipped her arm around his. "Now, I'm really going to miss her."

When The Clips took the stage, Elise's arm was still around Robert's until she pulled it away to join in the clapping and cheering that greeted the band.

The Clips ended their show with a second encore, a cover of the Material Issue song "What Girls Want." Janet singing about girls wanting love, drugs, sex, affection, and an impossible combination of features in a guy underlined for Robert the difficulty in knowing just what Elise wanted from him. She kept saying "yes" whenever he asked her to do something with him. Maybe she only wanted friendship. Who knew? He was sure of two things: 1) he loved her, and 2) he needed to tell her he loved her before she left Chicago for good.

78   SO THIS IS GOODBYE, AGAIN

The show was over. Robert and Elise stood on the sidewalk in front of the Metro. Jen and Jay were a few feet away behind Elise. Derek and Sherry were a few feet away behind Robert.

"Thank you for inviting me," said Elise. "I had a great time."

"You're welcome," said Robert.

"Janet shouldn't have done that to you in front of everybody."

"It's no big deal. I'm sorry I didn't say anything about that beforehand."

"You don't have to explain. She's a Rockstar!" She giggled.

Robert breathed a little easier. "That's just how she is."

"Still, that wasn't nice of her to do. I know she probably thought it was funny."

"She has a big mouth like me."

Elise wondered, why? Why this guy? With all his charms and flaws laid bare for her to see? Why now? Why was the attraction and desire so strong and so full? She lowered her head and closed her eyes. In her mind she saw Robert opening his mouth wide to bite into a big, juicy, giardinera-topped beef sandwich, the meat spilling out of the bun, the juice dripping down his chin onto the wax wrapper spread on the red formica table in front of him. That was Chicago. She opened her eyes and he was still standing there, as neatly groomed as always, with those calves of his made lean and muscular from running. Why did she think him sloppy? Why couldn't he be a slob, a jerk, a doofus, anything to make him unappealing, anything to make it easier to say goodbye to him?

"For what it's worth," said Robert. "I'm going to miss you, even if you hate this city."

"I don't hate Chicago. It's just that it's not Paris.

"So, goodbye. Or should I say, *au revoir*."

"*Au revoir*. I'm going to miss you, too."

Elise unclasped her hands and reached out her arms to Robert. His French pronunciation was clumsy, something she could help him fix. They embraced. She could spend the night with him. Have a last fling. If they were going to have sex she knew she would have to take the initiative. The geek in Robert wouldn't let him pounce. Even if she had let him pounce, and she might if he would. But she didn't want to just have a fling with him and become a joke or source of embarrassment or curiosity 10 years later like Janet. She wanted all of him.

Robert thought his arms fit perfectly around her and that she smelled sweet and that his boss Ted Allen was right that some decisions are more permanent than others, and that Janet was right, too, that Elise must feel something for him if she had chosen to spend her last night in Chicago with him. They broke their embrace, Robert putting his hands in his pockets, Elise folding her arms.

Robert looked over Elise's shoulder. Jen and Jay were standing about twenty feet off. They appeared to be talking and looking at Wrigley Field, which was about a half-a-block away. He glanced over his own shoulder. Derek and Sherry were talking near the entrance to the Gingerman Tavern. Derek caught his glance and winked, nodding at him and gesturing for him to "Go on! Do it! Make your move!" Sherry slapped his arm. Now is the time, thought Robert. Opening his mouth had gotten him a promotion. Keeping it closed for too long had led to the disaster at St. Vincent Ferrer.

"I just want to tell you," said Robert. "That what you're doing is pretty amazing. Most people are too afraid to go after what they really want."

"Thank you," said Elise. "Even if you don't think it's original?"

"I don't want to have an argument the last time I talk to you. Though it would be fitting, since that's how we met...I'm just glad I got to meet you and that you've spent so much of your time with me, especially when you have so little of it left to give."

"I've had a lot of fun hanging out with you."

"That's good. Because I know what this is. I don't have to think about it and I don't have any doubts about it. I love you, Elise."

Her placid face crumpled into pain. "Please don't do this to me."

"I'm sorry. It's done."

"Why? It's going to make everything so much harder." Her eyes began to well up with tears.

"It's already hard. It was hard trying to pretend I didn't feel for you the way I do. It's hard knowing you're going to be on another continent after tomorrow."

"I know. I'm so sorry. But I've been..." She curled in her lips and looked away, down Clark Street.

"Planning this for so long," said Robert. "I know...So here we are. I should probably leave it at that. I've already upset you enough. I don't want to upset you. It's the last thing I want to do. But I couldn't watch you go without letting you know how I feel."

She couldn't move her eyes in his direction. "I know I'm leaving you behind. It's not something I want to do. It's something I have to do."

"I'm just going to walk away now. Have a wonderful life, Elise."

"You, too, Robert."

After a few seconds, she dared a glance in Robert's direction. He was standing by Derek and Sherry. Derek slapped him on the back. Sherry put a hand on his shoulder.

Elise tried wiping the tears from her face as she stepped closer to Jay and Jen. Their troubled looks forced the bubbling pain in her heart to fill her body to her extremities.

"Please don't say anything," said Elise. "It's hard enough."

79   ONE RED LEAF

In the morning, Robert went on a run. Unable to sleep comfortably the night before, he had woken up feeling wound and frustrated that Elise was leaving. He would not be able to call her. He would not be able to bump into her by chance walking around the neighborhood. He had said what he had to say. He had no regrets. He just wished it had been enough to get her to stay.

As he was walking down Bob Fosse Way toward his apartment, he saw a leaf float down from one of the maple trees and land on the sidewalk. It seemed too early for the leaves to change colors and fall. He reached down and picked it up. He thought briefly that it might be painted, but it wasn't. The leaf was red, fall red. He looked at the ground around him, down the block and behind him, then the street, and the lawns on the other side. There were no other leaves on the ground. In the trees that lined the street, all the leaves were green.

He took the red leaf with him up to his apartment and set it on his dining room table next to the books and unopened mail.

80   SNOW IN AUGUST

Sunday afternoon the clouds piled in, set low and stopping above the city. They darkened with each passing minute from translucent white to asphalt gray. Many of the tops of the city's tallest buildings, like the Hancock and Sears Tower, were submerged in the clouds. Planes at O'Hare and Midway circled in sun, descended through white and landed under gray. Then the rain came and the temperature dropped.

At five o'clock, Elise was standing in line with the other passengers waiting to board the plane. She felt chilled, wearing a short-sleeve shirt and jeans. Through the floor-to-ceiling windows she watched the falling sleet outside become snow.

"This is crazy," said a male passenger behind her.

"Snow in August? Who ever heard of such a thing?" said a woman.

Elise gave her ticket to the flight attendant at the gate entrance. He fed it through the machine, handed it back to her, and said, "Enjoy your flight."

Elise thanked him and entered the passageway, which was very cold and caused her to shiver. She was doing this, she thought as she walked along the downward slanting path. She was leaving the U.S. She was leaving Robert. He could visit her. Yes, he could! As soon as she got to Catherine's she would send him an email. She would tell him...What would she tell him? "I love you and miss you? Would you come visit me?" Could she say those things? Or would that be cruel? Would that be playing with his feelings thousands of miles away?

The plane was cold, too. Once in her seat, Elise tried the air nozzle. The air coming out was cold. So she shut the nozzle and sat shivering some more, watching the seats on the plane fill up with people, who were also shivering and complaining about how cold it was on the plane.

Elise told herself that she was making the right decision to get out of Chicago and return to the city in which she had earned the right to live. She would arrive at Charles De Gaulle airport, take the train into Paris, and then the Metro to Catherine's apartment. Patrick would really be scared. He should be. In a matter of hours, all would be right with the world. She was getting on the right plane going to the right city. The snow and sleet could not stop the plane. The plane had to take off. She was not going to stay here. She was going to be happy. She wanted to be happy. The man who loved her was going to stay in Chicago while she went to Paris. Why couldn't love be more conveniently timed? Why did it pop up at the most odd times and drag you to another continent to break your heart? Or show up on your doorstep just as you were about to undertake long-prepared plans? Why couldn't love fit itself into your life more easily? Why did it insist on rearranging everything you had set your mind on?

Through the window the snow looked pretty as it fell. The first snow of the season always looked pretty to her. Not that the first snow ever happened this time of year...She could still get off the plane. Cancel her ticket. How much would she lose? Too late. She was in her seat. The money was gone regardless now. She took out one of the magazines she had bought, the *New Yorker*, and began to read to help her pass the time and not think about Robert.

An hour later, the plane fully loaded, a woman's voice on the plane's intercom said, "Attention all passengers. The tower has informed us that due to the intense weather, we are going to be delayed. Therefore, we are going to deplane. We will re-board the plane once the weather improves and the runways are cleared."

81   THE HAPPIEST PERSON IN CHICAGO

Robert was on his gaming computer when he heard something pelt the windows. It was after nine. He had been engrossed in a game of Quake 3 for a few hours and hadn't noticed much else other than his sudden need to pee. Killing things had made him feel a little better. Earlier in the day, he'd had to shut the windows it had gotten so cold. Not knowing what was hitting the windows and now becoming aware of the whir of the wind, he quit his game and raised the blinds on a window and saw the snow. It was melting on the glass. Down below, in the glow of the orange street light, he saw the snow falling and melting on the street. Since when did it snow in August, he thought. He had never seen that in his whole life. Of course, he had never seen the Chicago City Council go on strike either, so what was snow in August compared to that? It must be a record of some kind. He went to the bathroom, peed, and returned to the living room to turn on the TV. He sat in his recliner, and waited through the news stories on WCHI about a gang-related killing in the Lawndale neighborhood (officially breaking the one-week-old truce), a new Bose electronics store opening in the Gold Coast neighborhood, and how your toothbrush might be making you sick. Then came the weather report by Nathan Hunt.

Nathan looked giddy as his face came onscreen in front of a map of the Midwest. "It's amazing. We've got snow in August," he said. "I've never seen anything like it. There are numerous canceled and delayed flights at O'Hare and Midway airports. The roads are very slick. So be careful if you have to go out. You'll need your cold-weather clothes, too. It's quite chilly. The temperature has dropped over 40 degrees Fahrenheit since this afternoon."

"Boy, you seem very happy Nathan," said Chris Giancarlo the anchor.

"Sorry, but lately there hasn't been a whole lot for me to do. The only precipitation we've had in weeks has been moderate and occurring only at night. But today, I've hit the meteorological jackpot!"

"Good for you."

"And it's only going to get colder! Down to 21 degrees for an overnight low. We're going to set a record for cold temperatures in August!"

Robert switched off the TV, hoping for Elise's sake that her flight had gotten out before the snow had started falling so heavily.

82   WAITING

This could not be happening, Elise thought as she sat by the gate with everyone else from the flight. She could not be waiting for the runway to be cleared. This city had truly the most horrible weather of any city on the planet, because not only did it have the extremes of summer and winter, the seasons themselves felt no compunction to stick to the designated times of the year in which they were supposed to reside. Snow in August! De-icing a plane in August! How insane was this city?

She could get up, walk out of the terminal, and go to Robert's apartment. He loved her. She loved him. What more was needed? No, she was committed to seeing this through. Besides, her suitcase was already on the plane. Though she could have her suitcase removed now. It was possible. She did not have to get on that plane.

One of the flight attendants announced that they were re-boarding the plane, starting with the passengers in First Class and families with small children. Elise saw a couple that looked not much older than her with a girl no more than two years old. They were talking in French, the father guiding the girl along as she toddled. There were two other families with small children. Between the three families there were five children, two of them infants. The infants had been quiet during the first boarding. Now they were crying, their mothers trying to soothe them.

There was time to back out, she told herself. Time to cancel all her plans. She would have to get her suitcase off the plane. She would have to take a cab to Robert's. Would he accept her now? Could she stay with him? Or should she go to Jen's place and stay with her and Jay, or maybe a hotel? She couldn't just move in with Robert like that. Maybe for the time being, until she found another apartment. Not to mention a job. She would have to get her stuff out of storage and buy new furniture. She didn't even have a bed or futon anymore...Staying would be more trouble and work than getting on that plane. Getting on that plane was the only rational thing to do for a person like her in the position she was in. She couldn't just walk away from the gate for a guy she had only known for two weeks.

Elise's row number was called on the PA. She stood, holding her bags, and took her place in line.

83   ELISE RETURNS TO FRANCE

Tired didn't quite describe how Elise felt as the plane pulled into the terminal at Charles De Gaulle airport a little after noon, local time. Exhausted was better. Irritated, too. The two infants had not slept well. So no one on the plane had slept well. Elise took little comfort in the misery she had shared with her two seat mates; a history professor from Northwestern on his way to an international conference in Paris, who specialized in the history of food, and his wife, a grant proposal writer who consulted for non-profits. They had two sons, ages 17 and 15, old enough to leave at home while they went to France to mix work and pleasure. They sympathized with the parents of the infants, but traveling with small children was always a crap shoot. They had left their sons at home so they wouldn't miss school and, besides, the boys weren't interested in traveling with mom and dad.

"Adventures are nice," said the wife, "We used to have those."

"We're starting to have them again," said the husband.

"Enjoy the ability to travel at a whim while you can."

"Thanks. I will," said Elise, wondering how a lack of movement felt. Since undergrad she had been planning her next move or trip, always focused on the next big leap away from wherever she was residing. From studying abroad, to returning to finish her degree, to looking for a job, to applying to graduate programs, to moving with Patrick to Paris, to plotting in Chicago to return to Paris.

Elise had given the couple only minimal information about herself, resisting the temptation to ask if the professor had heard of Dr. Terry Lipton. Nor had she told them she once worked for him. She had not told Lipton she was returning to Paris. She had only exchanged a handful of emails with him since she had been deported. The most recent exchange taking place over a year and a half before. She had found shortly afterwards that he had been in Chicago for a book expo and he hadn't bothered to contact her. She thought it best just to leave him alone. She had apologized for any trouble she might have caused him regarding her employment status. He knew people, counting the mayor of Paris, various ambassadors, writers, artists, and journalists as friends. So for her to do what she did and get herself deported, shredding the work he had done on her behalf toward a work permit, was seen by him as an act of stupidity and ingratitude. He had told her as much, and she hadn't argued with that characterization.

Elise exited the plane and waited in line at immigration with everyone else. When it came to her turn, the indifferent French immigration official asked for Elise's passport. She handed it to her. The official flipped through the pages. They were all blank. No stamps. Elise had gotten a new one shortly after her deportation.

The official scanned Elise's passport using the scanner next to the computer. Then she put her hands on the keyboard in front of her and began typing. She read the screen for a few seconds, then furrowed her brow.

Elise listened to the Immigration Official explain how since she had been deported, she was on a list of U.S. citizens who could not obtain a visa to enter France. Elise's first feeling was disappointment. This lasted until the explanation was finished. Then a contentment settled into her, like she had lost a bet with herself that she hadn't wanted to make in the first place. She was Elise, the fluent-in-French former expat who should be in Paris. That was her, or what she had thought was her. Not an Expat Wannabe living in Chicago with a boyfriend named Grabowski. Yet, in that moment, she felt free to want to be back in Chicago with Robert, and no longer fending off her feelings for him. Robert was the brave one. He had been honest about his feelings. He had risked rejection. Why was she so dumb sometimes?

"I said, 'Do you understand?'" said the irritated Immigration Official.

"Je comprends," said Elise.

The official summoned two members of the National Police and explained the situation. The policemen nodded and took Elise into custody.

84   THE HOLE IN MONTROSE AVENUE

Through heavy fog Robert turned the corner that morning onto Montrose, headed toward the L station. The temperature had risen into the 50's shortly after sunrise. Warm enough to melt all the snow that had fallen the day before and cause a thick fog to cover the city. Just beyond the Metra tracks he saw the flashing lights of the construction crews and the barricades. Looking through the fog was like trying to look through layers and layers of cobwebs. Only the brightest objects shown through. The rest were dark with blurred outlines.

It wasn't until Robert had passed under the Metra tracks that he saw the people and the TV crews gathered around just beyond the L tracks. There was a huge hole in the street that had opened up shortly after two in the morning. An 85-year-old water pipe had burst, washing away all the sand and dirt under the street and flooding the basements of the buildings nearby. A drunk, who happened to be slouching by shortly after the hole appeared, saw it and said, "That's more like it," and proceeded to empty the contents of his bladder into the hole.

The hole, which took up the entire width of Montrose Avenue, had sucked in the sidewalk in front of El Torito, the burrito joint on the south side of the street. The sidewalk on the north side was spared.

Up on the L platform, Robert could see the hole in its entirety and thought, wow, there's a hole in Ravenswood.

Robert boarded the next L train. It was so crowded that Robert had to stand. He held onto a pole and wondered how long it was going to take to fill the giant hole. That section of street would have to be rebuilt and the foundations of the nearby buildings would have to be shored up. Not a simple job.

The L train stopped at the Irving Park Road station and only a few more people were able to cram themselves onto the train. After the train pulled out from the station, it stopped in the middle of the tracks before the turn near the Paulina stop. It was at that point when a thin man in a dark gray suit that looked about a size too large for his frame shouted a sermon to the riders about the need to accept Jesus Christ as their Lord and Savior. Robert wondered since when did these guys start doing this on the Brown line trains, when it was generally accepted that these feeble attempts to convert people were to be performed on the Red line trains, and occasionally on the Blue line trains. The man went on at length about the need to read the Word of the One True God as revealed in the Bible, and the life of His One and Only Son who died for Our Sins. At certain moments he paused and a collective sigh of relief was heard from the passengers on the train in their expectation that the unsolicited sermon was over. Then groans rolled through the car as the man continued with his attempt to save their souls.

Robert hadn't had any coffee yet. He had planned on stopping by Gloria Jean's on the way to the office. He was also thinking about how the woman he loved was in France, and how his father and brothers were headed to prison. The last thing he wanted to hear on a Monday morning was a sermon from someone he didn't know, on a topic he didn't care about, on a train he nor anyone else could exit.

"Just shut the hell up!" yelled Robert over the man. "Do you really think anyone on this train is going to hear you shouting at them and suddenly say, *Oh, you are so right. I've been living my life completely wrong. Yes, I want to follow you and learn how I, too, can go around on L trains shouting at people to get them to read the Bible.* Do you really believe this is the best way to get your message across?"

The car filled with cheers, laughter, and clapping.

"Sir, I'm just trying to spread the Word of God," said the man through the din.

"All of us are stuck on this L car that has stopped for no apparent reason, as L trains often do on this horribly run transit system, and the last thing we want to do is listen to you or anyone else go on and on about saving our souls.

Most of us are on our way to work. We don't need a sermon. We need quiet!"

"Sir, I feel sorry for you that you have so much hate in your heart that—"

"Right now the only thing I hate is having to listen to you."

"God bless you, sir. I don't mean any disrespect. I'm just here to help you understand the Word of God."

The man turned and exited the L car through the door at one end, and entered the next L car.

After the door had shut behind the man, Robert felt shameful and he wasn't sure why that feeling was in him. Maybe he had been too harsh, but dammit, he was sick of being subjected to that kind of crap.

The train jerked forward, then stopped, the riders jostling into each other and wondering when the train was going to start moving at full speed again.

85   NO LONGER AN EQUAL

The line at Gloria Jean's moved slowly thanks to a woman reading a long complicated order. Many of those behind her, including Robert, wondered why she hadn't called it in beforehand.

At the office a few of his workers greeted Robert with "hi" or "good morning." Nothing more. No one asked how he was doing. His own friendly inquiries were met with one-syllable or mumbled replies. It was not like it was before, just last week. Gone, so quickly, was the casual banter he'd had with all of them as co-workers. He knew he was now their boss and no longer an equal. They were looking at him differently and talked to him more guardedly.

Robert was inside his own office shortly after nine. He took comfort in the fact that he had what was now rare: a meeting-free morning. So he shut the door and concentrated first on returning the many unreturned emails he had received, and second, looking again at how the projects matched up with his resources. He did manage to make quite a bit of progress cleaning out his Inbox before there was a knock on his door.

"Come in!" shouted Robert.

"Hi," said Karen, peeking her head inside. "I hope I'm not interrupting."

"It's all right. What's up?"

"I wanted to ask you something."

"Sure. Have a seat. Close the door."

Karen sat in one of the chairs across from him on the other side of his desk. "Is there going to be a reorg? That's all anyone is talking about this morning."

"I haven't heard anything," said Robert. "My understanding is what it was before: there will be a reorg of some kind to consolidate the two banks' operations. I don't yet know when it's going to happen or who's going to be affected."

Karen nodded. "I see."

"I'm sorry. If I do find out anything, I will tell you, Karen. But you cannot tell anyone it came from me. Okay?"

"I understand. I don't want to get you into any trouble. Besides, you get yourself into enough trouble."

He gestured around his office. "Look at this trouble I'm in right now."

"You're a good boss."

"Thanks."

His phone rang. The LCD screen indicated it was Ted Allen.

"I've got to take this," he said. "It's Ted."

Karen got up to leave and Robert picked up the phone.

"Hello," he said.

"Robert, there's an emergency meeting in the Root Conference Room in five minutes. All VPs and managers," said Ted.

"All right. I'll be there." He hung up the phone. "Okay. Maybe this is it."

"What?" said Karen.

"An emergency meeting of all the managers and VPs."

"Not a good sign."

"No. Not at all."

86   FOR THE PEOPLE

The nine o'clock press conference at City Hall started late because Aldermen Campbell, Otter, and Jefferson were late. The media were gathered to hear from the mayor and the aldermen about the deal they had reached to end the strike. Aldermen Campbell, Otter, and Jefferson apologized for their tardiness and stood with Mayor Nash as the mayor's spokeswoman read a statement explaining that a study would be commissioned looking into adding a statue of U.S. Grant to Grant Park to fix the imbalance of statues to namesake parks. No comment was offered on whether microphones would no longer be shut off for errant aldermen. No comment was offered on the arrests in Operation: Greasy Thumbs.

"Now we can get back to the business of running the city for the people," said Mayor Nash.

"Are you saying Alderman Campbell and the other aldermen were wrong to go on strike?" asked a reporter.

"I'm not going to play the gotcha game with you guys. We're happy the strike is over. Everyone is happy the strike is over."

"But it sounds like—"

"The strike is over! Let's get back to work."

"Alderman Campbell, would you agree with Mayor Nash's assessment that by going on strike you haven't been working?"

"I didn't say that!" shouted the mayor. "How dare you say that!"

"We've all been working," said Campbell. "We're always working! The work of the people goes on 24 hours a day, 365 days a year."

"But if you were on strike, that means you weren't on the job, wouldn't you say?"

"We're not taking anymore questions," said Alderman Otter.

87   THE BOMB

Charles Fitzgerald, President of Fourth National Bank, informed the VPs and managers present at the meeting that the Merger Task Force had identified a number of redundancies and that the company-wide reorganization to address those redundancies would occur on Friday. There would be layoffs on both sides. The Marketing and Sales Departments were being moved to Raleigh, N.C., where BMC was headquartered. No retail branches were to be closed (as expected), since the banks competed in different markets.

So here it comes, thought Robert, sitting near the middle of the room. No wonder his staff had been wary of him. They were probably chattering about the possible outcomes of a reorg based on nothing more than their own suppositions. Because he had been through it so many times at a number of other companies, he knew their paranoia would increase at a rate directly proportional to their morale's decrease. The paranoia would only end once the reorg occurred. It was going to be a long week.

Then everyone in the room heard a loud boom from outside the building. A few looked around. Others shrugged their shoulders. Fitzgerald said, "I wonder what that was," then continued talking about the details of the reorganization, some of the long-term plans for the newly-combined company, and the expectations of increased revenues.

Nearly everyone else who was in or near the Loop that morning at 9:36 am heard the explosion. To some (like Robert), it sounded like a loud boom. Others described it as the sound of an extremely large pile driver pounding once. It was followed closely by dozens of car alarms shrieking in nearby parking lots, then the sirens of fire trucks and ambulances a short time later. Those closest to the Dirksen Federal Building saw the flames engulf what remained of the shell of the van Alderman Soldiamori had been about to exit. The alderman, his attorney, and two federal agents were killed. Three agents were injured.

There was immediate speculation in the media about whether the Outfit had planted the bomb and what this meant for Federal prosecutors and the cases they were building.

88   REORG

Ted Allen had summoned Robert to his office at the conclusion of the meeting.

"First," said Ted, seated behind his desk, "I really like your idea about the software for automating much of the testing on some of our projects. It's a great idea. It's something I think is long overdue for implementation."

"Thank you," said Robet, sitting erect.

"No. Thank you. It's the kind of thinking your department needs."

"You're welcome." This made Robert feel good. He sat back and rested his right ankle on his left knee. Finally, his department was going to get the tools it needed to work more efficiently and effectively.

"Unfortunately, given the current priorities, we can't go forward with such a large expenditure on software. I'm sorry. But you understand, right?"

Robert didn't like it and he wondered why he and Karen had even bothered doing all that research. "Yes, I do."

"Second, because of the reorganization you'll need to choose four people from your department to be laid off. Staff people. Not contractors. We can let contractors go any time we want. With the merger, we just don't need as many people. For the short term we're going to have a number of redundant departments. Eventually, that will change. In the meantime, we need to have the departments finish their current projects and then shift resources as those projects are completed. It will make for a smoother transition."

"Okay."

"I know you've just been promoted. This is not the kind of thing any manager wants to do, especially when you've barely been in the job. But, as they say, it goes with the territory."

"I understand."

"I'll need a list of people to give to HR by the end of the day, today."

"That soon?"

"Yes."

"Are there layoffs at BMC?"

"Yes."

"How many will be laid off in their QA department?"

"Robert—"

"I need to know."

"That's not your concern."

"It is my concern. How many?"

"None. But don't read anything into that. It's just a reflection of their resource needs. To tell you the truth, they're understaffed."

This was not the time to argue, or throw a fit, or rant, Robert told himself. He was the department's last resort. His own department was understaffed. Ted had seen that from the long report Robert had sent him explaining the department's need for automated testing software. He was barely being given a chance. How could he make do with a quarter less people? The number of projects hadn't been cut. The automated testing software was supposed to allow his people to catch up. Unless they were going to cut some of the projects. They would have to cut some of them. Now he had to pick four staff people and put on a calm face to his department. He was going to have to lie to Karen. He shouldn't have told her that he would be straight with her. There was no way he could be straight with her about something like this. It would put the department into an even greater panic.

"You don't need to explain," said Robert, "though I don't like it. We're understaffed. That's why I pushed for the software."

"None of us like it."

"I know. I know."

"I've taken a big risk promoting you, Robert. I had to justify it to a lot of people. Don't let me down. We are in a battle for our survival. You know how these things work. We're taking a hit for now. The only department I oversee that isn't going to lose people is IT. Documentation and Software Development are losing people, too."

Robert took a few deep breaths, his clasped hands resting on his chest.

"It's harder than you thought it would be," said Ted.

"Yes," said Robert.

"Get used to it...You might even feel like I threw you to the wolves. But given the circumstances, you were the best choice. I couldn't do an outside search, that would have given the decision-makers the excuse to simply shift the entire department to Raleigh. Internally, you were by far the best candidate. Take a look at some of your staff. I have a feeling that you already know who you can afford to lose."

Robert turned his eyes from Ted, to the view of the shadowed gray building across the street, to the book case filled with numerous industry-type awards and no more than a dozen books, all about managing people. Why was it the few offices of upper-level executives he had seen were always so clean while the average manager's desk was overflowing with paper? He glanced back at Ted before focusing on his own hands still folded on his chest. He opened and closed them before straightening himself in the chair.

There was no way Robert was going to lay Karen off. She was too smart and valuable to him. She was the person he trusted the most in the department. Since contractors were not to be let go, that meant he had to keep Wen, Dipti, Sanjay, and Nikolai. Which was fine, as they were all knowledgeable and hard-working.

There was Gary who knew a lot, was dependable, but worked as fast as an L train passing through one of the many slow zones in the system. So there was one.

The young guys Jeff and Bob were energetic and dependable. Jeff was the more detail-oriented of the two. He liked Bob better on a personal level, but he often missed obvious things. So Bob would have to go. Number two.

Anna was not the most thorough tester despite her intelligence. Number three.

That left Katrina, Timur, and Rakesh. Oh, boy. All three of them were very good. All three of them were smart and thorough testers. Rakesh, though, had rubbed more than a few programmers the wrong way. He had even gotten into an argument with a programmer (also from India) and the two of them had been heard shouting loudly in Hindi. Frank had complained to both Lisa and Perry about Rakesh, accusing him of going overboard in his criticism of some of the projects. Rakesh was brutally blunt. Robert didn't have a problem with that. But telling someone their software was a "piece of crap" was beyond what his job required.

So there were the four: Gary, Jeff, Anna, and Rakesh.

Robert would put their names in his email to Ted that he would send in the afternoon, and let Ted think that he agonized most of the day over his decisions. Not letting him know what a cold-hearted bastard he really was. That had been too easy. He did not like how quickly he had chosen the four. He didn't know whether this meant he was cut out to be in management. If it did, was it a desirable thing? To be able to figure out so quickly who you could do with and without was a skill he had never thought he would need, let along exercise. He had to admit that his father was right: you could not rule without spilling blood.

Ted leaned forward, his elbows resting on his desk. "We have a lot of work to do if we're going to keep our jobs, be they here or in Raleigh. You and I both know everything will be headquartered in Raleigh, eventually. You know how these things work. Mergers are never between equals, no matter what anyone says."

Robert had never even been south of the Mason-Dixon line, not even to his parents' Florida condo. Moving to Raleigh was an unknown. It was a big gamble Ted was making, a losing one in all probability. By promoting Robert he had protected one piece of his territory for the time being. For sure his department would have been given over to BMC's QA manager if Ted hadn't attempted to keep it for himself. Robert could see now that his promotion was a temporary one. When the time came to fold his QA Department into BMC's QA Department in Raleigh, he would either be offered a demotion and a move to Raleigh, or more likely he would be laid off. There was no way two QA Departments were going to be maintained in two separate parts of the country for one bank, when their operations could be contained and managed in one location. There was no other way to look at it. Robert's best bet was to keep his mouth shut for the time being, do his job the best he could, and take the exit that was sure to be offered him in a few months or more. Meanwhile, he would update his resume.

"Raleigh, huh?" said Robert.

"There's always the chance they'll keep Documentation, Development, and QA here, since you'll often be working on different projects than the people in Raleigh. That's not the most likely scenario. They always prefer to have things under one roof. So as projects are completed, you're going to see an accelerated shift of resources to Raleigh."

89   SIMMERING

The four people whom Robert had chosen to be laid off were now sitting in his office. An hour before, he sent the email to Ted Allen that included the names of Gary Majewski, Jeff Ryan, Anna Toporovsky, and Rakesh Sharma. He received a reply from Ted saying only, "Thank you."

Robert had been thinking about how he was going to face the people in his department knowing what he knew. Until the corporate reorganization was implemented on Friday, he knew the people in his department were going to keep simmering with anxiety and fear, partaking in the angry speculation that comes from not knowing whether you're going to lose your job. How could he look at Gary, Jeff, Anna, and Rakesh and keep a straight face? He had been in that position numerous times and he had hated it. He hated his current position even more.

Robert wasn't supposed to tell his workers anything, not even admit that a reorg was going to take place. Why? To prevent worker sabotage? His people weren't like that. That was the thing about firing people: companies didn't give people two week's notice that they were to be fired. He was going to be a different kind of manager. He was going to be honest. He wasn't going to spend the week telling them there were no layoffs or that no one in the department would be laid off or that he didn't know who was going to be laid off or what was going to happen. The best way to put their minds at ease, he thought, was to let the ones who were safe know that they were safe, and let the ones who were to be let go know that they were to be let go.

Robert's right hand rested on his now moist mouse. He closed all the windows on his PC monitor, leaving only the black and white White Sox logo that served as the desktop background. The clock on his computer screen displayed 4:34 pm. His left hand was shaking on the keyboard, lightly tapping keys in no particular order but not hard enough to register on the screen. His whole body felt jittery like it was going to run out of the office on its own. So with both hands he gripped the arms of his chair. Anna, Gary, Jeff, and Rakesh were looking at Robert, expecting him to say something. Their faces were mostly impassive, with a bit of the usual end-of-day fatigue in their eyes.

Anna yawned, covering her mouth and saying, "Excuse me."

"I know you're probably wondering why I called you four in here," said Robert. "You've probably heard the rumors about the layoffs. Well, they're true. They're happening this Friday."

"Okay," said Gary.

"Why are you telling us?" asked Jeff.

"Because the four of you need to update your resumes," said Robert. "Feel free to use me as a reference."

"Are you firing us?" said Gary.

"No. You're going to be laid off on Friday."

"How do you know it's us four?" asked Rakesh.

"I know."

"But how do you know?"

"Do you really want the answer to that question?"

"Yes."

Robert swallowed and looked Rakesh in his brown eyes. "Because I did the choosing. All right? They told the managers to choose X-amount of people in their departments. It had to be staff because contractors can be let go at any time."

"Why are you telling us now?" asked Gary. "I've never heard of a manager doing something like this. You choose us and then tell us four days before we're going to be let go that we're being let go?"

"He just doesn't want to feel guilty," said Rakesh as if spitting out a flavor-dead piece of gum.

"I don't want to lay off anyone," said Robert. "But I also didn't want you four and the others spending the week doing nothing but wondering what's going to happen. I figured a little notice might be good."

"Yes, that's wonderful," said Anna flatly. "It makes being fired feel so much better." She turned to the others. "Doesn't it make you all feel better about getting fired?"

Gary looked disappointed. Jeff looked dumbfounded. Anna and Rakesh glared at Robert.

"This sucks," said Jeff. He shook his head and looked down at the floor.

"Exactly," said Anna.

"It's total BS!" said Rakesh.

"Yep, it is," said Gary out of the right side of his mouth.

"I'm sorry," said Robert. "I thought being honest might be better than lying to you guys all week."

"Knowing the day you're going to be fired, excuse me, 'laid off,' isn't exactly a comfort. I wish I didn't know," said Rakesh.

"I don't care if you don't show up for the rest of the week. All I ask is that you tidy up things before you go. "

"So why us?"

"Rakesh, it's complicated."

"Don't, Rakesh," said Gary. "It's not like he wants to lay us off."

"No," insisted Rakesh. "I'd like to hear why I was chosen to lose my job. Why me?"

"I don't have to tell you that," said Robert. He knew he had just made a big mistake and was now about to compound it. He had dug a hole, jumped in it, and now it was collapsing in on him.

"Why not? You've already told us that you chose us to be laid off."

"Rakesh, it doesn't matter why. We're all on borrowed time here. The whole department is going to end up in Raleigh sooner or later. Which means we're all going to be without jobs."

"That's not the point. We were chosen to be laid off first for a reason."

"Wait, wait!" said Gary holding up a hand to Rakesh. "The department is moving to Raleigh?"

"Everything that can be moved will eventually be moved to Raleigh," said Robert. "It's been made clear to me that that is the direction the new company is headed. We're taking the brunt of the layoffs. Not BMC."

"I see," said Gary.

The four left Robert's office. Robert put his head in his hands, knowing they were going to tell their coworkers everything: who was being laid off on Friday, and what the layoffs meant for the future of the combined companies.

Less than five minutes later Karen knocked on Robert's door and asked if what Rakesh, Gary, Anna, and Jeff were all saying was true.

"Yes, it's true," said Robert.

"I'm glad to know my job is safe."

"At least someone in this department is happy."

90   THEY DEPORT AMERICANS?

Elise was sitting in a holding room with her head in her hands, staring at the dirty tile floor. She was the lone American in a group that included women from India, Ukraine, Mali, Algeria, and Morocco. The grimy room smelled of mold with a touch of urine and feces that emanated from the extremely messy toilet behind a door at one end of the large room. It reminded Elise that the public restrooms in French restaurants were often atrocious. With the exception of dog poop, the streets, museums, and parks could be immaculate at times, but the public toilets seemed wholly forgotten. It was one thing Chicago definitely had on Paris: cleaner public toilets.

The other women in the room were speaking in low tones in a mixture of fluid, heavily-accented, and broken French.

"I didn't know they deported Americans," said one.

Elise knew they had to be talking about her.

"She's an American?" said another. "I wonder what she did."

"You say they're deporting an American?" said a third woman with a chuckle. "That's funny."

"Yes. The woman over there."

"Why would they deport an American woman?"

"Maybe she's a prostitute."

"I'm not a prostitute!" said Elise.

"Then why are they deporting you?" asked a Moroccan woman. She was sitting across from Elise. She looked no more than 25 years-old.

"It's a long story. I was deported once before. They stopped me just now from entering the country."

"Twice now?! That is unbelievable." Then to the Algerian woman next to her. "Did you hear that? She's being deported for the second time."

"An American deported twice from France? I've never heard of that," said another woman.

"And her French is very good," said the Algerian.

"Your French is near perfect," said the young Moroccan woman.

"Thank you," said Elise. "Now I have nowhere to use my near perfect French-speaking skills."

"There is always Québec."

"It's much colder there."

"True, but they speak French. I hear it is a good country. You have not been deported from Canada, have you?"

"No."

"So where in the U.S. will you go? Where is your home?"

What should she answer? Technically, Elise didn't have a home. She didn't know where she would end up. They were going to put her on the next flight with an open seat headed toward the U.S.A. If she had to call somewhere home there was only one place, the place with someone who wanted her to return to that place.

"Chicago," said Elise.

"I have never been there. What is it like?"

"Wonderful. Lots of parks. A beautiful lakefront and skyline. Great restaurants, museums, and culture."

"Can you find a job if you go back?"

"Yes. Probably."

"Then that is not so bad."

"No. It's not."

"In Rabat, where I come from, there is not enough work. There is not enough work in all of Morocco."

"How long have you been in France?"

"Three years. Until a few days ago I was cleaning in an office building. Now I don't know what I will do."

Elise thought she had been acting like a spoiled brat. She had skills she could use in the U.S. to make money. At the very least she could probably go back to teaching high school French. Across from her was this Morrocan woman with excellent French skills, who had probably crossed the straits of Gibraltar and made her way through Spain to get to France, all so she could do janitorial work. The other women around her were probably in the same situation, either they or their husbands had no means of support back in their home country. None of them had probably ever tried to get an ex-boyfriend deported. None of them had made the trip to France simply because they wanted to. They made the trip because they had to in order to survive.

Elise folded her arms and went back to staring at the grimy floor.

91   BAD DECISIONS

Wednesday morning Robert arrived at his office building sweaty. He remembered why he hated wearing a suit; they made hot days feel more suffocating than they already were. After the snow had melted on Monday, the temperature had risen higher with each new day. Tuesday the temperature had reached a high of 85 degrees Fahrenheit. Now it was already 81 degrees with an expected high for the day of 93.

Robert entered the building, relieved to be in the comfort of cold, conditioned air, and got on an elevator. When the elevator doors opened on his floor, he headed to his office, greeting people in his department along the way. On Tuesday they had all seemed more relaxed. Gary had thanked him for his honesty. Anna and Jeff had arrived late and left early. Rakesh didn't show up at all. Today, his workers looked at him solemnly and avoided any morning chatter. As he got closer to his office, he saw that there was a security guard standing by the open door. Robert said good morning to her and she nodded back. He stepped inside his office to find Ted Allen and Rose Santos.

"Good morning," said Robert.

"You can shut the door," said Ted to the security guard.

The security guard entered the office, shutting the door behind her.

Robert thought that a security guard, your boss, and the head of HR in your office was a very bad sign. This had to be his last day at the company. Ted looked angry. Rose looked like she was playing poker. In her hands she held a manila folder.

"I have one question for you, Robert," said Ted deliberately. "Did you inform the people in your department that they would be laid off?"

"Yes," said Robert.

"Why on God's green earth would you do that?"

"I didn't want them to spend the week worrying about it. Everyone knew the layoffs were coming."

Rose coughed into her elbow.

"Do you know what this has done? If people didn't know for sure before, they do now. Plus, you've got people in other departments saying you already informed those who were to be laid off. Now other employees are asking their managers who among them is to be laid off. The other managers are in an impossible position. They're having to lie and they're wondering how their workers found out what's coming. Not to mention all the rumors going around about how everyone here is going to lose their jobs but not anyone at BMC."

Robert decided to explain his reasoning, despite knowing full well that not matter what he said, in a few minutes the security guard was going to escort him out of the building. He would get to take a few of his personal items. His email and server access had probably been locked by the IT department earlier that morning. He would sign some paperwork and that would be it. His career in management was over. All because by attempting to calm his own workers he had inadvertently put the rest of the company into a frenzy. This was the last thing he had intended to happen. Plus, he had made his boss look very bad.

"We were already in an impossible position," said Robert. "If I didn't tell them, they were going to spend the week worrying, sniping, bitching, and, above all, not working. And I'd have to lie to them over and over."

Ted rubbed his forehead. "I've made some bad decisions. But promoting you appears to be among the worst, if not *the* worst. You've thrown the entire company into chaos. Now, no one is working!"

"No one was working anyway. All they're doing is speculating about who's going to be laid off, who's moving to Raleigh, and why." The more he explained, the more he thought he sounded like a sullen teenager giving cheap excuses.

Ted raised his voice. "It was your job to keep them working despite whatever rumors they hear."

"So I'm fired."

"Oh, yes. You might have the intelligence and talent to be in management, but you don't have the maturity. You can't be trusted to do the job of a manager. You can't be trusted with information that is not intended for mass consumption."

"I'm sorry," said Robert.

"It's nice to hear. But it's far too late for that."

92   STRANDED

Elise was numb and groggy as she exited the plane at Newark airport at a quarter to noon. The next available flight for her had been a flight to the New Jersey airport on Wednesday. She didn't want to be in the New York City area. She didn't know anyone there. It was now up to her to get to Chicago. Her nostrils filled with a new, horrible smell. It was a dirty, industrial belching kind of smell. It was inside the terminal. It was inside the baggage claim area where she retrieved her suitcase. It was at the check-in desks. She wanted to get out of the airport and away from that smell.

If she had a cell phone, she could call someone, her parents, Jen, even Robert. But no, she had canceled the contract on her cell phone with less than two months on it, thinking there was no point in having it because she would get a new one in France. How stupid of her. Again.

Elise looked at all the counters. Which airline should she try? United? Continental? Northwest? American? She decided on United thinking they were headquartered in Chicago and therefore must have many flights to and from the city. She waited in line at the ticket counter with her bags.

When it came her turn at the counter, she said, "I need to get on the next flight to Chicago."

"Okay," said the woman as she typed on her computer. Elise readied her passport and credit card.

"The next flight, which departs at 1:15 pm, is full. But if you like, I can put you on standby."

"That would be great."

"Just one moment."

While waiting at the counter, the smell would not go away. How did people at the airport handle the smell? How long did it take before you stopped noticing it? Where did it come from? It was unlike anything she had ever smelled before. She had gone from the moldy-mildewy-urine smell of the detention room at Charles De Gaulle to the recycled air of the plane to the blunt dirt smell at Newark that was now shoving its way up her nose. Please, she thought, let there be an open seat on the next flight.

93   THE SPACE BETWEEN THEM

Robert had put off making a big trip for groceries for over a week, so caught up was he in his new job and Elise. He could have gone earlier, but since being escorted out of the

Fourth National Bank Tower he had spent the day sitting in front of his gaming computer trying not to sulk about his joblessness, his family's legal problems, and the fact that he had not yet heard from Elise. Robert knew that taking a grocery trip at that time of night (after nine) would make him lose his parking spot around the corner from his apartment. But there were no decent grocery stores within walking distance of his apartment and he couldn't put the trip off any longer.

On his way out of the building Robert was stopped by Logan, who was returning from his AA meeting. Though the night was muggy, it was more pleasant outside than inside his apartment. Robert had an air conditioner in his bedroom so he could sleep in comfort, but the rest of his apartment was bursting with heat. His window A/C unit was humming along with the many other A/C units hanging out of apartment windows.

"How are you doing?" asked Robert.

"Eh, not so good," said Logan. "Those idiots at the National Endowment for the Humanities rejected my grant application. Can you believe that? Our language is doomed Robert."

"Sorry to hear that." Robert tried to sound sympathetic.

"I know you don't believe me but our language needs to be preserved."

"Uh-huh."

"So how's your lady friend?"

"She's in France."

"For what?"

"To live there."

"You didn't scare her off, did you?"

"No."

"I'm just kidding, Robert."

With all the free time Robert had now, he could get on a plane and go to France. He wondered how Elise was doing, whether her flight had gone well, whether she had a job lined up. He hoped she would send him an email, soon, even a short one just to let him know that she was in Paris and that everything was going well there. He wanted her to be happy, even if she couldn't be happy with him.

"I know," said Robert. "Well, I'll talk to you later. I gotta run to get some groceries." Robert took a step toward the sidewalk. He didn't want to get stuck in another long conversation with Logan. It was late.

"Hey, before you go," said Logan. "I've been meaning to tell you something."

"What's that?" said Robert who was half-turned away from him.

"The cable should be up and running by the end of the week."

"Lot of good that does me. I already went and called to have them set it up for me, legitimately. They're coming by tomorrow afternoon."

"Suit yourself."

Robert took another step toward the sidewalk.

"One more thing!" said Logan.

Robert turned. "What's that?"

Logan stepped closer to him, glancing around as if he was checking to see if anyone was watching. In a low voice he said, "How's your family?"

"My father and brothers made bail. They're pretty shaken up and scared, and angry. Thanks for asking."

Logan nodded. "Whatever happens, I hope your father and brothers use the experience as a way to straighten themselves out. Especially your brothers. With small children..." Logan's voice faded away. He looked more grave than Robert had ever seen him. "When they're young, that's when they first get to know you. If you really screw it up, it's hell to try to fix later."

"I've wished they'd straighten themselves out too many times to count."

"People learn by doing, not just the right things, but the wrong things, too."

"This from the guy who was helping me get free cable."

"Ha. I never said I was perfect."

"True."

Logan put his hand on Robert's shoulder and squeezed a little. "I'm sorry, Robert, for you and your family."

The way he said it made Robert think it was Logan who had done something wrong. "Thank you," said Robert.

Logan pulled his hand away and they said goodbye to each other.

Robert walked down the block to his car. He drove to the Jewel on Lincoln Avenue and did his shopping. When he returned from the store, Robert took the obligatory drive down Bob Fosse Way even though he didn't think he had a chance in hell of finding a parking spot on his block at that time of night. The trunk of his car loaded with bags, Robert drove down his street just in case there was an outside chance of a spot. He cruised along slowly. In front of the entrance to his wing of the apartment building, he saw someone with a large suitcase and a medium-sized backpack sitting. That was all he could tell given the distance and dim lighting.

At the corner, he turned right onto Sunnyside. There had been no spots on Hermitage when he had come up that way minutes before, so he resigned himself to parking another block over on Ravenswood. After he parked the car, he popped open the trunk and unloaded the six bags and gallon of milk. He shut the trunk and looked at the bags. He figured out how to put four bags in his left hand, leaving the right to hold the gallon of milk, the bag of bread and pastries, and the bag of cereal boxes.

By the time Robert reached his apartment building, his arms and hands were tired. The person was still standing in front of his wing of the building. He stood by the gate and looked at her, and wondered how the heck he hadn't recognized her before.

"Robert?" she said.

"Elise?" he said.

She jogged to the gate and opened it. He stepped inside. The gate clinked shut. He set down the milk and plastic bags, then shook loose his pain-stiff hands.

"What? How?" sputtered Robert.

"I'm banned from France," said Elise.

"You're kidding, right?"

"No."

"How is that possible?"

"It doesn't matter. I want to be here."

Their minds whirled with the endless things they wanted to say about how they felt about each other, the things they wanted to do, the places they wanted to go, the things they wanted to see, together. Elise rose on her tiptoes a few times, almost jumping. Robert was flat-footed and swaying ever so slightly to the beat of his heart. An A/C window unit on the third floor turned off. A light in a window on the second floor went out. Cricket chirps echoed in the courtyard. The space between Robert and Elise dwindled to nothing as they eased closer, wrapped their arms around one another, closed their eyes, and kissed.

ACKNOWLEDGMENTS

My thanks go out to:

Tyler Craft Cormney for his encouraging words early on about this novel.

John Waller for his friendship and pointed comments about "clout."

Michael Getzlaff for his keen insights about the characters and the editing of the final manuscript.

Susan Compo (a valued teacher who became a trusted friend) for reading an early draft of this novel and providing invaluable feedback.

Jane Melnick, because without her I might never have made it this far as a writer.

Donald Freed for teaching me what it means to be an artist.

My amazing family for their love and support.

A special thank you goes to my wife Stephanie Nawyn, without whom this book would not have been possible. She has given me the space and encouragement to write. I love you.

ABOUT THE AUTHOR

Richard Hellinga was born and raised in the Chicago area. He worked for a dozen years in the IT industry and has a master's degree from the Professional Writing program at USC. He now resides with his wife and children near Lansing, MI.